Josh's Challenge

A KING BROTHERS STORY

TROUBLE IN TIMBISHA TOWNSHIP
BOOK THREE

ELISE MANION

I'd like to thank my husband for putting up with all my one-sided conversations and constant promises that I'd "be right there," only to be left waiting while I write one more chapter, or edit one more scene.

Tom, you are my prince, my heart, and sometimes my challenge. I love you with all my heart.

Contents

Josh's Challenge

CHAPTER 1

Mystery Chocolate

"How long have you had a stalker, Miss Theroux?" Timbisha County Sheriff Jarod King asked as he examined, with gloved hands, a white box filled with chocolates and a syringe filled with liquid.

"Cut the formal crap, Jarod. She's upset enough," said her landlord, Josh King. He was also the sheriff's youngest brother.

Missy stared, speechless as usual, while two sets of perfect blue eyes glared at each other. She took a cautious step back in case the brothers' reputation for fighting were to explode on her front porch.

"Excuse me, gentlemen, but I don't have a stalker," she denied in a shaky voice. Unfortunately, Harold's face flashed before her eyes.

"Who's Harold, Missy?" Jarod asked less formally, interrupting her thoughts.

Crap on toast, did I say his name out loud?

"Melissa?" Josh asked with so much concern in his voice it stole her breath. When he reached up to touch her shoulder, she moved out of his reach, and flushed with embarrassment.

"Harold Klein was my philosophy professor."

"You had an intimate relationship with one of your teachers?" Jarod's tone wasn't judgmental, but the question annoyed her anyway.

"Of course not. He asked me out and I said no. When he kept harassing me, we obtained a restraining order. He backed right off after that." She crossed her arms protectively over her chest, the reminder of the awkward situation making her feel small.

"Who's 'we'?" Jarod asked, not skipping a beat.

"Me and my roommate."

"So you *do* have a stalker," Jarod confirmed.

She let her shoulders fall. Did she? Harold didn't live anywhere near Timbisha Township. He didn't even live in Nevada. He'd never left "gifts" like the one found on her porch this morning. Shaking her head, she asked, "How do we know the chocolates are intended for me? I just moved in."

"She's got a point, Jarod. There isn't a name on the box," Josh said.

"Exactly," she agreed. "You see, Sheriff, I was just about to take a jog when I found it on the porch—"

"Don't call him 'sheriff' when he's acting like an ass," Josh interrupted.

"The only ass on this porch is you," Jarod answered.

Before Josh could counter his brother, Missy pressed on. "Maybe it was intended for the people who used to live here?" Then she turned to Josh. "Do you know how to find your previous tenants?"

Josh and Jarod shared a look with each other before the sheriff cleared his throat. "Well, that's an interesting theory, since I used to live here. Actually, it was my wife's townhouse before she was my wife... Oh, hell." Jarod rolled his eyes heavenward.

Josh turned to face Missy. "I bought the townhouse from Lauren but rented it back to them after they got married so I could remodel their suite at the estate."

"Oh, I see." She really didn't, and his vague explanation still didn't answer the question as to why someone would leave a potentially lethal box of chocolates on her porch.

As if reading her mind, Josh said, "The syringe we found in the box does suggest it could be tied to the drug dealers you cleared out of Timbisha Township, Jarod. Maybe this is residual fallout from some of Brad's associates?"

Missy shuddered at the reminder of the awful story her sister had recounted to her; the kidnapping of Jarod's wife and daughter, the meth, the murders; all things Missy never thought would happen in her small hometown.

"When you called you said there's a syringe inside the box, Missy. I don't see it," Jarod asked as he lifted the lid.

"Yes, but we didn't touch it. When we saw the syringe, Josh quickly closed it and called you. It's small."

Jarod tipped the box a little to the side. "Found it." He took the syringe out of the box, gave it a cursory glance before placing it in an evidence bag. He set it aside and then checked under the bubble wrap covering the chocolates.

"What the hell is that?" Josh asked. Missy didn't miss the anger in his voice.

"It looks like each candy has a paper letter pinned to it, but they aren't in order," Jarod said quietly.

"Like a word jumble?" Missy asked.

Jarod raised his eyebrows. "Yeah, maybe," he said, shrugging as if considering her theory. "Won't know anything until I can get this analyzed." He took some photos of the box, of the lettered chocolates and syringe, before replacing the lid. He then stuffed the whole thing into another evidence bag and sealed it. "I would prefer you not be alone. Can you stay with your mom for a while?"

"No!" Missy declared before she could catch herself. Jarod and Josh raised their eyebrows at her outburst. "I mean, of course I'll be careful, but no, I can't stay with Mom. Marguerite's moved home to take care of our mother while she's sick, and I don't want to impose on either of them. I'm sure this," she indicated the toxic chocolates, "will turn out to be nothing, right?" She hoped it would be nothing.

"Hey." Josh put his arm around her shoulders. She realized she was shaking with an oncoming panic attack. Surprisingly, his comforting touch stifled the onset. His next words, though, brought on a different sort of embarrassment. "Look, I'm right next door. You've got my number. All you have to do is call me, Melissa."

"Of course," she whispered. Missy had never been good at conversation with humans. She related more to animals than people, which meant she'd spent most of her life with creatures who communicated by behavior. Josh, handsome devil that he was, made her fumble for words with his amazing blue eyes, his easygoing personality, and lady-killing smile. She was always flummoxed when he was near.

The sheriff studied her for a moment before finally relenting. "Fine. I'll talk to Dane but in the meantime, Missy, I want you to keep your doors locked. Here," he handed her a card, "this is my personal cell. Don't hesitate to call me for anything, day or night. Understand?"

"Yes, sir." She took the card and tucked it into her pocket.

"Josh, that goes for you, too. I have a bad feeling about this."

"Yeah, me too."

She followed Jarod to his cruiser, the offending box of chocolates under his arm, while Josh tagged along on her heels. "Thank you."

"You're welcome, Missy. I'll be in touch." Jarod put everything in the trunk before getting in—ignoring his brother, she noted—and pulled away from the curb.

When he was out of sight, Josh turned her toward him. "I mean it, Melissa. Call me anytime, and don't be shy about it. It doesn't matter if the box was meant for you or not. Things got crazy around here last fall and, I swear, if anything happened to you..."

His sincerity took her by surprise. However, she wouldn't feel comfortable imposing on him, especially if he were entertaining one of his many female admirers. Now that Jarod had departed, the hideous awkwardness which had plagued her since childhood was creeping in. It was an unwelcome social anxiety that usually happened when she couldn't think of a thing to say to someone she'd known for most of her life. Before her affliction got the better of her, she cleared her throat and said, "Of course, Josh. Thank you."

That was a proper response, wasn't it?

His smile was beautiful as he patted her shoulder before leaving for his townhouse. She studied Josh's confident swagger until she felt the heat in her cheeks. Embarrassed, she entered her own townhouse and immediately tripped over a damn cardboard box, stubbing her toe.

"Dang it! I hate moving," she mumbled as she hurried to pick up her ringing iPhone. She snatched it off the counter and slid her finger over the screen. "Hello?"

"It's me. Are you all right? What happened?" Marguerite said in Big Sister Interrogation Mode.

"I know it's you, your picture was covering the home screen. I'm fine," Missy sighed.

"Oh, no you don't. Explain why Jarod had me call a courier to run a dubious box of chocolates, and a syringe for God's sake, to a forensics lab in Reno! Chocolates, I might add, found on your front porch?"

Missy rolled her eyes. Obviously, her sister already knew what was going on, so why was she making her rehash it? "We don't even know if they were meant for me, Marguerite. The message was jumbled."

"What message? Jarod was tight-lipped about the whole thing."

"It might've been meant for him. Josh thinks it could be a warning for finding the drug money in Vegas last year." *God, please let it be about the drug money.*

"Or," Marguerite countered, "it could be Harold's doing."

"Harold isn't stalking me!"

"Oh yeah? Then why did you get a restraining order against him?"

"Because he was a little too persistent," Missy explained weakly.

Marguerite's disgusted grunt came loud and clear. "Same difference." There was silence on the other end. Missy imagined the cogs rotating in Marguerite's brain. Her sister was a smart cookie who hid behind the false persona of a dumb blonde. Behind the Estee Lauder mask and salon-colored hair was a sharp, analytic mind.

Finally, Marguerite admitted, "I guess it could be possible some moron hadn't realized Jarod and Lauren moved out of the townhouse. What did the message say?"

Missy sighed. Marguerite wouldn't quit until she had all the facts. "You guys'll know before I do." She paused before she admitted, "Josh was the one who opened the box and called Jarod."

"Is Josh in the habit of stopping by early in the morning, or did he stay the night?" Marguerite asked in a knowing tone.

"No, he did not stay the night. Sheesh!" Her sister always assumed things were naughtier than they actually were.

"Keep going," Marguerite commanded, back to being all business.

"Okay, so I guess I was just standing on the porch not moving, holding this box of candy. Josh must've seen me. He came out of his townhouse and ran over to check on me. As soon as he saw what was inside the box, he called Jarod. You know the rest. Satisfied?"

"Not until I know for sure who that box was intended for, and what was in that syringe," Marguerite answered with some heat. "I'm calling Uncle Dane just in case."

"No need, I think Jarod's going to do that."

"Really?" Marguerite sounded surprised.

"Yes, why wouldn't he? He knows Uncle Dane is ex-FBI, and didn't you both say they worked together last fall?"

"Never mind about that." Marguerite was quiet for a moment. "Do you think Harold could've sent the chocolates?"

"Marguerite! I told you, I took care of him."

"We'll see," she said. "I have to go. Jarod needs help with the lab forms."

"Fine. I'll see you later. Please don't tell Mom about this. I don't want to worry her."

"I won't. I love you, Missy."

"I love you, too, Marguerite."

Missy ended the call and looked around her cluttered living

room. She hadn't unpacked a thing in two weeks except the necessities. Her bedroom furniture and clothes were in place, but she hadn't bothered with the rest of the condo, which currently resembled a storage unit. Not wanting to think about what needed to be done, she reached back to her messy ponytail and tugged at it to make sure it was secure. All she needed was her iPhone for music and her earbuds. Exercise was her drug and running was her preference. She did a few stretches before heading out the front door once again.

HE WAS STALKING HER.

Josh leaned his forehead against his living room window and groaned. How could he, Josh King, Timbisha Township's ladies' man extraordinaire, have been reduced to spying on his neighbor, his *tenant*? Full of self-disgust, he turned away from the window. Women had always come easy to Josh. Twenty-six years of dating earned him an ease with women even his brothers were jealous of, but only one girl twisted his guts in a knot and made him feel like an adolescent who was nervous about asking his first crush to the dance: Melissa Anne Theroux.

Josh had tried to ask her out many times in high school because she was unlike the other girls vying for his attention, but Melissa would blush an adorable shade of red before running away. Three years younger than him, he supposed the age difference had been the cause of her embarrassment, but the sting of her rejection followed him through his college years anyway. When he returned to Timbisha Township after graduating, she'd been out of state pursuing her veterinary degree.

He hadn't seen her again until six months ago when she'd been a bridesmaid in Jason and Julie's wedding. All grown up, she'd been elegant but still bashful. Unfortunately, the more he'd poured on the charm during the customary dance between groomsmen and bridesmaids, the further she'd withdrawn from his reach, daring him to win her over.

After the wedding, she'd immediately left home again to finish school and returned two weeks ago when she accepted an offer to work for Timbisha Township's one and only veterinary hospital. He hadn't believed his luck when she'd submitted her application to rent the townhouse from him. Accepting it on the spot, she'd moved in after going over the rental agreement, a document he'd paid little attention to because he'd been too focused on her dark, auburn hair, the light dusting of freckles dotting her nose and cheeks, and violet eyes which almost seemed purple.

Now she lived next door, where she spent a good portion of his day clogging up his mind with images of the two of them dancing together under twinkle lights and around ice sculptures. He couldn't get her out of his head. He was obsessed and it made him feel edgy — and a little creepy.

Melissa is the ultimate challenge.

Josh waited until she started her morning jog before he started his own run. He watched her lock her door and take off around the corner. He tied his shoes and stood. He usually jogged earlier, but the present left on her front porch had delayed both of their morning runs. He didn't like to socialize when *he* ran, so he never bothered her during hers. Jogging cleared his head, so hitting on Melissa during her workout would be hypocritical. Sometimes he followed her at a distance and sometimes he didn't. Either way, they usually made it back home at about the same time. It was in those moments while they caught their breaths, that he cherished. They'd both be coming off their post-run highs, and she seemed happy to smile and talk briefly.

She's just shy.

He'd waited a few minutes before taking off on his own and was now about three blocks behind her. *Just like a stalker.* God, he was pathetic, but the "gift" she'd found had him on alert, and he wanted to make sure she was safe. He usually ran about five miles. He wondered how far she would run today after everything that had happened earlier. He never used the same pattern twice in a row, for safety's sake, and was relieved Melissa exercised the same caution, especially in light of this morning's potential threat.

He wondered a lot about Melissa.

While his eyes enjoyed the lovely bounce of her soft behind, his mind was stuck on the box of chocolates. Was it just a prank sent to goose Jarod for breaking up the meth ring last fall? Josh had no answers, but he'd make damn sure Melissa stayed safe on his watch, which didn't make him a stalker at all.

He hoped.

By his calculation, they'd run almost two miles when something caught Melissa's attention. She veered off the road down into a ditch and out of sight. He immediately picked up his pace and sprinted to the point where she'd disappeared from view. As he got closer, he heard a low growl followed by Melissa's melodic voice quietly telling a small creature everything was going to be okay.

"What is it?" he asked quietly, not wanting to spook woman nor beast.

Judging by her raised eyebrows, his appearance had

surprised her. She pointed into the culvert. "It's a kitten, about six months old. Looks like it's hurt."

He ambled down into the ditch and, sure enough, a mangy orange cat with its leg twisted at a weird angle hissed and spit at Melissa.

"Need some help?"

"Um. Actually, yes. I've got a dozen boxes in my garage. Do you mind getting one? I'll stay here with the kitten and try to make friends. I don't like the look of that leg."

"No problem. I'll be right back." He ran to their complex, getting in a good sprint to finish off his jog. Glad to be her landlord, he quickly keyed the garage code, grabbed an empty box, and then headed for his pickup. He'd been gone under fifteen minutes but in that time she had, indeed, made friends with the kitten. It was curled up in her lap, crooked leg and all, while Melissa stroked its fur.

"Oh, thank you," she said when he handed her the box. With gentle precision, she secured the mangy creature inside the container and then gracefully stood up, looking at him expectantly.

"Where are we taking him?" he asked as he helped her out of the ditch and to his waiting pickup.

"Uh," she began, looking unsure, "I already called Doc Brown. I start work at the clinic tomorrow morning, but until then I'd like to take it home, if it's all right with you? I'll pay an extra pet deposit."

"Don't give it another thought," he reassured her. "This little guy needs our help. Besides, I trust you."

"Thank you," she said with a relieved smile. "I have a feeling the poor thing has been out here alone for quite some time. I don't know how it's managed to survive with its hind leg twisted so badly." She murmured the last part to herself.

Josh nodded while assisting her into the passenger seat and then placed the box on her lap. She was being uncharacteristically confident. She'd always been shy, but it seemed animals were the key to her heart. He made a mental note of this new information as he closed her door and headed for the driver's side.

"Excited about working with Doc?" he asked once they were on their way back home.

"Yeah. Doc's the reason I wanted to be a veterinarian," she said a bit wistfully.

"You specifically came back to work with him, right?"

She hesitated a moment, making him wonder again about the box of chocolates, before she smiled, "Yes. Of course, that's why I'm here."

Hmmm. She had a secret she didn't want to tell. Josh could spot a fibber a mile away, and now his curiosity was piqued. "Are you sure? Because there for a second it sounded like you weren't," he teased.

When she glanced his way, he saw her guard come up, and the awkwardness returned in a flash. He felt it like a slap. She was shutting him out again.

"Melissa," he began as he pulled into the driveway, but she ended the conversation before he could finish.

"Thank you for the help."

She quickly opened the door and jumped out, barely waiting for him to shift into park. Without a backward glance, she darted for her townhouse, keeping a tight hold on the box. She was inside before he could say goodbye.

Damn it. He'd felt the beginnings of a connection while she helped the animal, but as soon as he turned on the charm she bolted.

He hoped to figure her out soon because now that she was

back—all grown up and living next door — he wanted to get to know her a whole lot better.

He knew women better than either of his brothers. Grim determination took hold as he plotted his strategy. If he couldn't get past her skittish ways, no one else could.

He'd get her to go out with him by the end of the week or his name wasn't Josh King.

CHAPTER 2
Anxiety

Missy's mind ran on a continuous loop all night, leaving her exhausted the next morning. Dreams of orange Oompa Loompas with deformed legs injecting poison into candy intermingled with the vision of Josh in his running gear flitted from frame to frame. His skintight sleeveless tank showed off washboard abs. She'd counted eight through the white moisture-wicking material. She sighed heavily as she stared into her closet while trying to decide which color scrubs to put on for her first day of work.

A rustling caught her attention. Two amber eyes blinked at Missy from under the covers. The orange kitten had finally settled in after singing the song of its people until three in the morning. Missy had given in to her guest's needs by letting it sleep with her on the bed. Now, a loud purr ground through the bedroom, sounding like a Harley engine trying to turn over in the dead of winter.

"You're quite the personality, aren't you, Ginger?"

The kitten answered by licking its front paw in preparation

for a leisurely grooming, even though Missy had given her a bath the night before.

Just as Missy pulled her shirt over her head, the doorbell rang. Wondering who it could be so early in the morning, she jogged down the stairs to the front door. A glance through the peephole revealed Josh standing expectantly on her front porch, lady-killer smile in place. Though it thrilled her to see him, she was already running late because of the kitten's shenanigans the evening before.

Taking a deep breath to still her shaking hands, she opened her front door leaving the outer glass door locked in place. "Good morning, Josh." In her head she sounded sure of herself, but in reality it came out a whisper.

Stupid nerves.

"Hey, Melissa. Just wanted to see how you and the kitten are doing. Everything okay? You didn't jog this morning."

How could a man be so handsome? she thought to herself. *And kind?* She had little experience with men, other than Harold, and he was neither thoughtful nor kind. Just annoying.

"Everything is great." *There, that sounded more confident.*

"You're my first renter and well, after what happened yesterday, I thought I should check on you." He wore a concerned expression which reminded her of Marguerite.

The thump-thump in her chest preceded the flush crawling up her neck. Mustering up what little confidence she had, she replied, "Thank you for helping out with everything yester-day." She swallowed thickly. "I'm sorry, but I've got to run. I'm late for my first day at the clinic." Mentally she patted herself on the back. Most of the words coming out of her mouth actu-ally had some voice to them instead of a stupid whisper.

A crinkle hung over those gorgeous blue eyes. "Oh, sorry!

I'd better let you get going then. Please don't forget to call me if you need anything." He gave a mock solute and sauntered back to his townhouse.

Ensconced in a pair of well-worn jeans, Missy let her eyes linger on his behind, before she closed the door, turned the deadbolt, and let out the breath she was holding.

Josh King was a player.

Her experience with Harold had left her on guard against certain types of men. Time would tell if Josh proved to be someone she should avoid.

She returned upstairs to finish getting ready, trying to calm her nerves, which were frayed over her first day. Doc hired her on the spot after graduation. Lucky to have an in with the local vet in her hometown, she found working with animals, even large beasts with terrible attitudes, a lot safer than some humans. Animals didn't put her on edge—the people she'd need to interact with in order to help their pets, did.

It was times like these she really envied her vivacious big sister. Marguerite could handle herself in any social situation with grace and confidence, whereas Missy would rather stick her head in the sand.

Pushing aside her personal issues, she finished braiding her hair and wrapped the end in a cloth-covered hair tie, the tips touching the waistband of her jeans. She didn't wear makeup — that was more her sister's style — but today she wanted to show an effort in her appearance. She quickly drew a thin, dark line on her upper lid at her eyelash border and then brushed a few strokes of mascara over her lashes. It wasn't much, but it made her strange violet eyes appear normal.

Satisfied with the purple scrubs she'd picked out for the day and double-checking nothing was out of place, she picked up the box containing the kitten, grabbed her keys, and headed for the garage. She'd chosen this rental complex because each unit came with a single-car garage, which was rare in a small town. The rent was low but, in truth, it was her uncle who'd negotiated a great deal on the unit. He was the head of security for King Construction and James King's personal bodyguard. When she'd announced she was coming back to Timbisha Township, Uncle Dane worked out a deal with Josh, and all she'd had to do was sign the contract.

A beautiful June sun brightened the clear blue sky as she drove through town to begin her veterinary career. Trees lush with green leaves lined sidewalks, and spring bulbs had made way for roses, petunias, and marigolds to decorate window boxes in the town square. She checked her dash thermometer. It read 81. It would make ninety degrees by midday. She rolled her window down, letting a smile play on her lips as the fresh air blew her braid back and forth. The kitten sat in the box on the passenger seat, enjoying the sunshine as well, with sleepy eyes and a contented look on its furry face.

Dr. Brown ran the Timbisha Township Veterinary Clinic located in a square, plain building on the other side of the fairgrounds. It offered small-animal care in the hospital and on-call services to the local ranchers and farmers in the area who kept livestock. Abner Brown, better known as Doc (because the familiarized version of his name is Abby, and he'd just as soon shoot you as be called by a woman's name), was nearing retirement age and looking for someone from the community to take his place when the time came.

For now, Missy would be working in the office helping with... well, everything. If she was apprenticing to eventually take over the hospital, Doc had reckoned she should know all of the ins and outs of the business, and she had agreed with him. Today she'd be working with the office staff, establishing a rapport with his clients, hence her nervousness.

People just weren't her thing.

She parked in the back parking lot, as instructed prior to coming to work, and entered through the back door, which put her in the middle of the kennels. A dog barked from one of the cages and some rustling came from another. Her current patient, whom Missy cuddled in her arms, looked around warily but otherwise made no complaints.

She peeked at the barking dog, which turned out to be a young pup of neutering age. His tongue lolled to one side, and he whined his greeting when she showed him her face. He thumped his tail a few times before she headed toward the front of the hospital. It was early. The doors to the public wouldn't open for another hour, but the staff had already gathered.

"Ah, here she is," Doc said as Missy made her way to the staff gathered in a semicircle behind the client counter. "Everyone, I'd like to introduce our new veterinarian, Melissa Theroux. As you know, she'll be shadowing you this morning before we ease her into the exam rooms. And I see she's already brought us some business."

There was a round of hellos from the group, but when Doc eyed the kitten with a raised eyebrow, Missy was reminded she had the first patient of the day. She squared her shoulders and explained the situation as professionally as possible.

Doc gave a cursory exam of the kitten before determining it should be placed in the back. "Any empty kennel will do, and then I'll give you a full tour of the facilities."

Missy hurried to find an open kennel. It was hard to leave the kitten in a cold, steel cage, and she was given baleful eyes and a defiant meow for her effort. Once the kitten burrowed into the towel from the box, Missy felt marginally better leaving her alone. When she returned to the front office, a woman roughly the same age as Doc stood up to shake her hand. "Hi, I'm Doc's wife, Gale. It's a pleasure to meet you, Melissa."

Missy automatically took Gale's hand, surprising herself, not at all nervous. "Nice to meet you, Gale."

Introductions were made around the room. By the time the office doors opened for the public, she felt a little more confident. She made a note to herself to get her sister a gift for all of her coaching the past few months. Being socially awkward in a small town was an inconvenience at best and a curse at worst, but Missy was determined to overcome her anxiety once and for all. Her career depended on it.

JOSH TURNED DOWN THE DIRT ROAD LEADING UP TO Jason's property. Each of the King brothers had been given a section of their family's estate to be used as a homestead when he was ready to settle down. The oldest brother, Jarod, had no plans to use his plot of land, preferring to stay in the estate house. He lived in the newly renovated penthouse suite with his wife, Lauren, and their five-year-old daughter, Jessica. Lauren was expecting a baby in the fall. Josh had made sure there was plenty of room in the new suite for the growing family. Construction was the family business. Making renovations and additions to the estate were a dime a dozen.

Jason, the middle King brother, married Josh's longtime friend, Julie. They were expecting their first baby in July, and Jason was eager to get the house finished before their little King was born. Much to the family's chagrin, they'd opted to find out the sex of the baby but not reveal it to anyone until the birth. Their mother, Camille, was having a fit over the decision, which only appealed to Josh's impish sense of humor.

He stopped at the fence, got out, and swung the heavy metal gate open before returning to the pickup to move through. He'd have to talk to his father about replacing the gate with a cattle guard. He couldn't see Julie, once the baby was born, having to fight with it while taking care of an infant.

After he wrestled the gate closed and resumed his trek up the gentle slope to Jason's home, some purple prairie flax caught his eye. The color immediately reminded him of Missy's amazing eyes. They weren't technically purple but more of a violet hue. He'd be damned, though, if there weren't days when they were as purple as that summer prairie flax.

Maybe her eyes changed with her moods?

Or the color of her clothes?

The seasons?

Hell, he didn't know about such things, but what he did know was her eyes were strange and beautiful and just another mystery which made Melissa unique.

He rolled to a stop at the log used as a parking block and shut off the engine. Jason yelled from somewhere in the house, and his voice carried into the cab of the now quiet truck. Apparently, he was already on site terrorizing the crew. Josh tapped on the front door's frame before he stepped into the large entry of the newly constructed house. Jason was mean-mugging the electrician, who stubbornly stuck to his story. Josh could see the sparks begin to fly before he stepped between the two men.

"Jason, we've got it covered. Matt, make sure your men have the plans for the outlets. If they don't, I've got another copy with me."

"Fine, Josh. Tell your brother we are on schedule and keep him out of my hair."

Jason moved forward. "Why I ought to..."

But once again, Josh blocked his brother's progress. "Back off, Jason. Come with me. Now." He kept eye contact with Jason, knowing that backing down from him would be a mistake. When Jason finally met his stare with a stony one of his own, he relaxed his shoulders. "Yeah, fine. What do you have for me?"

He drew Jason to the other side of the house and smiled. "Nothing. I just don't want you to kill the only electrician around for a hundred miles."

"I'm not going to kill him, Josh. I'm trying to motivate him into finishing before my kids are born."

Josh laughed. "He'll be finished before Julie gives birth to this one, Jason, let alone to your future kids. No need to exaggerate."

His crazy brother grunted before they heard a loud crash.

"Oh, what now?" Jason groaned. Josh followed him outside where a delivery truck hauling windows was parked. Broken shards of glass glinted everywhere in the bright sunshine, and a man was bleeding from his forearm.

"What happened?" Jason snapped as Josh pulled his cell phone from his pocket. The blood gushing from the man's arm was no little thing, and he'd need to go to the emergency room. Josh wanted to make sure the hospital knew he was coming. Jason helped them get the injured worker into a vehicle, griping the whole time about incompetence and the lack of work ethics in America. Josh was sure the men were more afraid of Jason's mood than the blood gushing all over the cab of the work truck.

"I think I hired the Keystone Cops to build my house instead of professionals," Jason muttered.

"They aren't that bad, you're just a prickly ass these days. How's Julie doing?"

"She's tired. She can barely fit in that damn food truck she insists on working in every day."

"And you're letting her?" Josh had known Julie forever. She could be reasonable most of the time. Then again, she was pretty damn stubborn, just like Jason.

"I have to. If I say anything, she bursts into tears. I'm kind of done with the baby hormones. They've taken over my Jujyfruit. I want my wife back."

Josh could only grin. Julie had been increasingly difficult lately due to the size of her belly and the swelling of her ankles, which he'd heard her complain about for the last two weeks.

"Let's go over these plans so you can get home to her. I need to meet up with Dad in thirty minutes anyway."

Josh explained his recent ideas to make things easier for Julie and the baby, including the installation of a cattle guard. The conversation took longer than either of them had planned, but when they were finally done, Josh had to roll the windows up in his truck so the dirt clouding from Jason's speeding truck didn't choke him to death on the way back to the main road.

AT NOON, MARGUERITE BREEZED INTO THE veterinary hospital looking overdressed in a red blazer and pencil skirt with matching stilettos. Thankfully, her poster girl smile was enough to wash away Missy's embarrassment over what had occurred earlier in the office.

After taking a new patient's information for a sick cat, Missy unintentionally mentioned to the pet's owner that the cat may need to be put to sleep. The woman proceeded to cry, which also put the animal in additional distress. Gale had quickly taken both the client and the cat into an examination room to wait for Doc, who later lectured Missy on the importance of keeping her medical opinions to herself before performing a thorough examination. He'd then sent her out to walk the puppy which had been neutered the night before. That should've bolstered her spirits, except she'd ended up fighting with the waste baggies, spilling them to the ground and accidentally stepping in the puppy's deposit.

Marguerite's smile was infinitely better than dog poop.

"Are you ready for lunch? My treat."

"Yes. Need to grab my purse and I'll meet you out back." Missy left the front office, took her bag from the hook next to the back door, and stepped into the hot, fresh air. As she reached for her lip balm, a sporty red convertible came around the building, stopping in front of her. Missy hopped into the passenger seat and Marguerite hit the accelerator. Her sister soon had them parked at Molly's Diner.

"I hope this is all right with you. I have a hankering for a veggie melt," Marguerite said with relish as she gracefully got out of the car.

Missy admired her sister, the Lady in Red, grateful Marguerite had rescued her from her professional failures. "Anything is good because I'm starving."

Molly's was a local diner boasting a U-shaped counter surrounding an open kitchen in the center of the building, with booths lining the outer three walls of plate glass windows. It had been remodeled many times over the decades, but each time retained the feel of the original décor. It was now decorated in blue vinyl with white piping, and chrome-and-white Formica counter tops.

They found seats at the counter surrounding the grill. Before their tushes had time to warm up the vinyl-covered stools, their orders were taken and two iced teas were placed in front of them.

The sisters discussed what the next step would be in their mother's treatment, which put a damper on the day. Changing the subject before either of them broke down and cried, Marguerite asked, "So? How has your morning gone?"

Missy explained the day's events in detail from her most recent embarrassment to this morning's interaction with Josh. By the time she'd finished her tale their order arrived.

"Uncle Dane got me a great deal on the townhouse, but I'm not sure I want to live that close to Josh King, let alone have him as my landlord."

Marguerite stared at her for a moment.

"Why ever not?"

How could she explain her feelings to a vixen like her sister? Marguerite wouldn't understand because she was so self-assured. Missy liked Josh, but she just didn't know how to act around him and it made her uncomfortable.

"He's too nice," she said miserably.

"And good looking," Marguerite added.

"Yeah," Missy agreed on a sigh. "There's that."

"Look, not every man is like that creep you had to file a restraining order against." Marguerite took a drink of her tea. "Out of all three King boys, Josh is the sweetest. You could do worse than having a rich, good-looking guy as your landlord. Besides, he really does like you. I can tell." Marguerite winked for emphasis.

"He's okay, I guess," Missy mumbled.

"For heaven's sake, Missy. Josh isn't the type of man to take advantage of his tenant. Unlike your professor, Harold Klein, slimeball," she muttered the last.

"I don't want to talk about this." Missy held up a hand to terminate the conversation.

"Well, not every man is a possessive liar who harasses young women, especially not *Josh*." Marguerite declared the last bit with finality before she picked up her veggie melt and took a hearty bite.

It was Missy's turn to change the subject. "How do you like being Jarod's secretary now that all your undercover informant business is over? Has he forgiven you?"

A few months prior, their uncle enlisted Marguerite as an informant for an FBI task force to uncover the drug ring which had been plaguing Timbisha Township. Sheriff King hadn't appreciated being left out of the loop. In order to gain trust, Marguerite sullied her reputation in order to get the information they'd needed. According to Marguerite, one of Jarod's deputies had been involved, and Jarod was still upset about not recognizing what had been happening right under his nose.

"Jarod, Lauren, and I have an understanding," Marguerite explained. "If we all behave in a professional manner and keep our personal business to ourselves, everything will work out fine. So far it has, and Jarod even asked me where I was headed for lunch today, which surprised me. When I said I was meeting you, he asked me to tell you hello. That's progress, isn't it?" Marguerite raised her perfectly plucked eyebrow.

"Please tell him I said hello back," Missy chuckled, pleased her sister's professional relationships were on the mend, but she declined mentioning Jarod had already broken the rules regarding Marguerite's personal business by asking where she was going for lunch.

Just as Missy began to dig into her own sandwich, Josh and his father, James King, sat down at the counter to their right. All of Missy's new confidence fled her the moment she heard Josh's voice. She risked a glance in their direction and immediately got snared by his dazzling blue eyes. He seemed as surprised to see her as she was to see him.

"Hello, ladies," he said with a wink and his infamous lady-killer smile.

"Hey, Josh," her sister lilted. Marguerite was as big a flirt as Josh, and most people mistook her confidence for arrogance, which sometimes broke Missy's heart.

Other times, Marguerite asked for it.

Missy gave him a weak smile before focusing on her grilled ham and cheese. Unfortunately, the sandwich now made her stomach churn. She picked at some fries and tried to pretend Josh wasn't there, which turned out to be impossible because Marguerite struck up a conversation with the two men.

"I've been hearing rumors about this place, Mr. King. Is it true you're trying to buy Molly's now that Derek Lawlor is facing bankruptcy and jail time?"

Missy rolled her eyes. Her sister was such a buttinsky, but to Missy's surprise, Mr. King smiled.

"Yes. King Construction had been under contract with Lawlor to renovate the establishment. Since my company already completed a large portion of the work, it seemed like a waste of manpower to leave it unfinished. Besides, Molly's is a landmark. So the paperwork's come through, and you are now speaking to the joint owners of Molly's Diner and Casino."

"Joint owners?"

"I'm partnering with Josh," Mr. King said proudly.

"So it's true? Molly's sign will come down?"

Josh shook his head. "We met with the town council. The

old sign will have to come down because it no longer meets code. However, since Molly's is so well known, we don't want to risk losing her customer base. The new up-to-code sign will be a replica of the original, only adding the word 'casino' to the establishment's name."

"Look at you, Josh King. With the two townhouses, and now Molly's Diner, you're becoming quite the real estate mogul in Timbisha Township. Any other ventures to add to your bachelor status?" Marguerite shamelessly flirted and, for reasons Missy didn't want to examine too closely, she didn't like it one bit.

Josh only smiled, looking truly humble. "No, nothing at this time. My family keeps me so busy with our various projects and renovations that I'll barely have time to work on Molly's, which is why we're doing this jointly."

Mr. King said nothing, but Missy didn't miss the unmistakable look of pride on his face. Then Josh claimed Missy's attention, making her stomach drop and the food on her plate completely unpalatable. "How's our kitten doing? Any news?"

"*Our* kitten?" Marguerite asked. "You and Josh got a kitten together?"

"No, *we* didn't get a kitten. I found it while I was jogging yesterday. I thought her leg was broken, but Doc did x-rays and it's a birth defect. She's getting her vaccinations today, and then I can take Ginger home."

"Ginger?" Josh's smile was radiant and filled the coffee shop with sunshine, almost making her lose her breath. "'Cuz she's orange, right? I approve," he said, raising his cup to her.

"Yeah. Only twenty percent of orange cats are female and I wanted her name to reflect that fact." Missy blushed but needed to secure Ginger's living arrangements. "It's okay if I bring her back to the townhouse, isn't it? I'd really like to keep her, and I'll pay a pet deposit, if you'd like."

"Tell you what. I'll waive the pet deposit on one condition."

Missy swallowed. "What's the condition?"

"That you let me visit her whenever I like," he said with a wink.

"Th-thank you." Missy turned to Marguerite. "Uh, I think it's time for me to go back to work now." Marguerite threw her an understanding look and paid the check. Relieved, Missy stood.

"Goodbye gentlemen. See you next time," Marguerite sing-songed as they walked out the door to her sporty convertible.

CHAPTER 3
Unscrambled

J osh tapped the remote clipped to his visor as he made the turn into his driveway. The last of the sun's burning rays had just been doused by the western mountains, and stars were beginning to blink in the eastern sky. As the earth cooled, the desert air filled with the scents of hardy sage brush and barbecue grills. June was usually too warm to cook indoors, so most folks in Timbisha Township were inclined to have their dinners outside. Josh usually ate with his family at the King Estate, but tonight he'd worked on the plans for the casino renovation well past dinner time. He also wanted to check on his tenant.

Every window in the townhouse next door was lit. When he'd checked on Melissa this morning, moving boxes still filled her front room, even though she'd been living there for two weeks. Remembering those boxes made him wonder if Jarod had discovered anything about the weird package left on her front porch.

Maybe she needed help unpacking? Personally, he was a little OCD. Living out of boxes for two days — let alone two weeks — would've driven him to the funny farm. But helping with the care of her ailing mother, preparing for a new job, and now the kitten to tend to, Josh reasoned Melissa hadn't had time to put everything away. It couldn't be easy for her living in such disarray.

Yeah, he needed to help her get organized.

Having made the decision to see her again, he wasted no time with a quick shower and an even faster primp. When he was done, he ran back downstairs and swiped a bottle of red wine from the kitchen counter, not wanting to arrive empty-handed since he was showing up uninvited. Helping her unpack would be the perfect opportunity to get to know her better, but he had a backup plan in case she refused to let him inside — encourage her to talk about Ginger as she seemed comfortable discussing animals.

This plan better work.

From her front porch, he could see directly into the living room through the storm door. She wasn't downstairs, so he rang the bell. He heard her yelp and then some clattering from above before her loud footsteps tromped down the staircase.

Long legs and bare feet were the first things his eyes landed on as she stepped off the bottom tread of the stairs. He'd already broken out in a cold sweat before she stood there in a t-shirt, and shorts emphasizing those sleek stems.

He'd always thought of her as willowy, but *damn*. She was taller than most of the women he knew, around five feet ten inches. He was only a head taller, and he remembered how they'd fit together perfectly while sharing their wedding dance. Her thick auburn hair was in a jumbled pile on top of her head, instead of the usual French braid she seemed to favor. Loose tendrils teased her face, curling at her temples and sticking to a fine sheen of perspiration dotting her forehead. Her eyes widened in alarm when she recognized him through the storm door. Tonight their strange color had a bluer tint, matching the color of her shirt.

Unfortunately, the anxiety on her face reminded him of a panicked filly. He raised the bottle of wine. "Can I come in?" She looked around as if to seek help, making him wonder what had happened in her past to make her so jumpy. He'd known her forever, for heaven's sake. She had to know he wasn't a deranged lunatic. "I thought you might need some help unpacking — and I wanted to see Ginger," he rushed to say.

Bingo.

At the mention of the kitten, she straightened her shoulders and reached for the door handle. "Sorry. Yes, of course. I wasn't expecting anyone." Her voice was quiet, almost a whisper, but as she opened the door for him, she cleared her throat and asked, "How was your day?"

"Long," he answered. "Have you eaten?"

She raised her surprised eyebrows even further. "No, I must've lost track of the time. Have you?"

"Nope." He glanced at the boxes scattered around the living room. "I think a pizza is in order. I'll call Pizza Factory and have one delivered. What kind do you like?"

"Any kind of pizza is my favorite," she said with a smile.

A smile! Definitely making progress.

"I'll surprise you, then. While we wait, where do you want to start with these boxes?"

"Honestly, I have no clue, which is why they're still full," she said with disgust. "I hadn't realized I'd accumulated so much stuff while I was at school."

"How about the kitchen? Is everything unpacked in there or does it need work?"

"Needs work. I think all the kitchen boxes are stacked in

there already. If you want to start, I can go through these." She indicated the pile stacked in the living room. "Are you sure you don't mind?"

"Not one bit. I'll order dinner and then tackle the kitchen."

She excused herself and jogged back up the stairs. He watched her disappear before hitting the Pizza Factory number on speed dial on his cell phone. He ordered a large combination pizza for delivery, and because he was extra hungry tonight, he also got an order of chicken wings and a two-liter bottle of cola to wash it all down. When he put his cell phone back in his pocket, he began opening up boxes marked with a *K*.

Because this unit mirrored his own floorplan, he put her things away in the same places where he'd put his own: drinking glasses in the cupboard next to the sink, silverware in the drawer below that, etc., but she was only upstairs for a few minutes before returning with the kitten under her arm. It had been bathed and purred happily.

"How's she doing?"

Melissa smiled. "Ginger's doing great. Doc and I talked about it, and amputation of the deformed limb is an option, but I'd like to wait and see how she gets around before putting her through a procedure like that."

"Can she walk on it?" Josh asked, concerned the poor creature might have to have surgery.

"Pretty well. Here, I'll show you." She set Ginger on the floor. The kitten looked up at both of them for a minute and then limped to a bowl Melissa had designated as a water dish.

"She was probably dumped out in the ditch because of the deformity. I'm surprised she's so friendly." Josh squatted down to give the kitten a soft stroke down her back. Ginger immediately started purring, a rough sound reminding him of his ski boat, and wove herself around and between his feet while he was in his precarious position. He gently picked her up to prevent the unthinkable. She weighed less than a pound. Then he stood and cradled her in the crook of his arms, feeling the rumble of her purring against him.

"She likes you," Melissa said, sounding a little surprised.

"Of course she does. What's not to like?" He smiled as Melissa blushed a pretty pink.

When the doorbell rang signaling the pizza had arrived, he sauntered over to the door.

"I caught your shift, huh?" Josh asked the kid holding his dinner, grinning ear to ear. "I guess you'll expect a large tip."

Charlie laughed. "I don't expect anything, Josh. Cute kitten." Charlie Armstrong was Julie's little brother. The Kings had helped Julie raise Charlie when Mr. and Mrs. Armstrong were killed in a car accident six years ago. Julie had just barely been able to support herself and her brother, but with the emotional support of Josh's family, the boy had grown up strong. The eighteen-year-old now lived with the rest of the family at the King Estate.

Josh opened the door for Charlie, directing him through the maze of boxes to the kitchen where he placed the food on the counter. "Hey, Missy!"

"Hey, Charlie." Melissa returned his smile with one of her own. "What are your plans now that you've graduated high school?"

"I've been accepted to the University of Nevada. So I'll be heading to Reno in the fall."

"What are you studying?"

"I'm undeclared for now. I'll take all my prerequisite classes before I decide, but I've narrowed it down to either animal husbandry or criminal justice," he said with a chuckle.

Josh gave Charlie a pat on the back, then bro-hugged his shoulders. "My man here received a full ride scholarship. We couldn't be prouder."

"Congratulations, Charlie!"

"Thanks." He seemed to be embarrassed and began to back away from them toward the door. "Good to see you, Missy. You're my last delivery so I'm heading home."

Missy smiled at Charlie's embarrassment. She remembered when she'd gotten so much praise for her scholarship. She hadn't wanted to be the center of attention, either. She caught Josh's look of pride before she opened the door for the young man.

"Drive home safely, Charlie. Tell your sister I said hello."

"Will do, Missy." He yelled into the townhouse, "See you later, Josh!"

"Back at ya, kid," Josh answered around a mouthful of pizza.

"I think you embarrassed him," Missy said as she shut the door and followed the drool-worthy scent of pizza back to the kitchen.

Josh turned the box around revealing a fine pie loaded with all kinds of goodies. Missy closed her eyes and hummed, "Combo?"

"Yup. No anchovies, though. I hope you aren't disappointed."

"I only like anchovies in my Caesar dressing."

"Agreed." He rummaged through a paper sack and retrieved a carton of hot wings and some soda pop.

"I don't think I have any paper plates."

"No worries, we'll eat right out of the box. They supplied us with napkins, red pepper packets, and parmesan cheese. Oh, and I found your glasses... here." He set two on the counter and began to pour some fizzy brown liquid into each one.

Watching him move about her kitchen, Missy was overcome with the strangest feeling of comfort. She'd never felt anything like it, not even with her college roommate. It was like he belonged in her kitchen. Josh's reputation as a ladies' man around Timbisha Township should've been enough to warn her away, but tonight she felt strangely at ease with him. *Maybe it's Ginger's fault*, Missy wondered as the kitten continued to weave in between Josh's feet. She giggled when Josh stumbled for the third time while doing the cat waltz. Ginger seemed to be leading the dance.

Without permission, she heard herself ask, "Who are you dating these days?"

Holy hell, where did that come from?

Of course, the cad smiled at her as if pleased by her question. "No one at the moment. How about you?"

She shook her head. "Not enough time to date." She had a career to focus on and her mom to worry about.

Men to avoid, she thought with chagrin. She had no time for romance.

"There's always time to make friends, Melissa," he said quietly before taking another bite of pizza. She stared while he chewed, fascinated by the small muscles working in his jaw and then in his throat as he swallowed.

She hadn't realized she was staring until he said, "Like what you see, honey?"

Embarrassment took control and sweat beaded on her forehead as the telltale blush bloomed from her neck to her hair. She quickly turned away, not wanting him to see how flustered he made her. Anger wasn't far behind as she realized she had no clue what she was doing socializing with Timbisha Township's most sought-after bachelor.

"Hey," he said, concern in his voice, "Melissa, I'm just teasing. I didn't mean to offend you."

Honest to God, he sounded like he meant it. Of course, she was being silly, which embarrassed her more. Why couldn't she be more like Marguerite, or her ex-roommate who had helped her through so much while being away from home? She fought the uncontrolled tears forming in her eyes and used a napkin to buy her some time to get a grip. Mustering up confidence she didn't possess, she whispered, "You didn't offend me."

He briefly patted her shoulder, making things worse because his touch sent her body into an electrified spiral. "Are you sure?"

"Mm-hm," was all she could get out.

He studied her for a second until he finally asked, "How's the food?"

Grateful for the subject change, she smiled. "Pizza Factory is always good. Thank you for thinking of it."

There was a loud meow from the other side of the bar, followed by the sound of a bowl being swatted around on the linoleum. "I guess Ginger's hungry, too," Josh said with a laugh. The kitten limped around the empty bowl, swatting it every few seconds. Missy chuckled at her before putting a scoop of dry food in the dish. The purring began immediately, only stopping when Ginger dug into her dinner.

"She'll be right as rain in no time with an appetite like that," Josh said.

"Do you have pets?"

"Not in town," he said. "We had lots of animals growing up. There's more room on The Estate and someone's always around. I'm not home enough to care for it properly here. It wouldn't be right to keep one with the hours I work."

"No, it wouldn't, would it?" she murmured to herself while staring at Ginger. Maybe she should find a good home for the kitten, but it had been lovely having another soul in the house at night, and Ginger was really good in the car. Maybe she should talk to Doc about bringing the kitten to work with her on a daily basis.

"Don't worry about her, Melissa. Between me, you, and the clinic, she's going to have lots of company. I'm sure Doc would let her hang out there once she's had all her shots." Not only was Josh a mind reader, but he seemed confident it would work out. She hoped so.

"Well!" Josh suddenly clapped his hands, rubbing them together. "These boxes aren't going to empty themselves, are they?"

She chuckled despite everything. "No, they're not." She opened a box and began handing him some pots and pans.

MISSY AND GINGER RODE IN SILENCE TO THE Timbisha Township Animal Hospital, both enjoying the warm breeze and warmer sunshine, a routine they'd formed in the past week. Doc had declared Ginger to be in good health considering her abandonment. She was treated for parasites and dosed with a round of vaccines. She seemed to be functioning fine with the deformed leg, so surgery wasn't a priority at this point. Both girls were satisfied with life.

And then there was Josh.

He'd also become a part of Missy's daily routine. She could count on seeing his handsome face daily for their morning jog. He made their runs seem coincidental, but Missy knew otherwise.

She parked her Jeep in the usual spot. She struggled to unlock the back door while holding Ginger and not letting her bags drop from her shoulder to her elbow. Finally, she stepped into the kennels and said hello to the newest patient, a Rottweiler who'd gotten into a tussle with a porcupine. Luckily, the owner intervened before there was too much damage, but the poor beast had needed some stitches placed in his sweet face.

The dog wiggled his tailless butt and panted happily at her in greeting. Ginger became mute in her arms, pressing herself closer to Missy's body. "Don't you like dogs, Ginger?" The kitten blinked wide eyes at Missy before her motorboat purr started up again.

"Good morning, Missy."

"Good morning, Gale," she answered, feeling more comfortable with the staff every day.

"Doc's got a couple of appointments lined up this afternoon at nearby ranches. He'd like you to join him," Gale informed her as she took Ginger from her arms and placed the kitten in a playpen behind the counter. Missy barely contained her grin as Ginger sniffed around the contraption and finally gave a meow of approval.

"Gale, you know she can get out of there, right?"

Gale stared at the kitten for a moment before saying, "Ginger and I have an agreement. She stays in the pen, and I give her attention and a little bit of catnip."

Missy sucked in a breath, appalled. "You do not."

Gale giggled. "No, I don't, but she hasn't tried to escape yet, either. I think she feels safe in there."

"Probably." Missy gave her a grateful smile before pulling a chart from the holder. "Beelzebub?" she called out to the waiting room.

"It's Bebe for short," an elderly woman said, picking up a pet carrier from her feet. As she drew closer, a sinister hiss issued from the cage, followed by a deep yowl.

Missy looked at the chart again. "Is this Bebe's first time here, ma'am?"

Gale snickered behind her computer screen. Missy raised her eyebrows, wary.

"Oh, no, dear. We've been seeing Doc since he was a kitten."

"Huh. Well, what can we do for you today?"

Gale looked up from her computer, all traces of mirth erased from her face. "Vaccinations," was all she said.

"Oh, well, all right. Then come this way and we'll get your Bebe all fixed up," Missy said, leading the way to an exam room.

"Aren't you going to suit up, dear?" the woman asked.

"Suit up?"

"Yes, dear. I wouldn't want you to get hurt like the last newbie Doc hired," she explained as she entered the exam room, leaving Missy horrified in the corridor.

<hr>

"WHAT'S WITH THE BANDAGES, MELISSA?" JOSH asked with concern as he opened her driver's side door.

Missy rolled her eyes. "Hazards of the job, I'm afraid." Bebe turned out to be a true spawn of the devil. After Missy emptied the first-aid cabinet, she'd seen to the rest of her morning appointments. Doc absconded with her at lunchtime, and they'd been visiting area ranches for the past few hours. She was relieved the last call of the day was at the King estate.

Josh gave her a puzzled smile before lifting Ginger from her box on the passenger seat. "I'm glad you brought the kitten. Jessica's been dying to meet her." Then he turned to Doc, who sat in the backseat after having insisted Missy drive to their various calls this afternoon in order to know how to get from ranch to ranch — *as if I haven't grown up around here.*

"We've got the heifer prepared as best we can," Josh told Doc.

Missy was impressed. Josh and Jason had prepared the pen where a cow was laboring. Not all of their calls had been this organized. Doc made his way over to check on things before he said, "Looks like we're just in time, Missy. We need to perform a cesarean or else they'll lose both cow and calf."

Missy had practiced the procedure before and knew what to expect. It would be performed while the heifer stood upright in a squeeze chute. Numbing agents were administered to the area before the surgical incision was made. The tricky part would be getting the calf out safely. Josh and Jason would serve as the muscle needed to remove the calf from its mother when the time came.

"How many of these procedures have you participated in, Missy?" Doc asked while he began to prepare the instruments. The heifer had already been shaved.

"This will be my third."

"Great. Show me where you'll make your incision," he instructed. She pointed out the area. Doc injected the numbing agent and discussed variables while she gloved up. He was going to let her perform the procedure. Missy nodded, trying not to show too much glee at the prospect.

Josh helped her put on her apron while she and Doc conversed, and Jason readied the chains for the calf. Everyone seemed to understand what was about to happen.

When it was time, Doc handed her the scalpel. With little fanfare, she made her cuts, first through the dermis, and then the uterine wall, careful not to damage the calf inside. Completing her incisions, she reached inside to find a hoof. Jason was ready with the chain while Doc guided them through the procedure as they went.

Jason stepped onto the rail of the chute for leverage, ready to pull the calf up and out of its womb. Josh stood behind Jason, ready to catch the baby after it cleared the mother's body. When Missy secured the chain, Jason asked, "Ready?"

"Go," Missy said, and the brothers pulled. The poor calf hit the ground with a thud, and Josh immediately dragged it to the front of the chute, where its mother could bond with her baby. The brothers patted the calf, encouraging it to get up.

Meanwhile, Missy began triage of the incision by first closing the uterus with dissolving stitches, then running a long suture down the mother's hide. Within twenty-five minutes of Missy and Doc's arrival, the calf finally stood up on all fours, and both mother and calf were secured in a freshly prepared pen in the barn.

"Well done, Missy," Doc said.

"Thank you," she replied as she removed her gloves and plastic apron. She was on a high, feeling the confidence which only came when she helped animals. It wasn't until Jarod approached with his daughter, Jessica, that the familiar anxiety began to form.

"Looks like it went well," Jarod said. "Come see the new

calf, Darlin'." He set his daughter, who was carrying Ginger, down and led the little dark-haired beauty to the pen.

"What's on Bella's side, Daddy?"

Doc knelt down and explained to Jessica, in children's terms, how the calf had needed to be born. Missy listened to his very simple explanation while she rinsed her apron and began putting the medical instruments back in their cases.

"That was some good work, Dr. Theroux," Jason said, surprising her.

"Thank you," she answered in a shaky voice while Josh helped her store her things. Now that she thought about it, he'd been assisting her the entire time, except for when he helped Jason with the calf.

"She's a natural," Doc called from across the barn. Missy tried hard not to blush, but some things were impossible to control.

Jarod made his way over to them, looking serious. "Have you received anymore gifts from your stalker?"

"I don't have a stalker," Missy mumbled as she loaded Doc's bags into the back of her CRV. Her high had officially been buzz-killed.

"We figured out the jumbled letters. Do you want the message?"

"Quit screwing around with her, Jarod, and just tell us." This from Josh, who looked ready to punch his brother in the face.

Missy stepped between them and sighed. Her need to stop potential violence overshadowed her social anxiety issues. "Yes, please, Sheriff. I want to hear the message." It had been in the back of her mind since she'd found that stupid box.

"'You can never hide from me, Missy,'" Jarod quoted.

"So the chocolates were definitely meant for her." Josh muttered before cursing vehemently under his breath.

"Who would send you that message? Who are you hiding from?" Jarod asked, acting as if she'd done something wrong, and it made her mad.

"I'm not hiding from anyone!" she shouted, losing her temper. Josh put a hand on her shoulder and she moved out of his reach. She didn't appreciate the sheriff's accusatory questions, as if it were somehow her fault someone had tried to poison her. She jerkily finished putting everything away before storming back to the barn for her kitten.

Jarod gently took her arm and spun her around. "The preliminary lab report found animal tranquilizers in the candy, Missy. The fact is, you do have a stalker. It's someone who obviously knows your occupation, and who possibly works around animals or, at the very least, has access to animal medicines."

She remained mute, afraid to say anything. Her mind raced. She didn't know anyone who would do *this*. "If I had a stalker, why would he leave the syringe inside the box, guaranteeing I wouldn't eat the candy?"

Josh and Jarod shared a look. "We don't know," was all Jarod said. "But most stalkers get off on terrorizing their victims. The unsub wants you to be afraid."

"He's succeeding," she whispered.

Jason suddenly appeared with Jessica and Ginger in his arms, and Doc following along. Missy felt a little overwhelmed surrounded by all three brothers at once.

"Hunkle Jase let me pet Ruby," the child announced.

"She's named the calf already," Jason said unnecessarily before a rumbling purr was heard from the kitten. "And she's made a new friend."

Ginger nestled into Jessica's arms, eyelids heavy. "I kept 'er safe," Jessica said. "That's why she likes me so much."

The gentlemen chuckled at the child's pronouncement, putting an end to the dark cloud which had formed around Missy a moment ago.

"Ginger likes to be loved because she didn't get any when she was born," Missy explained. "I think you're very good at giving out love, Jessica."

"She sure is," Jarod said softly. "Let's give the kitten back to her owner, Darlin'."

Jason kissed Jessica's temple, then gently handed over Ginger. Jessica's empty hands went around her Uncle Jason's neck, looking comfortable in the big man's arms. Missy barely contained her sigh. There was just something about a big man holding a child.

"Why all the serious faces?" Doc asked. "Missy did very well, and mother and baby are doing fine."

"You should know Missy has a stalker, Doc. I'd appreciate it if you could accompany her to any visits requested by unfamiliar callers," said Jarod. "I'll also need to ask you and your staff a few questions."

"Now, wait a minute," she argued as all her recent soft feelings vanished into thin air.

Doc held up a hand. "Yes, of course, Jarod." Then he put an arm around Missy's shoulders. "Get used to it. Once these boys take to you, you're in the family for life."

He'd barely finished that shocking sentence when Charlie arrived.

"Char-lee!" Jessica squealed, putting her arms out for the handsome young man.

"Jess-eee," Charlie replied, scooping her from Jason's arms.

"Where did you come from?" Josh asked.

"Camille sent me out to invite Missy and Doc for dinner. Plus, I wanted to check on the heifer."

"She's officially a cow," Jason said with a smart aleck grin.

"Ruby's budahful," Jessica explained as she led Charlie, who'd set the child on the ground, by the hand back into the barn.

"I need to get going," Missy said, walking back to her Jeep.

"Please stay," Josh said. "Jason's putting on some steaks, and I'm sure Julie's got something yummy to go along with it."

"Quit making my wife cook for you, asshole. She needs to stay off her feet," Jason yelled as he sauntered back to the house.

CHAPTER 4
Matchmaker

Josh relaxed when his best friend, now sister-in-law, looped her arm through the crook of his elbow. Lauren struggled to whisper in his ear because her baby bump pushed into his side, preventing her from getting too close.

"You know, I've always liked Missy," she whispered conspiratorially.

"Don't get cute," Josh warned. "Melissa's skittish enough. I don't need you scaring her off."

Lauren leaned back to get a good look at his face. "You do realize you're the only person in this town who uses her given name."

Josh narrowed his eyes. "So?"

Lauren, being the sassy-pants she was, narrowed her eyes back. "So... either you don't know her well enough to call her Missy, or you're trying to get her attention. Which is it?" She raised an eyebrow for effect.

Josh pressed his lips together, debating whether he should tell her. "Do you remember Mom's Yorkie?"

Lauren nodded, rolling her hand for him to hurry up and get to the point.

"Her name was Missy, and the damn thing yapped constantly."

Lauren burst out laughing. "You won't call her by her nickname because it reminds you of the dog?"

"Yup."

"Well, you're right. Missy is no dog. Her sister, on the other hand, could be described as a female dog, but I won't go there."

Josh rolled his eyes. "Please don't. Dane's in the house, and I know your opinion of his niece hurts his feelings."

Lauren folded her arms with a pout. Josh noticed the perspiration on her temples and led her to some shade under the pergola where wisteria vines, thick with green leaves, covered the steel structure. A few purple blooms still hung here and there, despite it being the middle of June. Nevada's growing season was often thrown off by harsh springs and late frosts. Established plants, like this wisteria, often acclimated themselves, blooming whenever the hell they felt like it. A warm breeze lifted one of her blonde tendrils, and Lauren stuck it behind her ear. "How long have you had a crush on Missy?" she asked quietly.

Josh wasn't willing to admit how he felt about Melissa Theroux. He always got the girl in the end, but maybe with this girl, he'd gone about things the wrong way.

Lauren gave him a kiss on the cheek, startling him. "Jeez, Josh, you should've said something sooner. We could've been commiserating together all these years," she said with a chuckle. "Me over Jarod and you over Missy."

"Fuzzy slippers and wine coolers while we did each other's hair and makeup? I love you, Sassy, but no thanks."

Lauren punched him in the arm. "I'm totally insulted right

now. You should know I take my frustrations out at the firing range."

Surprised by her outburst, he gave her a quick hug. "You're right. I should've told you how I felt sooner."

Lauren was about to speak when she was carefully removed from Josh's arms. "Will you quit manhandling everyone else's wives and get one of your own, please?" Jarod asked with a warning glare no one took seriously anymore.

"I think he's working on it," said Jason, who shoulder-checked Josh after coming through the French doors behind them. He carried a platter of steaks, followed by Melissa, who carried her own platter of foil-wrapped potatoes. She smiled shyly at them on her way to the grill.

"Izzat right?" Jarod drawled, a wicked gleam in his eye.

"Shut up, Jarod," Josh warned.

Lauren, God bless her, poked her husband in the ribs. "Don't blow it for him, honey. He's got his work cut out. I have faith in you, Josh."

"Thanks," Josh muttered, rolling his eyes heavenward, praying Melissa hadn't heard them.

Jarod finally moved Lauren to the patio table, giving Josh a moment to study Melissa. She seemed to interact easily with Jason, who was by far the most intimidating of the brothers. She'd been confident while performing the procedure on the cow, but now her hands shook. He wondered if whether the news of the stalker bothered her, or just being around his big family.

"Are you mad at Missy, Huncle Josh?"

Jessica wrapped herself around his leg while trying to get both of her tiny feet on top of his large, booted foot. When he shot her a grin, she released his leg to lift her arms in the universal signal that this child would like to be picked up.

Happy to oblige, he lifted the little beauty into his arms and kissed her soundly on the cheek. She settled herself by putting her small arms around his neck and graced him with her sweet smile. Even though she'd put on weight since arriving last October, she was still small for her age, no doubt a consequence of her biological mother's drug addiction. Josh made himself ignore the ugly thought. Thankfully, Jessica was now with his family, safe and loved. When the kitten hobbled between Josh's legs, he realized the pair had a lot in common.

"Why would you think I was mad?"

"'Cuz yer lookin' at her like you look at Char-lee right b'fore ya bop him one."

Josh couldn't contain his laugh. Jessica's personality was bigger than all three of the brothers put together. "Well, I promise I'm not thinking of bopping Melissa."

"Good. 'Cuz she saved Ruby, an' her mama."

"She sure did, princess."

He carried Jessica to the table and deposited her in the seat next to Lauren. Julie was sitting closest to the barbecue, directing her husband on how to cook the steaks. Even in a cushioned chair with her swollen feet on an ottoman, she looked uncomfortable as her hands rubbed circles around her large belly. His father and Dane conversed at the other end of the table with Doc and Jarod, who had his arm around the back of Lauren's chair, while Lauren helped Jessica get settled. Josh suspected the empty chair on the other side was for Charlie, whom Jessica adored. Charlie was helping Camille set the table. Each time one of them passed Julie, they'd pat her shoulder or kiss her head.

She looks miserable. Her belly was too big for her size, and he worried about her.

His brothers had each married one of Josh's best friends,

and now both were pregnant with his nieces or nephews. Josh was lucky he had such a loving family, but recently he'd felt a little left out, which wasn't something he was used to.

The outdoor kitchen was as big as the one inside, complete with all the amenities, including a set of cupboards for dishes. Camille King, his mother, was a stickler when it came to gatherings and events. She was prepared for any scenario, including outdoor family barbecues. Speaking of which, Jason and Melissa were still working together at the grill, and it ticked Josh off that his brother got to spend so much time with her today. Shouldn't Jason be more attentive to his pregnant wife?

He pulled out a chair for himself, but when his mother subtly cleared her throat and indicated with her chin he should sit one chair over, next to Melissa's seat, he quickly switched. He caught his mother's eye and she winked. Hmm, her record for matchmaking was two for two, so he'd take whatever help she'd give him.

Maybe he wasn't so left out after all.

AFTER THE MEAL, GINGER LAY CURLED ON MISSY'S lap while Doc, her Uncle Dane, and the Kings conversed around her. The kitten's stuttering purr was therapeutic, hypnotizing her out of the social anxiety always lurking close by. How she'd ended up at the grill with Jason, she wasn't sure. She'd remembered her manners and asked if she could help, assuming Camille would task her with setting the large patio table. However, that hadn't been the case. Julie immediately began instructing her on how to fix the potatoes. Honestly, if a person didn't know how to wrap foil around a potato, they had to be an idiot. Before she could tell Julie she had it handled, Jason leaned into Missy's ear and whispered, "She's a chef who's on the DL, doctor's orders. Just go with it. Charlie will distract her in a minute." He'd winked, sending a beet-red blush to Missy's cheeks. Josh wasn't the only handsome King in the bunch. The three brothers together were overwhelming to the senses. *Eye candy* didn't quite cover it.

Melissa's expertise was with animals, not humans. However, judging by the size of Julie's burden and the weary expression clouding her pretty face, either her due date had been miscalculated or she was going to give birth to a very large baby King. Considering Jason's size, the latter was most likely the answer. All of the brothers were big, muscular men who resembled their father, but Jason was the biggest of the three and looked more like his mother with those amazing green eyes. Whether the baby came early or was just large, their child would be beautiful.

Sitting next to Josh, Missy covertly studied him while he engaged in a discussion about sports with Charlie, who sat across from them. Josh, too, was a big man who filled his padded chair to the limit with solid, tattooed muscle. Sunlight poured through the vine-covered pergola, creating stripes across his eyes, making their sapphire blue color blaze like fire. Josh was by far the most handsome man she'd ever known. Sitting this close to him made her sweat. Thank God for the summer heat. She could blame the unwanted perspiration on the season and not on his heavenly cologne floating on the breeze, or the way his voice hummed over her ears, or how his shirt clung to his hard chest. She continued to pet Ginger with shaking hands. Thankfully, the kitten was affectionate and not one of those cats that wanted precise petting, biting you if you stroked its fur one too many times, or not enough. Missy wouldn't have made it through the meal without Ginger's calming presence.

"She is the cutest kitten." Josh's breath caressed her neck as he leaned in to murmur in her ear.

"Yes, she is," she whispered back stupidly.

Why am I so nervous around him?

"Do you watch sports?"

His random question took her by surprise. "Uh, sometimes."

"Really? What do you watch?"

It was hard getting her eyes off his dimple. She shifted her gaze to Charlie, who was getting ready to lob his napkin at Josh. The evil grin on the young man's face distracted Missy enough to answer, "I watch a little baseball when I have time, but honestly, I prefer football season." As she finished her sentence, the napkin hit Josh in the chest. He ignored it.

"Yeah? Which teams?"

"Well," she began, but was interrupted by her cell phone. Just as she reached for hers, Doc's phone also went off. They eyed each other, knowing this bit of relaxation was over and they'd been called to another emergency.

After thanking James and Camille for the meal and apologizing for rushing off without helping to clean up, Missy and Doc headed to her car, followed by Josh. Doc got in back, while Missy secured Ginger in her cat crate on the front seat. When she turned, Josh was right there, looking at her with a strange expression.

"Thank you again for inviting us to eat. Everything was so good," she said, ignoring the thundering of her heart.

"Anytime," he answered with a smile. "We do this a lot in the summer. What time do you think you'll be home?"

Whoa.

"Uh. D-depends on the emergency."

"I'll look for you, and if you're not too tired, maybe we could share a beer on the front porch. What do you say, neighbor?"

Wow. "Maybe," she hedged. It was flattering to be asked, but surely Josh had other women in his life who needed his attention?

Not trusting her voice, she smiled one last time and clambered into the driver seat. She felt awkward again, and Ginger was locked up in her crate in the passenger seat. It was best to get moving before her antiperspirant quit working. She turned the key in the ignition and put the CRV in reverse with purpose before turning around and starting down the long driveway to the main road.

"He's a good man, Missy." Doc's comment scared the hell out of her. He'd been so quiet she'd nearly forgotten he was back there.

When her heart stopped racing, she peeked at Doc in her rearview mirror. "I know."

"I'm not trying to pressure you, but he likes you. You should give him a chance."

He liked her? Like... LIKED her, liked her? She refused to ask Doc that ridiculous question, so instead she admitted, "I wasn't lying. If it's not too late, I'll get a hold of him tonight when I get home." She wanted to end this discussion before it got too personal. "Remind me again how to get to the Ferrero Ranchero," she said, hoping that would signal an end to his relationship advice. She ignored his chuckle as he gave directions to the next emergency call.

It was a little past eight o'clock when she pulled into her driveway.

Home at last.

Grimy and needing a shower, she leaned over to unlatch the cat door. Ginger looked around and seemed to sigh in relief. She gave Missy a pathetic meow, stretched, and climbed into her lap, ready to leave the vehicle. Giggling, she scooped up the kitten and headed for the front door. She glanced Josh's way and, sure enough, he was sitting on his front porch drinking a beer. He held it up in salute.

Should I go over there?

"What do you think, Ginger?" she whispered.

The kitten meowed, then made a move to be let down. Missy complied, and once Ginger was earthbound, she hobbled quickly to Josh.

"I guess that answers my question," Missy muttered. Sucking in a deep breath, she slammed the car door and headed to his front porch to retrieve her wayward cat.

As she approached, Josh reached into a cooler behind him and produced a cold bottle of beer. Ginger rubbed herself on Josh's legs while purring to her heart's content.

"'Bout time," he chided as she sat down next to him and accepted the bottle.

She took a long pull and sighed. "Thank you." She held up her beer, and he clinked his bottle to hers. They sat quietly for a few minutes staring at the lawn in front of the building. A mixture of honeysuckle and freshly cut grass hung in the cool night air, soothing her tired soul.

Josh nudged her shoulder. "So, you never told me who your favorite teams are." He lifted an eyebrow.

It made her giggle.

"What's so funny?" he asked with a puzzled grin.

Squinting into the dark, she took another drink.

Screw it.

She'd been called lame before, it didn't matter now. She turned her head, resting her chin on her tired shoulder, and looked him straight in his gorgeous blue eyes. "I like to have a game on when I'm alone. It doesn't matter what team, but I usually end up rooting for the frontrunner by the end of the season." There, she admitted to being a sports fraud.

Josh looked at her a minute before taking another drink. He pulled Ginger, who'd been curious about his beer, into his lap. He let her sniff the opening and she purred louder. Her rough tongue snaked out to take a quick lick on the glass, making him grin. "I don't really like being home alone, so I do the same thing. Keep the games on, I mean. Helps me concentrate on my work."

"You? Lonely? I don't believe it."

He huffed. "I never said I was lonely, Melissa. I like to hear voices when I'm working alone. There's a difference." He looked at her strangely. "Wait, are you saying you're lonely? Hell, girl, I'm usually here. Just come on over, even if I'm working. I won't mind."

His offer seemed genuine, but she'd never invade his privacy.

Suddenly his big chest expanded on a breath before he muttered, "Or maybe not," before taking another swig. He was in a strange mood tonight.

She finished her beer and handed him the bottle. "Thank you for the drink, and the lovely afternoon with your family. I really did enjoy myself." She reached for Ginger and headed home. Once she was inside, a sense of melancholy unlike she'd ever felt pressed upon her.

God, am I going to start my period?

What the hell was wrong with her?

Gotta be exhaustion, she thought, as she climbed the stairs to her bedroom and a long, overdue hot shower.

MARGUERITE WAS SO FOCUSED ON HER COMPUTER screen she didn't notice the man standing at the counter. It wasn't until he'd cleared his throat when she looked up into eyes so brown they were almost black. He had a rugged face and his hair was too long for her taste.

"I'm here to see Sheriff King," he stated with a slight twang in his speech. His aftershave floated over the counter, a perfect blend of spice and man. Marguerite silently thanked God she'd worn a high-necked blouse because it covered the blush creeping up her neck. She really didn't like the way her words had gotten stuck in her throat, either. When she continued to stare, he leaned over the counter on his elbows. "Honey, are you all right?"

Losing her ability for speech hadn't happened since she'd been a teenager facing a very handsome Josh King.

"Ma'am?" His second question brought her back to reality. She quickly stood, giving her a better view of the man and inadvertently caused her mouth to water.

Swallowing, she put on her most professional smile. "Please excuse me. Can I tell the sheriff your name?"

His answering grin drew her eyes to twin dimples buried in the beard stubble growing on his cheeks. His complexion was dark, and a few pieces of silver interspersed in his whiskers. The contrast was striking. He didn't look old enough to have gray hair.

"Declan McKinley, U.S. Marshal. What's your name, honey?"

"Marguerite Theroux." She averted his piercing gaze by checking Jarod's schedule on her computer. "He's not expecting you, but his schedule is clear. I'll just go check if Sheriff King will see you." She could've buzzed Jarod over the phone, but she needed to get some distance from this disturbing man. "I'll be right back."

"I'm countin' on it, Miz Theroux." Her name rolled off his tongue in his delicate drawl, sending shivers down her spine. She hightailed it to Jarod's office without looking back. *Never show a predator your fear*, her uncle's words rang in her ears. She tried her best to moderate her pace so she didn't appear to be running.

She knocked on Jarod's doorframe and quickly stepped into his office. "There's someone here to see you." God, she hated the way her voice came out all breathy. "He says he's a U.S. marshal."

Jarod glanced up with his usual annoyance but widened his eyes when he got a good look at her. "What's wrong? Are you all right?" He seemed genuinely concerned for her welfare, which threw Marguerite further off balance. It wasn't long ago the two of them could barely tolerate each other. Her rapport with Jarod had only gotten better when Lauren, the previous administrative assistant, had married the good sheriff — and she and Uncle Dane had promised to keep him in the loop with regard to federal investigations.

Unfortunately, Jarod's uncharacteristic display of concern rattled her, and Marguerite felt her eyes well with tears of embarrassment.

Unacceptable!

They were at work and nothing serious had happened,

except for the predator who'd just walked in the door making her hormones go all wonky.

She cleared her throat. "Nothing's wrong, Jarod," she assured him, schooling her features. "I was caught off guard is all." It was honest and didn't go into personal detail.

He gave her his special interrogative eyeballing, the one he used when he didn't believe a word a suspect said, prompting the suspect to fess up. It made her smile. "Really, I'm fine. He's waiting in the reception area."

"Did he give a name?"

"Declan McKinley. Were you expecting him?"

"No," he said thoughtfully. "Let's go see what the marshal wants."

It was not normal protocol for Marguerite to sit in on an interview, but Jarod insisted she stay. The sheriff's station was testing out some new office policies. Things had been slow since *The Big Drug Bust*, as the people of Timbisha Township liked to describe it. It'd been Marguerite's idea to have the in-house deputies man the counter if she was away. Her uncle hinted he wanted to keep her on retainer in case something came up with the FBI again. It was his way of keeping her out of trouble, and Jarod liked the idea. After the initial shock of discovering she'd been the informant by gaining a close relationship with Brad Anderson and thereby putting herself in danger, Jarod quickly made a deal with both Dane and Marguerite. They promised to keep him in the loop at all times, and in return he'd share information on any cases that crossed over into federal jurisdiction. It would've worked out well, she thought, except nothing exciting had happened in Timbisha Township since *The Big Drug Bust*.

Jarod opened the conference room door for the marshal,

and Marguerite followed him inside. "Would you like some coffee or water before we start?" she asked Marshal McKinley.

"No, thank you," he replied, taking a seat. "If you don't mind, I'll get right to it. I'm looking for a fugitive and believe he's hiding out in Timbisha Township."

"How can we help in the search?" Jarod asked.

Marguerite settled next to Jarod, who was across the table from the marshal. She got out her legal pad and began to take notes. "What's the fugitive's name?"

She'd get as much information on the suspect as possible in order to run a computer search. It probably wouldn't give her any more leads than the marshal already had access to, but she'd also use her uncle's contacts if she ran into any roadblocks. He had access to databases unauthorized by the marshal.

Marshal McKinley raised his eyebrows at her. "Are you a deputy, honey? I thought you just ran the desk out front."

Jarod sighed, and from her periphery she noticed him shaking his head. She narrowed her eyes at the marshal. "I'm the sheriff's assistant. I'm trained in more than just administrative duties, Marshal."

"You don't say."

Jarod interrupted before Marguerite could take the marshal to task. "Give Miss Theroux the name, and we'll see what we can do to help you out."

The marshal nodded before giving her a wink which she chose to ignore. "His legal name is Harold Schurke, but he has other aliases. His latest is Klein."

Marguerite's head came up from her pad. "Are you talking about Professor Harold Klein?" All the hairs on the back of her neck stood on end.

"Yes, ma'am. You know him?"

She shared a look with Jarod, who excused himself from

the room. He left the door open and she could hear him issuing a B.O.L.O. When he returned to his seat, he nodded for her to explain what had happened to her sister in school, and recently in Timbisha Township.

When she finished, U.S. Marshal Declan McKinley sat back in his chair. "I'm on the right trail, then," he muttered to himself.

"What's he wanted for?" Marguerite had to know what kind of danger her sister was in.

"He was charged with fraud, identity theft, and money laundering when he was in his early twenties. He was captured when a girl he worked with accused him of sexual harassment. She filed for a restraining order. The investigation uncovered his true identity and his crimes. He stood trial and was convicted of all charges. Unfortunately, he never made it to prison. Some sort of computer glitch that we believe he had something to do with let him out the front door. His trail went cold almost immediately. He's a clever son of a bitch."

Jarod asked, "You're working a cold case, then?"

Marshal McKinley nodded. "My predecessor retired and all his cases were handed to me. This one caught my eye and stuck with me though, like a true mystery, and I like to solve those. My research uncovered Harold Schurke to be one bad hombre who needs puttin' away."

Marguerite swallowed. If Harold was in town, they needed to warn Missy.

The marshal continued. "I'll follow up on his position at your sister's college, and the restraining order she put on him. If y'all come up with anything in your own research, I'd sure appreciate a head's up." He smiled at her, making her stupid blush appear again.

What is going on with that?

She took the card he handed her and put it with her notes.

Jarod asked a few more questions as they continued to discuss the best way to flush out Harold Schurke, or Klein, or whatever his name was.

When they finished with their interview, Jarod shook the marshal's hand and headed back to his office, where she noticed he immediately picked up his phone. Hopefully, he was calling Uncle Dane.

Marguerite escorted Marshal McKinley to the front doors, stopping at the reception desk. He turned and smiled. "I'm sorry if we got off on the wrong foot, Miz Theroux. Obviously, you're vital to the sheriff's operation here."

She studied him for a moment, deciding whether the compliment was genuine or not.

"Thank you."

"I meant what I said. Please call me if you find anything more. Now that I know this guy has another mark — your sister — I want him off the streets for good."

"You and me both, marshal."

"Call me Declan, honey. I'm not the formal type." Before she could take him to task for the endearment, he winked and sauntered out the glass doors into the blinding sunshine.

CHAPTER 5

Graffiti

O n Saturday, an urgent pounding had Missy running downstairs. She wasn't expecting company and puzzled over the aggression her visitor inflicted on her poor door. Delight instantly replaced wariness when she faced a quirky, familiar face through the peephole.

"Angelica Daemon! What in the world are you doing here?" Missy asked as she embraced her college roommate in a fierce hug.

"Surprising you!" Angelica's bright smile, big blue eyes, and kinky blonde curls matched her given name to a T. A sweet button nose completed her cherubic face but somehow didn't take away from her vixen's figure. She wasn't tall, but she definitely could compete with Marguerite on sexiness.

"Well, you've succeeded," Missy said as she led her friend into the living room. "Seriously, what gives? Why are you here instead of someplace more exotic?"

"Well, it's a very strange story. My recruiter placed my name with several hospitals around the country. However, Timbisha

Township Medical Center had an opening for a registered nurse, so here I am! Can you believe it?"

No, Missy couldn't. She and Angelica had shared a dorm room in school and become fast friends. Even though Missy studied animals and Angelica studied humans, they'd bonded over medicine. They were worlds apart, otherwise. Missy's social awkwardness made her an introvert, but it hadn't deterred Angelica from befriending her. She'd gotten Missy through her worst panic attacks while living on campus. She'd become a protective mother hen when Harold began harassing Missy. If it hadn't been for Angelica, Missy never would've filed the restraining order.

Excited for her friend, Missy asked the first question on her mind. "Where are you staying?"

"With you?"

They both laughed before Missy confirmed, "Of course you are!"

Both girls proceeded to squeal like preteens at a Justin Bieber concert. Missy felt lighthearted. She'd always been comfortable with Angelica in a way which rivaled her sisterly relationship with Marguerite, with one exception—Angelica never made her feel insecure. There was no sibling competitiveness between them. Missy loved her sister with all her heart, but sometimes Marguerite was just... Marguerite.

Suddenly, Missy couldn't wait to introduce the two. It would be like a social experiment between vixens.

"What are you plotting, Melissa Theroux?" Angelica asked, her voice laced with suspicion.

"I was just wondering if you'd like to go with me to Mom's so you can meet her and my sister."

If Missy hadn't been paying attention, she might've missed

the brief look of concern crossing Angelica's face, but in a flash it was gone. "Sure!"

"Great! I'll call and let them know I'm bringing a friend—"

"Can I get my things settled first? It was a longer drive than I expected and I'd like to freshen up."

"Oh, jeez! Of course." Chagrined, Missy headed out the door. "Let's get your stuff."

They spent the next hour getting Angelica settled into the spare bedroom. Missy hoped to one day use the room as an office, but with her less-than-ambitious attitude toward interior decorating, she supposed a roommate to help with the rent was a better option. Looking for a roommate was hard work. Finding a compatible roommate was mostly luck, and with Missy's shyness, she hadn't even considered searching for one. Doc paid her enough, but she had student loans to pay off, and saving money would be a problem for a while. She'd been willing to cut out frivolous activities in order to save her funds. Angelica's sudden appearance would give her budget more wiggle room.

"I hope you don't mind sleeping on a futon."

"Anything is fine. I'm just glad to have a place to lay my head at night," Angelica said a bit tiredly. Her belongings consisted of clothes and a few textbooks packed in boxes. Even when they'd shared a dorm room, Angelica lacked in the personal items department. Maybe because she was a "military brat," as she liked to refer to herself. It made sense. Moving from place to place kept her from accumulating too many possessions, and since Angelica's original plan had been to become a traveling nurse, she'd obviously continued the minimalist lifestyle.

Missy hated moving with a passion, which is why she'd waited so long to unpack. All she'd ever wanted was to come home to Timbisha Township and be a veterinarian. Moving from place to place was about the worst thing Missy could think of.

By the time they got Angelica settled into the spare bedroom and she'd taken the time to freshen up, they'd missed lunch with Missy's mom. Marguerite informed her their mom was napping. Missy wasn't only disappointed but starving too.

"We can go grocery shopping, or we can go get something to eat and then go grocery shopping, since I have nothing in my cupboards anyway. You pick."

With a laugh, Angelica said, "Let's eat first. It's not wise to shop on an empty stomach."

"Booth or bar?" Missy asked once they were through the familiar glass doors of Molly's Diner.

"Booth. I want to watch people go by as we eat. This town is definitely charming." Angelica's eyes were everywhere. Since Missy had always loved it here, she was glad her friend appreciated her small town, too.

Speaking of small towns, Josh walked into the diner just as they were handed menus. He was alone this time, looking a bit haggard, Missy thought, but his eyes brightened when they landed on her. He immediately headed their way.

Missy panicked.

"What is it?" Angelica asked.

"Nothing," Missy whispered as Josh arrived at their booth.

"Hey, Melissa," he said in that smooth voice which gave her goosebumps every time it was directed her way. Her heart dropped, though, when he eyed Angelica with interest.

Clearing her throat, she introduced them. "Josh, this is my

friend from school, Angelica Daemon. Angie, this is Josh King, my landlord." His title reminded her she'd have to go over the terms of her lease again; first a pet and now a roommate. She hoped Josh would be agreeable with letting Angelica stay.

He was in full charm-your-panties-off mode when he reached for Angelica's hand. "Pleasure to meet you, Angie," he said, smooth as silk.

Predictably, Angelica's reaction to Josh was just as flirtatious. "The pleasure's all mine. Won't you join us?" she asked with a sweet smile, gesturing to the seat next to her. To Missy's surprise, Josh slid into the booth next to her instead of Angelica. Maybe he wanted to be able to stare into her friend's eyes. Yes, that made sense. Angelica was beautiful.

"What brings you to Timbisha Township?" he asked, oozing charm like melted butter. Thinking of melting butter, a grilled cheese sandwich sounded good. Really, Missy was starving. Even Josh's proximity hadn't affected her hunger, but when he slipped his arm on the back of the booth around her shoulders, little tingles shot down her arms.

Angelica explained her circumstances to Josh while Missy studied the menu she knew by heart. She needed time for the lightning to stop zipping down her limbs.

"I hope it's all right if I stay with Missy for a while."

"No problem. I'd feel better if she wasn't living alone anyway. I know my brother will be happier about the situation."

Missy was having a hard time following the conversation. God, he smelled good.

Angelica tilted her head in the cutest way at Josh. "What situation bothers your brother?"

"Melissa has a stalker. My brother, the sheriff, isn't happy about it. None of us are."

"I do not have a stalker," Missy denied behind her menu.

Josh ignored her. "He left a box of drugged chocolates on her doorstep with a note telling her she couldn't hide from him."

"Harold's back? Oh my God, Missy!"

This is getting out of hand. "We don't know that for sure—"

"Jarod's investigating this Harold person's activities for the past few months," Josh admitted, anger lacing his voice.

Missy sat back and listened as Angelica reiterated what had happened at school after Josh retold the chocolate tale in detail. The two of them had a lot to say to each other, and the more they talked, the more Angelica flirted with Josh. Missy told herself she wasn't jealous. She'd almost convinced herself of that when her food arrived and her appetite vanished.

JOSH EYED THE LITTLE SPORTS CAR PARKED IN Melissa's driveway and frowned. The roommate was the reason his tenant hadn't jogged this morning. Angelica Daemon's flirtatious demeanor hadn't fooled Josh, either. He'd known plenty of women who wore the same predatory look in their eyes and had the same alpha female attitude. He didn't doubt her concern for Melissa, but she had an agenda and he wanted to know what it was. He grimaced at how he might have to attain it. He did not want to get that close to Angelica Daemon.

He'd just jogged past Melissa's driveway when he got a good look at the back of her Honda CRV. Anger immediately redirected his feet to her front porch and made his fist pound on the door. "Melissa, open up!"

He heard a pan clatter in the kitchen and feet stomping down the stairs. Before he could pull the master key from his pocket, the door swung open revealing Angelica in a long t-shirt, and nothing else. His eyes made an involuntary perusal of her form, strictly out of habit, before she made her ire known by asking, "What is your drama?"

As Angie's annoying question floated in the air, Melissa came up behind her. "Josh!" she said breathlessly. "Is everything all right?"

Melissa wasn't wearing much more than her houseguest. His anger boiled into lust, causing his tongue to stick to the roof of his mouth and his eyes to home in on her exposed flesh. Her tight white camisole left nothing to the imagination. It only came to the top of her belly button which — surprisingly — was pierced with a tiny purple jewel. His eyes zeroed in on the gem before traveling down to the briefest pair of spandex shorts he'd ever seen. He forced his eyes back up her luscious body to her eyes. Her hair was bed-tumbled and her makeup-free face showed off those adorable freckles.

Is this how she sleeps? He had to mentally shake his head as the picture of her sprawled out on his bed distracted him from the purpose of his being there so early on a Saturday. Unfortunately, all he could get out of his mouth was a stupid, "Nuh."

Angelica cocked a hip. "Shame on you, Missy. You didn't tell me your townhouse came with a little morning man candy."

Melissa elbowed her friend in the ribs. "Angelica."

"Come on in, handsome." Angelica reached for Josh's hand and gave him a yank. "Breakfast is almost ready."

Josh'd seen that sly look a million times before. It said she wanted him. He'd be flattered if Angelica weren't a man-eater —cold and calculating. Josh could spot one a mile away. He wondered how Melissa managed to befriend a woman like this. A woman, he noted, who was older than she let on. Josh's radar raised red flags all over the place.

Melissa shut the door and led him to a barstool. All thoughts of her roommate vanished as his eyes landed on Melissa's heart-shaped rear end in those itty-bitty boy shorts.

"She's cute, isn't she?"

"Angelica!" This time Melissa's voice was loud, startling a chuckle out of him.

"She sure is," he admitted. Melissa immediately turned to the coffeepot and began pouring mugs while shaking her head. He wanted both of them to know he was attracted to *Melissa*, even if she wasn't attracted to him.

God, the thought burned his ass. Had she liked her professor before things went bad? Josh wondered about the men Melissa was attracted to. Were they handsome? Was she into the academic type? Josh wasn't an idiot, but his interests were more outdoorsy, like camping and sports.

"Why did you bang on my door so hard, Josh?" Melissa asked, business-like as she placed a mug of hot coffee in front of him.

"Shit," he muttered, before he pulled his cell phone out of the zippered pocket of his running shorts and speed-dialed Jarod's number. He'd been completely distracted by the opposite sex. Now that he'd confirmed Melissa was safe, it was time to call in his brother. The girls looked at him like he was crazy before looking at each other, shrugging.

He listened to two rings before the line opened. "Sheriff's office, Marguerite speaking."

"Hey, it's Josh. Can you send Jarod over to Melissa's?"

"Of course. Why?"

He took a breath and looked Melissa in the eyes. "Because your sister's stalker left another message."

Melissa gasped and put one hand over her mouth and the other over her heart. Angelica's reaction was to get up and put her arms around Melissa while giving him a glare.

Marguerite, on the other hand, was fierce. "I'll have him there in ten minutes."

"Thanks, Marguerite."

"What does it say?" Melissa asked in a panicked whisper.

He gritted his teeth before growling out, "'I'll never let you go.'"

Angelica squeezed Melissa's shoulders. "It's gotta be Harold."

Melissa stood in a daze for a moment before she straightened her spine. "No, it can't be. Not after all this time."

"He wasn't subtle before, Missy. It doesn't sound like he's changed much."

Josh gave Angelica a thoughtful look. "You knew him?"

She turned her big eyes on him. "Yes, I'm the one who helped Missy get the restraining order. He was pretty creepy."

"I'm getting dressed," Melissa announced as she unwrapped herself from Angelica's hug, then stomped up the stairs.

Josh followed her with his eyes until she was out of sight.

"You're in love with her, aren't you?" Angelica's shrewd eyes narrowed in accusation.

The L-word took him by surprise and had him stammering. "What? No, no, no. It's not like that at all," he began. Lauren might've guessed, but his feelings were not public knowledge.

She tilted her head at him. "Yeah? Then what's it like? By

the way you just looked at her, there's no doubt you have the hots for her."

"I've just never seen her dressed like—" A knock on the door interrupted his confession. Knowing Jarod had saved his ass from explaining himself, he hurried to the front door.

"It's not permanent. I was able to rub a bit off with my finger after taking some photos," the sheriff said without preamble, typical of Jarod when he was in cop mode.

Melissa rushed down the stairs dressed in shorts and a t-shirt. She was still barefoot, though she'd put her hair back into its usual French braid. "Where is it?"

Jarod held the front door for her, and everyone but Angelica, who was still sporting only a long t-shirt, stepped outside. Melissa stopped short, causing Josh to bump into her back as she read the cryptic message on the back of her Honda. He caught her shoulders in a light touch, holding her steady as she gaped at the sight. "Are you all right?" he asked quietly.

He felt her shoulders slump for a moment before her spine went ramrod straight. There was no shyness in her voice when she said, "No, but I will be. You're right, Jarod. This isn't new to me. This is the kind of crap Harold used to pull at school."

Josh gave her shoulders a slight squeeze before dropping his hands to step beside her. "Jarod says it will wash off, Melissa."

"That's a relief, although Harold never did any permanent damage to my property," she explained. She shook her head for a moment. "Why now? I haven't seen or heard from him in years. None of this makes any sense."

Josh had no response while Jarod took some more pictures for evidence. "It's hard to know what triggers this kind of behavior, but this is a small town. If a stranger's lurking around, chances are someone's going to notice."

Josh knew Jarod was right, but he still had an uneasy feeling that whoever was doing this was just getting started.

MISSY'S UNEASE OF THE PAST FEW WEEKS QUICKLY turned to anger. She had a temper when she was pushed too far, and if Harold thought he could frighten her away from her home, he was sadly mistaken. Fortunately, her anger made her think clearly, distracting her from her social anxiety.

"I'll get a bucket with soap and wash it off for you." Josh took off for his garage.

"I'll grab some towels and a sponge," Missy added before she turned to Jarod. "Thanks for coming out so quickly."

"Are you kidding? My new secretary would've chewed off half my ass if I hadn't hightailed it over here." Jarod chuckled. "I was two streets over when I got her call."

"Sorry about that. Marguerite can be," she struggled for a word that wouldn't disparage her sister in front of her boss.

"Tenacious?" Jarod suggested.

"That's putting it mildly," Missy admitted, relieved he understood. "Do you want some coffee before you head back to the station?"

"Please." Jarod followed her back into the townhouse. "No one ever refills the damn pot at the office," he muttered under his breath.

THE SUN WAS SHINING BRIGHTLY WHEN JOSH TURNED the hose off. Missy couldn't take her eyes off of him. He seemed to grow more handsome each time she was with him.

He'd shown up in his running shorts and sleeveless running shirt. His clothing emphasized every muscle, and his tattoos glistened underneath the fine mist of the spray. When she moved to pick up the bucket, he was beside her in a flash, removing the handles from her hands. "I've got it." He took the bucket and dumped it in the grass.

"Thank you." She picked up a towel and began drying off her car. Through her lashes, her eyes followed him as he set down the now empty bucket, grabbed a towel for himself, and began drying the other side of her car. A minute passed before he broke the silence.

"How long does Angelica plan on staying with you?"

Ah, he was interested in her sexy friend which explained why he'd helped with the car. He wanted to pick her brain about Angelica. It pained Missy to think about it, but they'd make a handsome couple. "I'm not sure. She's starting a new job this week."

He popped his head up over the roof. "Where's that again?"

She didn't believe for a second he didn't remember the circumstances of Angelica's visit. "Timbisha Township Medical Center."

"And what will her hours be?"

If he was trying to figure out a convenient time to ask Angelica out, why didn't he just ask her himself? Missy was sure her roommate would be more than willing to go out with him, but she grudgingly answered anyway. "I don't know what shift she'll have, but I know she'll work ten or twelve hours a shift. Why?" Man, she was a glutton for punishment. She already knew why. He wanted to take Angie out on a—

"Because I want to know how often you'll be alone. With this creep on the loose, I want you safe," he said, surprising her.

"You don't want to ask her out?" Missy cringed as the words formed an embarrassing bubble in the air above their heads. His dimple appeared in his cheek before spreading into the killer grin he was known for. She wanted to kick herself, or him, she wasn't sure which.

"Uh, nooo. I don't have time for a woman like Angie." He shook his head and continued to dry his side of the car.

Offended on her friend's behalf, she demanded, "What do you mean, 'a woman like Angie'? Angelica is terrific!"

He'd already worked his way down the passenger side and dried the rear of the car and was now working his way up to her. He stood and looked into her eyes, the epitome of seriousness. "She's not my type, Melissa."

Caught in the spell cast by those amazingly blue King eyes, she merely whispered, "Oh," while time stood still. He raised his hand to rub his thumb over her bottom lip, making her body tremble. When he brushed a tender kiss to her surprised mouth, she murmured out another, "Oh."

"Yes, 'oh,'" he confirmed with a knowing look. Just as he leaned in for another sweet kiss, they were interrupted.

"What'd I miss?" Angelica asked as she bounded down the porch steps.

Missy was so startled she jumped back guiltily from Josh. "Nothing."

Josh snagged the wet towel from her hand, a scowl on his face. "To be continued," he whispered before gathering up the bucket and heading to his townhouse. "I'll be right back," he threw over his shoulder.

Missy schooled her features but still couldn't keep her eyes off Josh's retreating behind.

"What's wrong?" Angelica asked.

"Nothing," Missy repeated while waiting for Josh to disappear into his garage. A giddy feeling came over her and she squealed, "He kissed me!"

"Really? Wow, he works fast."

"Fast? I've known him forever, Angelica."

"Exactly, and he's just now showing an interest?" She shook her head. "Maybe he's a damsel-in-distress kind of guy. I wouldn't get too excited over it."

Missy frowned, a little offended at Angelica's dismissive comment. But hadn't she tried to ignore her attraction to Josh over the years because of his reputation with women? Maybe her roommate was correct. Missy wasn't Josh's type, based on his previous attractions. Angelica knew men a heck of a lot better than she did, and Angelica had also been correct about Harold. Missy would take Angelica's advice to heart and try not to read too much into Josh's kiss. He was Timbisha Township's favorite bachelor, after all.

CHAPTER 6
Excuse

With the exception of brief hellos before work, it had been two days since Josh had seen Melissa.

Two days since I kissed her.

Every morning either one of them had an excuse not to jog. For him it was meetings with his father. and for her it was a vet emergency. When he'd gone back to his townhouse to drop off the buckets, Jason had called, needing Josh's help with some lighting on the new home. Then, yesterday, while picking out a bottle of wine for Melissa at the grocery store, Josh received a text from his mother asking for help with a display for her catering business. He'd finished it in time to eat dinner and deliver the bottle of wine to Melissa, but when he called her to confirm if she was home, she told him she'd gone out to dinner with Angelica. It seemed their busy lives were conspiring against him.

He was going crazy for another taste.

I miss you, Melissa.

"Son, what are you doing?" James asked, annoyance personified.

"Sorry, Dad, I'm just a little distracted. What were you saying?" They were sitting around the conference table in the trailer King Construction set up as an office behind Molly's Diner. It was just the two of them, since Jason was still working on the new house. Thinking of it reminded him he was also worried about his best friend. Julie's pregnancy wasn't going smoothly. She'd been put on bed rest after her last doctor's appointment due to her developing pre-eclampsia — sudden onset of high blood pressure in pregnancy — and edema. For now it was being controlled with rest and medication, but the entire family was concerned for both mother and child. Jason was on the ragged edge, and Josh prayed his brother refrained from killing any of their subcontractors before Julie gave birth.

James raised a concerned eyebrow. "Has something else happened to Missy?"

"I wouldn't know. I haven't seen her since her car was graffitied."

James set his pen down and leaned back in his chair. "Jarod said there was no permanent damage."

"No, but the message was clear. Her stalker is here in Timbisha Township, and he's not letting up one bit," Josh tossed his own pen onto the table and stood to pace the small confines of the trailer. "What kind of man gets off on frightening a beautiful young woman, Dad?"

"The kind who isn't a man at all," James said with conviction. The Kings didn't tolerate bullies or cowards, and a stalker was both. "I've had a few discussions with Dane on this matter. He's looking into this Harold person. Apparently, he went missing a few weeks ago, just packed a bag and left without a word to his colleagues at the university or what little family he had in the area."

"Does Jarod know?"

"Of course. Don't forget Dane is Missy's uncle. Family comes first, and Jarod understands that all too well. Besides," James chuckled, "Jarod appreciates Dane's expertise after last fall, and Marguerite is running the show at the sheriff's office. Jarod doesn't really have a choice in the matter."

Picturing Marguerite and Jarod duking it out at the station brought a devious grin to Josh's face. Marguerite was not a woman to be trifled with. She'd always known how to get what she wanted. There'd been a brief moment in high school when he'd thought Marguerite was attracted to him, which had scared the hell out of him because he'd been a little attracted to her. Back then he'd been a little attracted to all the girls, but Marguerite was high maintenance and, although she was beautiful, she just didn't compare to Melissa's gentle elegance.

"If you're finished mooning over Missy, can we get back to work now? The hotel isn't going to build itself." James once again let his irritation show.

Josh chuckled as he resumed his seat. "Yeah, old man, we can. Keep your shirt on."

They spent the rest of the morning poring over the building inspector's reports, comparing them to various plans, and weighing architectural pros and cons on style with regard to structure. Though King Construction had built its business doing work for Timbisha Township and the State of Nevada, Molly's Diner and Hotel would be the first project Josh had a personal interest in, and one he'd share with his father. Molly's was a landmark and it needed to be preserved. He wanted to get it right.

They left the trailer for the comfort of the diner by lunchtime. When they pushed through the glass doors, Josh's face split into a grin. Melissa was sitting at the counter with Marguerite. Before he got the chance to say hello, his father caught their attention. "Hello, ladies. Would you care to join me and my son for lunch?"

Marguerite smiled while Melissa's endearing blush colored her cheeks. "Thank you, Mr. King, we'd love to." Marguerite took her water and nudged Melissa off her stool.

"I'll let Karen know you're moving," Josh said, flagging their waitress behind the counter and gesturing to his father's normal booth. To Josh's delight, Marguerite faked out her sister, letting Melissa slide into the booth first and just as she was getting ready to sit down, Marguerite sat on the opposite side of the booth facing Melissa. His father, God love him, sat next to Marguerite leaving the space next to Melissa open for Josh. It was the smoothest move he'd seen in a while. He was still chuckling when he slid next to her, bumping his thigh into Melissa, who, he noted, glared at her sister.

The time apart had amped up his attraction to her, and he wanted to get his lips back on hers. Unfortunately, he couldn't think of a single excuse to kiss her in the diner.

"What are you two handsome devils up to today?" Marguerite asked. Josh caught the wink she'd sent to her sister.

"Working on the plans for the hotel, Ms. Theroux. How are things down at the station?"

While James engaged Marguerite in small talk, Josh leaned in to Melissa's ear. "How's our kitten?" That was the other thing which sucked about being apart from her. He'd missed the damn cat as much as the woman.

"She's great." Melissa gave him a relaxed smile. Talking about animals was the key to her heart, and Josh would work that lock every chance he got.

"I was thinking of putting some steaks on the grill tonight. Wanna bring her over?" *In for penny...*

"The usual, Mr. King?" Karen interrupted, as she set down two plates in front of the sisters.

"Yes, that sounds great."

"How about you, Josh?"

He stared at Melissa's plate and drooled. She'd ordered the deluxe double cheeseburger with fries, his favorite. Truly, he was falling for her more every day. He pointed at her plate. "I'll have what she's having."

It was no wonder half the town's female population was in love with Josh. He made ordering food sound naughty. Here he was eyeballing her cheeseburger like it was a filet mignon and asking her to his place for dinner, which she hadn't agreed to yet. She felt giddy, which was a dangerous way to feel, but she couldn't help herself. He was good at short-circuiting her senses.

"You don't already have plans again, do you?" he asked with what sounded like frustration.

Melissa realized Mr. King and her sister were now listening. She swallowed. "Uh, no."

She felt him relax again. "I'll put the steaks on the grill around six-thirty. Sound good?"

When she still didn't answer right away, Marguerite kicked her in the shin. *That hurt!* She gave her sister the Death Stare. Marguerite sat innocently as if nothing had happened under the table. "Angie will still be at the hospital, but I should be home by then. What should I bring?" Missy asked while Marguerite nodded with approval.

He flashed that infamous smile of his. "Just you and the cat."

"Who's Angie?" James asked.

"Angelica Daemon is my sister's new roommate," Marguerite explained. "She lived with Missy while she attended school, Mr. King."

"Ah, so she's someone you can trust," James proclaimed.

"Angie's great. I'm really glad to have her, and it beats trying to find a roommate," Missy added.

"Why do you need a roommate?" Josh asked.

"I don't *need* one, but every little bit helps." She shrugged. Angelica hadn't been with her long, but she'd already pitched in with the groceries.

Karen returned to the table with the rest of their order. The look on Josh's face when his meal was placed in front of him was almost indecent. "These are the best burgers," he said with reverence as he took a huge bite.

Missy only ate half her meal because she spent the rest of the time watching Josh devour his. When she caught her sister's eye, Marguerite wore that knowing look she got when she was proud of herself, the look which meant she'd manipulated Missy in some way to her liking. It usually annoyed Missy, but this time she'd gotten what she'd wanted, too. Missy had a date with Josh later that night, and she would make it no matter what crisis tried to wreck it.

"I can't make it for dinner," Melissa said.

"Why not?" Josh failed to keep the whine out of his voice. He swore the universe conspired against him.

"Angie's car won't start and she needs help getting home. I'm sorry, Josh. I was really looking forward to those steaks."

She sounded as disappointed as he felt. Would they ever get a moment alone?

"I could tag along, maybe see if I can get her car running?" If he went with her, he might be able to fix Angelica's car and then Melissa could still come over for dinner.

"That's a great idea, but I'm already on my way to the hospital."

"Why don't I meet you down there anyway? It'd spare having to call a tow truck if I can fix whatever's wrong with it." He almost kicked himself. He sounded desperate even to his own ears.

"That's sweet, Josh, but Angie's already called one. She just needs a ride home. If... if it's not too late, maybe I could still come by," she suggested.

He was proud of her for not shying away from their date. "I'll keep the steaks warm."

"Sounds good," she said with a hint of relief in her voice. It gave him hope she wasn't purposefully avoiding him.

Frustrated, he clicked off and tossed his phone on the kitchen counter. She was all he could think about anymore. Tonight's dinner was supposed to have been the beginning of a relationship with her, one made of deeper kisses, and hand-holding in public. Now he was forced to wait another day because he had a bad feeling he wouldn't be seeing her tonight.

Guts, I hope you're wrong.

He covered the steaks with tin foil and left them on the stove to keep warm. He put the bottle of wine back onto the rack and headed to the living room to wait. If she didn't show up, then he'd go to her. Melissa had a shy nature, but he'd already proven he could get around her awkwardness. The problem was the more time they were apart, the more he felt he'd lose ground and have to start over. He didn't want to give her time to change her mind about him.

He found the Giants game on television. The hotel plans for Molly's sat untouched on the coffee table. If Melissa didn't show in another hour or so, then he needed to pull his head out of his butt and focus on work. He slid the rubber bands off the rolled-up plans and spread the diagrams out before him, making notes where the inspector found problems. It was an old building, and if they were going to tear down portions or open up walls, they'd be dealing with asbestos abatement. The whole electrical system needed to be upgraded in order to handle the new circuitry for modern equipment. The inspector also found roof damage caused by a bad storm last winter. The roof would have to be replaced, along with repairs to the foundation. Everything had to be brought up to code. Josh needed to incorporate the upgrades while still keeping the integrity of the old landmark. It was like solving a puzzle. He loved what he did for a living, and it had the added benefit of distracting him from the constant distraction of Melissa Theroux.

He worked until his eyes grew heavy. The game went into extra innings, ending in a Giants win, but time had gotten away from him. It was after eleven when he looked at the clock. He hadn't heard a word from Melissa. Surely, they were home by now. He checked his phone but found no texts and no missed calls.

He got up and stretched his legs, which led him to the window. There were no cars in her driveway. Had they run into more trouble with the tow truck? Two beautiful women with a stranded vehicle late at night was a predator's dream. He dropped the blinds and picked up his phone. Just as he was about to hit her number, headlights flashed through the window indicating someone was pulling into the driveway next door. He pulled the blinds aside again in time to see the girls exiting Melissa's CRV.

He rushed out the front door and caught up with them on their porch. "Hey, did everything go all right with the tow truck?"

"What do you think?" Angelica grumbled irritably.

Melissa juggled with the key and the cat carrier. Josh took the key from her hand and unlocked the front door. "Thank you," she said with a relieved smile.

Angelica continued to curse under her breath as she stormed up the stairs in her nurse's scrubs. Josh followed her with his eyes until she'd cleared the landing upstairs. "She's had a rough day, huh?"

Melissa laughed. "She's one of the moodiest people I've ever met. Keep in mind, I grew up in the same house with Marguerite, which makes me an expert."

"Wow. That is moody." They chuckled a moment as she unlatched the door on the carrier. "Has she eaten?"

"Angie? Who knows. She was so grumpy about her car I didn't bother asking."

"No, I meant Ginger," Josh clarified. The confusion made them laugh outright as he scooped some cat food into a dish on the kitchen floor. The kitten happily hobbled over and dug in at the same time Angelica stomped halfway down the stairs.

"I don't know why everyone is laughing. Can you keep it down so I can get some sleep?"

Josh didn't care for her attitude and was about to tell her his thoughts on the matter when Melissa brushed it off like it was no big deal. "Sorry, Angie. We'll keep it down."

"He's staying?"

Melissa looked at him for a split second, "Um, no. It's late and we all have to work in the morning." She raised her eyebrows indicating he should agree with her statement.

It pissed him off.

He didn't want to leave. He'd been waiting for her all damn day, and now her rude roommate was cutting him off. *Again.*

Before he could disagree, Angelica said, "Goodnight, Josh." She stood there waiting for him to leave, eyebrow raised.

To his surprise, Melissa took his hand. "I'll walk you to the door."

He took a good look at her and realized she was exhausted. Resigned to wait one more day to be alone with her, he allowed her to lead him away. When they reached the door he leaned in and kissed her cheek. She smelled good, and it took everything he had not to linger a bit longer. "I'll see you tomorrow," he confirmed before he returned to his own empty townhouse.

CHAPTER 7
Stalker

Missy waited until Josh cleared her walkway before turning her irritation toward Angelica. "There's no need to be rude, Angie."

"I wasn't rude. I'm tired. This new job is kicking my butt," she mumbled, looking a little pale.

Missy took pity on her. "Do you want me to fix you some herbal tea before you go to sleep? It helps me unwind when I've had a crazy day."

Angelica smiled and descended the rest of the way down the staircase. "That would be great. You're so good to me." She sighed as she sat on a barstool. "I don't know what I'd do without you."

Missy turned on the electric kettle before gathering mugs and tea bags. "I don't know either." She giggled once and then faced her roommate. "And you'll apologize to Josh in the morning." She wasn't asking. As she'd reminded Josh, she'd lived with Marguerite her whole life. The secret to dealing with grumpy alpha women was to show no fear.

Angelica's smile dropped a bit. "Yes, I'll apologize to him. I promise."

"Good, because he hasn't done anything to justify your rudeness. He's my landlord, and having a roommate was not part of my lease. Be thankful he's so easygoing."

Angelica studied the mug in front of her before bobbing the tea bag up and down in the hot water. "You're right, Missy. He's been good to us. I'm just worried about Harold is all. I don't want you to get hurt, and I realize it was stupid of me to have you come get me this late at night. It was foolish to be out by ourselves. Harold could be anywhere. He could be watching right now."

"We aren't sure if it's even Harold who's after me. It could all be a prank."

Angelica pinched her lips with disgust. "You can be so stubborn, Missy. You know it's not a prank. But you're right, it could be anyone. It could be Josh."

"That's insane."

"Is it?" Angelica asked while sipping her tea. "You were fine until you moved back to Timbisha Township. Josh could've given you those chocolates. Doesn't his family have a small ranch? He could've easily gotten access to the animal tranquilizer, and he could have graffitied your car at any point in the night. Heck, he could've done it before he banged on the door."

Missy shook her head in denial. No way was Josh stalking her.

Angelica got up from the barstool and put her empty teacup in the dishwasher. "Think about it. I was right about Harold. If it weren't for me, who knows what he'd have done to you? I'm going to bed, Missy. You should, too. Hopefully, when you wake up, your common sense will have returned."

Missy sat dumbstruck as Angelica trudged back up the stairs to her bedroom. Could Josh be stalking her? He certainly had the opportunity to place the chocolates and tag her car, but what was his reason?

The kitten had long since finished her dinner and now rubbed herself against Missy's legs. "What are we going to do with her, Ginger?" she cooed as she picked up the kitten and carried her upstairs to her own room. Angelica was right about one thing: Missy needed to get a good night's sleep so she could think of a rebuttal for what Angelica had said about Josh.

MORNING DAWNED HOT AND BRIGHT. MISSY WOKE with the sun like she did every day. She was tired from the late night but decided on a quick jog anyway to clear the cobwebs from her mind. Angelica still slept, evident by the snores coming from her room. The image of the petite beauty snorting and snuffling the night away made Missy giggle like it had when they'd lived together. Some things never changed.

Downstairs, Ginger managed to get herself onto the back of the couch and into a ray of sunshine. Missy gently patted her head before opening the front door and stepping out into the new day. The air was cool in the shade, but the sun's rays were beginning to send their blistering heat across the landscape. After a few warm-up stretches, her feet began to pound the pavement, taking her on the same route which had led her to the ditch where she'd found Ginger. It was an older road, not well-traveled by cars at the busiest times of the day, especially in this small town. It could be argued any route she took at dawn would be without traffic, but the real reason she chose this one was because of the scenic vista at the end. It led up onto a hill overlooking the valley and Timbisha Township below. When she got to the top, she could see the rural valley beyond the town, the river, and the green fields of alfalfa growing in perfect circles where irrigation sprinklers offered water to lush plants. It was quiet on the vista, only the occasional birdsong could be heard, along with the stomping of her tennis shoes on the old asphalt and the intake of her rapid breaths as she ran.

All of her senses came alive when another set of foot stomps came from behind her. She'd been in denial, not wanting to admit her stalker was real, but now someone had followed her up this lonely road in the early dawn where nothing stirred except for a few ground squirrels and the occasional lizard seeking sunlight to warm its cold blood. Fear and adrenaline flooded her body, ratcheting up her already accelerated heart rate, and sweat poured down her face as panic flowed through her veins. Should she face her attacker or attempt to outrun him? She'd thoughtlessly left the house without any sort of weapon to defend herself. Hell, she didn't even own mace!

Just as she'd decided to make an all-out run for it, Josh's familiar voice filled the morning air. "Melissa, wait up! Are you trying to kill us?"

The familiarity of his voice made her angry as suspicion and relief spread throughout her limbs. She turned to find Josh bent at the waist, his hands gripping his knees as sweat dripped onto the crumbling pavement. "Are you trying to give me a heart attack?" she shouted back.

His eyebrows lifted in surprise at her rarely raised voice before consternation filled his. "I'm sorry, honey. I didn't mean to scare you."

Was that true or was he pretending to be someone he wasn't? Was Angelica correct to assume Josh was behind her worry? She'd known him all her life. He had a reputation as a player, but also as a prankster. Surely he wasn't so cruel? He'd never pursued her before now, and she'd never considered he'd ever be interested in her. She was plain, uninterested in playing dress-up or doing all the girlie things Marguerite, or even Angelica, liked to do. She definitely wasn't like the other women he'd been known to associate with. Yes, she'd dated, but it wasn't her favorite thing in the world because she never knew what to say or how to act. She'd never thought of herself as shy, the way the rest of the world did. She was awkward, which was worse. Missy wasn't Josh's type, and his interest in her made no sense at all. He could have anyone, so why was he so eager to start up a relationship with her?

His behavior didn't add up, especially with him following her up here so early in the morning. It occurred to her Angelica might be right. Josh might be her stalker after all.

"WELL, YOU DID SCARE ME! I DON'T LIKE BEING followed."

He hadn't expected her anger. *Damn it*. She was shaking from head to toe. He'd truly frightened her! With placating hands raised, he said, "I'm sorry, I wasn't thinking. I should've called out to you sooner."

"Yes, you should have."

At a loss for words, which was something new to him since he always knew what to say to a lady, he gestured toward the valley below. "Pretty view," he said a bit lamely.

She closed her eyes and chuckled. "Yeah, Timbisha Township looks idyllic from here. What made you follow me, Josh?"

He sighed, still hearing defensiveness in her voice. He'd

really, really scared her, and now she thought he was dangerous. He saw it in the way she stood back from him, the way her eyes darted in all directions as if she were looking for a way to escape him. Unfortunately, he couldn't control the honesty coming from his mouth.

"I missed having dinner with you last night. It seems like I can never get you alone." He wanted to kick himself for two reasons. First, for admitting how desperately he wanted to be with her. Second, for sounding like he was, in fact, stalking her. He wasn't, of course, but he was truly at a loss on how to handle this shy, intelligent woman. She was becoming quite the challenge. If he pursued her too aggressively, his actions could be misconstrued as something sinister. Shit, he was screwed.

She cocked her head, mistrust in her purple eyes. "You missed me? You saw me last night."

"Barely." He stuck out his bottom lip in a pout. "Look, I'd already intended to run this morning. When I saw you up ahead of me, I thought it was a good idea to catch up. I didn't follow you like a stalker, I swear." He crossed his heart hoping a little levity would gain him some trust.

She looked at her watch and frowned. "I need to get back before I'm late for work."

"I know, it's getting late for me, too." He could feel the wariness radiating off of her. She was still frightened. "I'm heading back down the hill, and since you're heading back down the hill too, we are going to have to go together." How was he ever going to get over this wall?

She eyed him for a second before her shoulders slumped. She muttered under her breath about being crazy, but he didn't catch it all. She gave him a nod before she started down the hill. To his surprise, when he started jogging next to her, she didn't shy away or try to outrun him. Maybe she'd figured out that he wasn't there to hurt her. If anything, he'd protect her. She'd made a good point, though. If her real stalker were around, this would've been the perfect opportunity for an ambush. The thought had him scanning the area for any sign of the creep. He didn't feel so bad for scaring her anymore because she shouldn't have been up here all alone in the first place.

They were silent as they descended the hill. Once the road leveled out, their strained silence became a comfortable one while they breathed in and out in unison. Josh kept an appropriate body-length distance from her, not touching her but letting her know he wouldn't abandon her if they were attacked.

When they arrived at their row of townhouses they stopped at the lawn in front to catch their breaths. Josh saw a curtain move in Melissa's upstairs window. "How's Angie getting to work today?"

Melissa shrugged. "She's calling someone. Charlie's friend, Marco, I think. Apparently he hires himself out giving rides to people around town as a part-time job."

Josh raised his eyebrows. "Really?" He thought about it a minute. "Makes sense. There's no taxi service here, but people still need rides." He admired the kid's ingenuity.

"Yeah, it surprised me too," she said with a reluctant smile.

Before he could ask her to lunch, God help him, she cut him off. "I need to get going. I'll see you later, Josh." She was inside her door before he could wish her a good day.

Feeling like a total ass, he headed to his own townhouse for a quick shower before getting himself to work. Hopefully he wouldn't take his anger out on anyone. Come to think of it, though, Jason needed a good beating.

JOSH'S MOOD WAS COMPLETELY FOUL. AFTER HIS less-than-ideal morning with Melissa, he'd been called out to Jason's, who apparently was having trouble installing the kitchen cabinets. The company sent the wrong color and he was on a rampage. Julie was still on bedrest, causing Jason to snap at everyone and everything. It wasn't like him to get so riled up over something so trivial. Errors happened in construction, not very often with King Construction, but they did happen and were usually handled in a professional manner. There was nothing professional about Jason's behavior this morning.

When Josh arrived, his brother was red-faced and itching for a fight. He was squaring off with one of the installers, who apparently had no clue he was about to get his block knocked off. Josh rolled his eyes at the cocky young bastard. "Back off before you get killed, Lane."

The young kid turned to Josh. "He called me stupid. No one calls me stupid."

Josh sighed. The kid was dyslexic and had a chip on his shoulder about it, but Josh's idiot brother wasn't helping matters by pummeling the help.

"You're either stupid or color blind. The paperwork clearly stated 'gray lowers' on the invoice, so which is it?" Jason accused.

Josh got between them when Lane charged. "THAT'S ENOUGH!"

Jason's chest bumped up against the palm of Josh's hand trying to push his way toward Lane. Lane, on the other hand, backed off a bit when he got a good look at the maniacal amount of rage in Jason's eyes.

Reaching for a calm he didn't really have, Josh ordered, "Lane, get in your truck and go back to town. Obviously, the order was mixed up. I'm sure you didn't load the boxes into the truck, right?"

Lane huffed, "No, sir."

"That's what I thought. Go on and get the correct cabinets. I called in before I got here, so the order's on the dock waiting for your truck. It's a mix-up. Nothing to get your face bashed in for."

"He should've checked it before he left—" Jason began before Josh pushed him back.

"Get a grip, will you? We're all worried about Julie. Pulling the heads off everyone around you isn't going to get this house built," Josh said into his brother's face while keeping his voice low enough so that their crew couldn't hear the exchange.

Jason's shoulders sagged on a resigned sigh before he sat his ass on the front porch steps. "They're killing her."

"Who's killing who? What are you talking about?"

Jason looked up and around at his surroundings. "Uh, the doctors."

Josh swore that wasn't what Jason was talking about, but before Josh could question him, Jason's phone rang. He answered and listened to the caller a moment before suddenly jumping off the porch and running to his truck. Josh followed on his heels. "What's going on?"

"Julie's been taken to emergency. She's in labor!" And with that, Jason was gone, tires flinging gravel everywhere, dust flying in the wind.

Josh left brief instructions with Dennis, their longtime foreman, before he got into his own truck and headed for the hospital behind Jason's trail of dust.

THE WAITING ROOM WAS FILLED WITH HIS FAMILY. Lauren paced back and forth, one hand on her throat, the other on her lower back as she mumbled her silent prayers. Lauren wasn't religious, but she'd been attending Mass regularly with the family. Josh's mother, on the other hand, had her rosary out and fingered the beads in well-practiced fashion. Next to her sat James, who had one arm around her shoulders in loving support; his granddaughter sat calmly on his lap with her blue blanket. For once, Jessica wasn't sharing her smiles with the family. Jarod hadn't arrived yet, and Josh assumed he was still on patrol. When Lauren saw Josh, she quit her pacing to hug him. She'd been crying.

"Oh, Josh, I'm so scared. Her water broke, but then she'd began to bleed and..." she cried before she covered her mouth.

Josh's heart stopped. He pulled Lauren in for a hug and saw the fear in his mother's eyes when he glanced over Lauren's shoulder. Jarod arrived at that moment and carefully removed his wife from Josh's arms. "What's happening? Marguerite said Julie'd been rushed here in an ambulance?"

James calmly explained the situation. "She went into labor early, but there are complications. Jason's with her now. The nurse said she'd keep us informed." Josh heard the fear in his father's voice and knew things were pretty bad.

"Has anyone told Charlie?" Josh asked.

Just then, Charlie arrived with Marco, his best friend from school. They were both in swim trunks and t-shirts. It looked like they'd been tubing in the river, as two high school graduates should be doing the summer before heading off to college. "Where's my sister? How is she?" Charlie's voice was tinged with fear and rage. They'd all worked with him to control a temper that could be fierce when life's challenges threatened Charlie's self-control.

Josh knew how to handle the kid because he'd practically raised him. You didn't baby Charlie. You gave him the blunt truth. The cruel past had done something to the boy. Josh explained what little he knew about Julie and they were all waiting to hear from the nurse. Charlie's Adam's apple bobbed up and down a few times before the kid got control of himself and resumed the pacing Lauren abandoned earlier. Marco leaned against a wall out of the way, showing support for his friend simply by being there.

Soon, a nurse gave them the news Julie had been prepped for surgery and her husband would be with her during the caesarean section. That was it. Nothing about her condition or the baby. Josh wanted to drag the nurse back and demand she give them more information. She left without a backward glance, as if it were nothing at all for a pregnant woman to be rushed, hemorrhaging, to the hospital. As the idea formed, Charlie punched one of the vending machines sitting in the waiting room. Two colas rolled out and hit the floor. He stared at the cans for a few seconds, breathing in and out through his nose, before picking them up and handing one to Marco. The young men popped the tops as if nothing had happened. Charlie took a long drink before he resumed his pacing.

Forty-five minutes later, a haggard-looking Jason entered the waiting room wearing scrubs, tears falling down his face. Everything in Josh's chest squeezed tight. Lauren swallowed a cry and Jessica asked, "Where's my Joojee, Huncle Jase?"

Smiling as he cried, Jason announced, "Boys! Two healthy boys!"

The room remained in shocked silence for about three seconds before everyone started asking questions.

"Twins?"

"What the hell? Are you kidding?"

"You hid this from me?"

"How's my sister?" Charlie asked the most important question of all.

Jason wasted no time in engulfing his young brother-in-law in a bear hug. "She's beautiful, wonderful! She's doing great! They're sewing her up now, and when they move her to a room you can all come see her." He didn't let go of Charlie, and the smile on his face seemed to grow wider.

Josh sat down in relief before it dawned on him those two had kept a pretty big secret from the rest of the family. "You guys lied to us!"

Jason sighed. "It was Julie's idea. She wanted to reveal the ultrasound pictures at the baby shower."

"That is the dumbest idea she's ever had!" Lauren declared. Tears of relief were still wet on her cheeks. Josh had to agree. No wonder Julie had been so big. She'd been carrying his two nephews. Lauren hiccuped and asked, "She's really fine?"

Jason let go of Charlie to give Lauren a kiss on the forehead. "Yeah, Sassy, she's perfect."

CHAPTER 8
Here Kitty

Ginger wasn't in the house when Missy returned from her jog with Josh. Though it wasn't a habit to let the cat out on her own, she'd gotten out a couple of times by accident. Ginger always kept close to the townhouse when she did make her "escapes." She was a people-cat after all, and Missy was sure the kitten had abandonment issues. However, Missy was going to be late for work if the kitten didn't reappear soon.

"Angie, have you seen Ginger?" she shouted as she readied the cat carrier. Her keys and bag were on the table next to the carrier, and all she needed was the damn cat so she could get going.

"No!" came a returned shout from Angie's bedroom upstairs.

Missy opened up the front door again and scanned the lawn, but found no sign of Ginger. Josh had left about five minutes ago. She'd heard the big engine of his Dodge Ram turn over and rev down the road. She walked all the way out to the sidewalk calling, "Here kitty, kitty, kitty," to no avail. She checked her watch again, then went back inside, grabbed her keys and bag, and yelled up the stairs once again to Angelica, "Can you look for her before you leave this morning? I can't find her."

Her roommate appeared on the upstairs landing, answering with concern, "Of course I will." She smiled down at Missy. "I'm sure she's off exploring. I promise to look before I leave, and when I find her, I'll bring her inside." Feeling only slightly satisfied, Missy thanked Angelica and dashed out the front door. She was late!

The drive to the clinic was lonely without Ginger. Missy had become attached to the kitten in the short time she'd had her. A pet was therapeutic, providing comfort when her anxiety came creeping in. Ginger was a very friendly cat, comfortable around people even though she'd been abandoned early on. The kitten should've been feral after living in the wild for so long. It was a miracle she was so sweet, and Missy prayed Angelica would find her before the end of the day.

Maybe she should call Josh. Ginger was half his, after all.

No, if Josh was her stalker, then encouraging him wasn't a smart idea. But what if Josh wasn't the stalker and the real one had stolen Ginger? What if he hurt her cat?

Maybe she should call Jarod. He was the sheriff, after all, and he'd made her promise to call if anything out of the ordinary happened. Would he take her missing cat as a sign of a possible threat, or was she being paranoid?

Splitting the difference, she dialed the sheriff's office anyway. Marguerite would know if Jarod could help find her cat.

"Hey, it's me," Missy said after Marguerite's formal greeting from the sheriff's station.

"Hey, *Me*! Oh, guess what! Julie's in labor. They're all at the hospital now," Marguerite informed her. As the town crier, Marguerite loved sharing community information.

"Wow, she's early, isn't she?" Missy thought about Julie's large belly and remembered thinking they'd miscalculated her due date.

"Yes, there are complications, though. Apparently she was hemorrhaging and needed to be taken by ambulance. I'm still waiting to hear from Jarod."

Missy parked her car in the back lot of the animal hospital. She reached over to get the cat carrier before she remembered she didn't have it with her. "I lost Ginger this morning. Do you think I should bother Jarod with finding her?"

There was a pause on the other end of the line. Missy swore she could hear the cogs turning in her sister's head. Finally, Marguerite said, "I'll let him know as soon as I hear from him. He's got good instincts, Missy. Can you tell me the last time you saw Ginger so we can puzzle out when she went missing?"

That's why she loved her sister so much. Marguerite could be superficial and nosy, but she was rational in times of crisis, and losing Ginger felt like a crisis to Missy. She explained about seeing Ginger on the back of the couch before she left for her jog, about Josh scaring her and possibly being her stalker, and about Angelica's car not working and their late night. Marguerite took it all in and before Missy knew it, they were ending the call with Marguerite's promise to call with any news at all. Marguerite didn't debate her suspicions about Josh, which surprised her. But, again, that was Marguerite. She only disagreed with you when you needed to hear it.

After the call, Missy grabbed her bag and rushed through the animal clinic's back door. The kennels were full. She was greeted with happy barks and a few whines for attention, which she gave to the most demanding patients before hurrying to the main area of the hospital. Doc and the staff were well into the morning meeting.

"Missy, there you are. We were beginning to worry," Gale said.

"I'm sorry. I couldn't find Ginger this morning."

Her announcement was met with sympathetic looks from everyone before they resumed going over the day's schedule. When the meeting finished, the day began to fly. Patients filled the waiting room. Doc had left on an emergency, which left Missy to hold down the fort while he was out.

The Timbisha Township's phone tree had been activated, and the news of the twins being born to Jason and Julie King was met with both joy and relief. She hadn't been the only person worried about Julie's size. Gossip spread about how the young couple had known they were having twins but chosen to keep the knowledge a secret. The town now speculated Camille King would have something to say about it. Missy couldn't imagine anyone going up against her. Camille was easy to get along with, and was well known for her kind heart and generosity in Timbisha Township. However, when it came to her family, Camille was a lioness protecting her pride. Missy hoped the deception wouldn't cause the lioness to eat her young.

MARGUERITE DRUMMED HER FINGERS ON THE DESK next to her keyboard while she decided what to do about Ginger. A missing kitty was a small matter, but the cat was important to Missy and therefore it was important to Marguerite. Add to it the mysterious and threatening messages left by her sister's stalker, and a missing pet felt like much more than a coincidence.

Missy thinks Josh is responsible?

Marguerite rolled her eyes at that stupid theory because it was obvious to anyone who'd been around them the past few weeks that Josh was in love with her, but Missy was too close to the situation to see it. Josh, God bless him, lost his famous charm whenever he was around her. It was just too cute.

"What's got your brow furrowed up, honey?" came a deep Southern accent from the other side of the counter.

She looked up into warm, brown eyes and cursed. *Something* about Declan McKinley rubbed her the wrong way. He wasn't rude, per se, but he wasn't polite either. "My sister's cat has gone missing."

Warm eyes widened with lifted eyebrows. "When?"

That he would take an interest in a missing cat was disconcerting since she'd been worried about it herself. "This morning, after her jog. Why? What do you know?" Her heart beat a little faster at his change in demeanor.

He adjusted his cowboy hat and stared out the plate glass window. "Have you told her about Harold yet?"

"You said not to."

"Hm." He drummed his thumbs on the counter and Marguerite swore she saw the gears moving in his head. "Have you told your sheriff about the cat?"

"Not yet, he's at the hospital with his family. His sister-in-law went into labor. Should I call him now?" Her anxiety amped up with every question he asked.

The marshal shook his head. "No, let's wait. Family comes first."

"Missy is my family, Marshal. She comes first for me, so is she in danger or not?"

He sighed. "Look, honey, I meant no disrespect to you or your sister. I'm gonna take a ride over to her condo. You wanna tag along? Maybe assure yourself she's safe?"

He'd done it again. Patronized her concern for her sister and treated her like a dumb blonde. "No, thanks. Missy's at work." She turned her chair to face her computer, ignoring Declan.

"Suit yourself. Let the good sheriff know I was in, would ya?" he drawled as he sauntered out the door. She was glad he was leaving for two reasons. First, simply because he was going, and second, because he gave her a fantastic view of his backside in those jeans.

Hell.

She knew herself too well. That pain-in-the-ass marshal was going to be on her mind until he left Timbisha Township. She could only pray they'd catch Harold so Declan would get out of town — and her head.

GOD HELP HIM, BUT THAT WOMAN CHAPPED HIS HIDE. There was no getting around her stuck-up attitude. Declan sighed to himself. Who was he fooling? She was way too young for him. She had to be in her mid-twenties and he was... not. Dismissing the delectable Ms. Theroux, he clicked the key fob to unlock the driver's side door of his pickup. He cursed the blazing hot handle as it burned his fingers before he hopped behind the wheel. Black was not a good color choice for a Nevada summer. Even the steering wheel was hot. He turned the engine over and cranked up the air conditioning. The radio was set to an eighties station, which suited him just fine. Van Halen's "Panama" beat through the speakers as he headed out onto the main road on his way to Melissa Theroux's condo.

Declan thought Timbisha Township was an interesting little place. He drove by the town's landmark, Molly's Diner, and noted the construction equipment filling the parking lot behind the restaurant. Signage emblazoned with *King Construction* covered the temporary chain-link fence surrounding the work site. His investigation of the town revealed the sheriff's family connection to the largest construction outfit in the state. He wondered why Jarod had chosen law enforcement over the family business — something he'd have to discuss with Bainbridge.

Declan shook his head thinking of the man formally known as *Special Agent* Dane Bainbridge of the Federal Bureau of Investigation. The man had connections Declan could only dream of tapping into. He wouldn't be on this case if it hadn't been for Dane. After Melissa filed the restraining order against Harold, Bainbridge had reached out to Declan because Harold Schurke/Klein's case had been the last one Bainbridge worked before he'd come home to take care of his sister and nieces.

Declan had told Jarod he was working a cold case left to him by his predecessor. He hadn't lied; he'd just left out the part about Bainbridge. He'd been apprised of their history, and neither Declan nor Bainbridge wanted Jarod's outlook on the case to be biased by their connection. Harold Schurke/Klein had ties to drugs, fraud, money laundering, and sex trafficking. He was a slippery son of a bitch and Declan couldn't wait to get his hands on him.

He turned onto Melissa Theroux's street and parked down the block from her townhouse. Five minutes later, a beat-up Honda Civic drove past him and parked out front. Two young men sat in the vehicle; one behind the wheel, who was texting, and the other in the back seat. The front door opened and a blonde woman wearing hospital scrubs rushed out of Ms. Theroux's front door and hopped into the Civic. The driver made a U-turn and sped back into town.

She must be the roommate.

Declan picked up the file folder next to him and scanned for her name: Angelica Daemon. A preliminary check found she'd shared a dorm, and later an apartment, with Ms. Theroux while in school. No priors. He tossed the folder back onto the passenger seat after he'd jotted down the Civic's license plate number. He'd run a check on the driver, and a deeper check on the roommate, when he got back to his room. They looked like a couple of teenaged boys, and his gut didn't send out any alarms to his brain, so he settled himself deeper into his seat. No need to be uncomfortable for a day's surveillance in the hot Nevada sun.

CHAPTER 9

Warning

Michael James King cooed sweetly in Josh's arms as he stood in Julie's hospital room holding the baby and gently swayed back and forth. Gabriel Charles King lay in the tiny arms of his cousin Jessica, who was sitting on her mother's lap. It said something about the smallness of the little girl that she still fit into Lauren's lap after her own pregnancy caused her lap to shrink significantly.

"...An' your daddy is my hunkle Jase. We have another hunkle, too. His name is Josh. He's holdin' your brother now, so ya don't hafta worry we lost him," Jessica said to the tiny infant. Gabriel struggled to keep his eyes open while the little girl spoke to him.

Michael was awake, his baby blue eyes taking in the new world. Josh smiled into his nephew's angelic face while listening to Jessica. The room was filled with hushed voices as the adults held up their cell phones to capture the babies' first moments of life.

Suddenly, Julie giggled from the bed. "Is this how their

lives are going to be? Camera lenses and cell phones in their faces twenty-four seven?"

Camille hovered over Josh's shoulder with her camera. "Of course, dear. We have to start on the baby books right away," she murmured, clicking the shutter.

Josh couldn't help but laugh. "I'd be taking my own pictures if I wasn't holding this little one."

"Oh, do you need me to take him?" his mother asked as if it were a burden, but they all knew otherwise. She wanted to get her hands on one of the twins.

"Missing him already, Mom?"

"Well," she said, handing the camera to James, "if your back is hurting, I wouldn't mind holding him." No, Josh's back was just fine, but he wouldn't deny his mother the pleasure of holding her first grandson. *Again.*

Josh placed a gentle kiss on Michael's forehead before handing the baby to Camille. Once she had her grandson in her arms, Josh kissed her cheek as well. The whole family was in the room. This wing had been paid for — and built by — King Construction. Therefore, Julie and the twins were enjoying one of the suites. Camille insisted on having a few built in the maternity ward. Timbisha Township was made up of large families. The births of new members were joyous occasions, and the birthing experience, she felt, should be as comfortable as possible for mothers, babies, and their extended families.

Jarod's cell phone chirped. He lifted it from his belt and scanned the screen. When his forehead crinkled, Lauren asked, "What is it, babe?"

"Missy lost her cat."

That got Josh's attention. "Ginger's missing?"

"Daddy, what happened to the kitty?" Jessica was all ears now.

Josh put a hand on Jessica's tiny shoulder, careful not to jiggle Gabriel. "I'm sure Ginger went for a walk, sweetheart. She'll come back. She's a very smart cat."

Now he had to convince himself of the same thing. Ginger hadn't left Melissa's side since they'd found her. He studied his brother's face while he read the text on his phone. Jarod was holding something back and Josh didn't like it. "What?"

Before Jarod could answer, Charlie and Marco returned to the room carrying three large pizza boxes and a couple of food sacks. "Sorry we're late, but Marco had to pick up a fare," Charlie said with annoyance while Marco smiled an apology. "Anyway, I got a combo, a cheese, and a Hawaiian. There's a big salad, some cheese bread, and chicken wings in the bags." He and Marco spread the food out on the table.

Anyone not holding a baby or confined to a hospital bed crowded around the table. "What do you feel like eating, Jujifruit?" Jason asked.

"She's asleep," Josh said.

"Can I feed Gay-brell?" Jessica asked excitedly.

"No," Lauren said with finality.

Charlie wrestled Gabriel from Jessica's arms so Lauren could eat. Jessica, knowing by the look on her mother's face an argument would get her nowhere, skipped over to the table where her daddy filled a plate for her. Josh snickered at her antics. She was small but deceptively ornery.

"Holy cow, this is a big family," said a familiar voice from the doorway.

Josh turned to see Angelica pumping some hand sanitizer into the palm of her hand as she looked around the room from the doorway. When she met his gaze, she laughed. "I thought I might run into you up here."

"I didn't know you worked the maternity ward."

"It's my rotation this week." She dismissed him after that to make her way over to a sleeping Julie. "Mrs. King, I need to take your vitals," she said softly while wrapping a blood pressure cuff around Julie's arm. Jason and Charlie stood back as the nurse worked but refused to leave the bedside.

"That nurse is a hottie," Marco whispered.

Jarod chuckled. "You think so? She's kinda old for you."

"Exactly," Marco said with a slow grin. "She was the fare I picked up today."

"How'd you finagle that?" Josh asked.

"Didn't Charlie tell you? Here," Marco said, pulling out a homemade business card emblazoned with the words *TIMBISHA TOWNSHIP TAXI SERVICE* and handed it to Jarod. "My grandmother always needs a ride to church. When I turned eighteen, I asked the four churches in town and the community center if I could post my card on their bulletin boards. I offer rides to people who need them. I charge two bucks a mile. A ride in town averages around five bucks, but I get more if folks need rides from the surrounding farms and ranches. I'm only doing it for the summer until I leave for college. So far, I've made over fifteen hundred bucks! There are a lot of people who're without wheels. I stay pretty busy."

"Can you pick me up tonight after my shift?" Angelica asked when she'd finished with Julie. "My car's still in the garage."

"Sure thing, ma'am," Marco said with as much charm as an eighteen-year-old could muster.

She was about to leave, but Josh caught up with her. "What happened to Ginger?"

"I have no idea, but I'm sure she's just out cat carousing.

She'll turn up, Josh." Angelica pumped more hand sanitizer, rubbed her hands together, and exited the room.

"Looks like you've lost your touch, little brother," Jarod said.

"I'm not attracted to Angie."

"Interesting, since she's a physical representation of every woman you've ever dated since you started dating."

Josh didn't like the smug look on his oldest brother's face. "What are you getting at?"

"Nothing. Unless, your tastes have changed recently."

Josh picked at a fingernail. "You know they have," he said quietly. Jarod had no clue Josh's taste had always been for Melissa, and Josh wanted to keep it that way. He'd never hear the end of it if his brothers knew the truth. "What have you found out about Melissa's stalker?" he asked to distract Jarod from any further interrogations.

All teasing left Jarod's eyes and was replaced with disgust. "Not a damn thing."

It was after seven when Missy opened her front door after a long day at work and a visit with her mom. The living room was completely silent. No stuttering purr greeted her as she lay her bag on the counter. Angelica wouldn't be home until after eleven. She had the whole townhouse to herself.

It was lonely.

She opened up the refrigerator and scanned its contents. Nothing looked good, so she opted for a hard cider instead. She popped the top, turned on the television, and flopped onto the couch with a dejected sigh. Just as she was getting comfortable, she heard the beefy growl of an engine winding down next door.

Her stalker was home.

Gosh, the thought of telling him she'd lost Ginger had her eyes filling up. She swallowed to keep the tears from falling, but it was useless. Josh had just met his nephews. She didn't want to ruin his day by telling him the bad news about her negligence with the cat. She was a veterinarian, for crying out loud, and she'd lost her own pet!

How embarrassing.

Missy wallowed in self-pity for five more minutes before there was a knock on her door. She knew who it was before she even got up to look out the window, and she couldn't help the smile forming on her lips, despite the situation. She took a deep breath and opened the front door. Josh stood there holding a pizza box and a six-pack of beer. It was the best thing she'd seen all day.

"Hey," she said, trying not to pout.

He stepped through the threshold and leaned in to her cheek, giving her a soft kiss. "Hey, yourself."

She wanted to throw her arms around him and cry. She'd never felt so needy, especially when the person she was attracted to could be stalking her. The thought made her step back. She couldn't erase the smile from her face, though.

"Is that for me?" She indicated to the pizza box.

He grinned, showing off his dimple. "It is. I thought you might be hungry. Don't get too excited, though. It's only the leftovers of what Charlie brought for lunch at the hospital," he explained as he took the food and beer to the kitchen.

"Oh, how is Julie?" She listened to him intently as he

explained how scared they'd been and how Jason and Julie had kept the truth about the twins a secret, and then gave a long description of each baby. The love he felt for his nephews was obvious. As he spoke of his new family members, Missy's guard slowly came down. Did crazy stalkers love children? She didn't think so. There wasn't a mean or crazy bone in this man's body.

Still, before she could stop herself, she asked in a dazed whisper, "You aren't my stalker, are you?"

Josh lost the grip on a glass he'd been holding. He ended up catching it after a cartoonish juggling act ensued. Beer dripped off the counter where it sloshed out of the glass. He turned to her with incredulous blue eyes. She felt the beet-red blush crawl up her neck and cursed herself for the question. He shook his head, put down the glass, and stepped into her personal space. Gently, he cupped her cheeks with his warm hands and stared her down. "No, I'm not your stalker," he said clearly before placing his lips on hers. He kissed her with so much tenderness her knees went weak. He continued to caress her mouth, licking her lips until she moaned, giving his tongue access to hers.

White hot heat shot through her body. This man could kiss, and Missy's body responded to his sensual demands. As she was about to wrap herself around him, he gently pulled his mouth away, leaving her desperate for more. Breathing heavily, he touched his forehead to hers. "But I am pursuing you."

"Thank God," was all she could manage to say. She'd never wanted a man as much as she wanted Josh King right this second. Still on fire, she leaned up to kiss him again, but he leaned away.

"We have plenty of time *for that*." To soften his rebuff, he kissed her lips — chastely this time — then both of her cheeks and finally her forehead. "Tonight I want to get to know you better. You look tired. Tell me about your day." He grabbed a rag, sopped up the beer from the counter, then got another one from the fridge. This time he took care pouring it into the glass and handed it to her. He filled his own glass, took the pizza box into the living room, and patted the seat next to him on the couch. While he waited for her, he changed the channel to the Giants game.

She laughed in disbelief. "You are so confusing."

"What? You don't like hanging out with me?" He was teasing her. It would be funny if he hadn't just kissed her silly.

Maybe he's a sadist.

Deciding to be bold, she told him the truth. "I love hanging out with you."

"I hear a 'but' in there."

"I don't understand why you'd want to hang out with me." There, she'd admitted it. He was *Josh King*, Timbisha's Ladies' Man Extraordinaire, and she was plain ol' Missy Theroux, nerdy kid sister to the homecoming queen. He'd been confounding her since she'd moved into the townhouse and found the damn box of chocolates on the front porch. No, before that, since he'd flirted with her at Jason and Julie's wedding. She couldn't get their dreamy dance out of her head, or the way he'd tenderly held her. He'd been so sweet, but she'd been too scared to let him know how she felt, and she'd clammed up like a ninny. Was he messing with her or did he really care for her? She hoped it was the latter because she really wanted to kiss him again. Maybe even do more than kiss him.

Doing more would be a first for her.

"You don't have to understand why, you just have to know that I do." He took her hand in his and held it while he settled back on the couch facing the television. "Now, tell me about your day," he repeated.

She cocked her head. "You really wanna know?"

"Yes," he said with conviction. "I want to know everything about you, Melissa."

She waited for him to admit he was kidding around. He didn't.

"Fine, here goes." She described her day in detail, from the time he'd left her to losing Ginger, and everything leading up to when he'd shown up with the beer and pizza. She left no detail out. He listened to every word, expressed his concern for the missing cat, and vowed to help her find it. They settled into a comfortable conversation, and she enjoyed his company so much she forgot to be worried about saying something awkward. He flashed his dimple more times than she could count, and soon her heart was full of something she was afraid to name. He was still on the couch holding her hand when Angelica walked through the door at midnight.

"You two look cozy," Angelica announced after closing the front door.

Josh gave her a knowing smile. "We are, thank you. How was Marco's driving?"

"Gentlemanly," she answered with a conspiratorial smile. "And convenient."

"Oh my God, Angie. You did not put the moves on that sweet boy," Melissa accused.

She was so cute Josh couldn't stand it. "Of course, she didn't." He chuckled. "Marco probably put the moves on her."

Angelica winked slyly. "He's a bit too young for me, Missy."

"Hey, how was Julie when you left? Or can you tell me?" Josh asked with concern for his sister-in-law. She'd seemed fine when they'd said their goodbyes, but he'd noted the paleness of her skin and remembered the fear in Lauren's voice when she'd explained about the ambulance and the hemorrhaging.

"Mother and babies are doing fine. I'm worried about Daddy, though."

"Jason? Why?" He'd seemed okay when Josh left the hospital, totally smitten by his new family but getting back to his normal, domineering self. Jason had been a real crabby bastard for the last month. Josh had to talk three of their subcontractors out of quitting in the past week alone.

"Honestly, I think he was more exhausted than his wife. When I checked Julie's vitals before I left, your brother was asleep in the chair next to her bed with a baby on his chest and holding Julie's hand. The man is a multitasker even in sleep," she said around a delicate yawn. "Listen, I'm beat. I'm heading upstairs for a shower and my own bed. You two behave, now," Angelica lilted as she schlepped up the staircase.

Josh turned to Melissa, whose eyelids were a bit droopy as well. "I should get going. Tomorrow is a workday for both of us." He kissed her forehead as he stood.

"You... you don't have to leave if you don't want to." She blushed adorably, testing his resolve and making him regret his decision to wait, but he pulled her into his arms anyway.

"I told you, we have plenty of time for that." He smoothed the hair from her face. "When I make love to you, I want you to be fully conscious. You're dead on your feet, babe," he whispered before stealing a soft kiss. As he pulled away, she leaned into him demanding more. Not one to deny a beautiful woman, Josh let her have what he'd been holding back earlier. He tilted her head for a deeper fit and plunged his tongue into her sweet mouth. She tasted so damn good, and he made sure to pour how much he cared for her into the kiss. Melissa wasn't a one-night stand — would never be with him. If she let him keep her, he would get down on his knees and thank the good Lord every night. He had to gain her trust. She'd accused him of stalking her only just today and she needed time. He needed her to trust him one hundred percent.

When he released her, she hummed softly, her eyes at half-mast with exhaustion and arousal. He had to cut his losses now before she attacked him. "We'll look for Ginger tomorrow morning before we go to work. Thanks for spending the evening with me."

"Goodnight, Josh," she said a bit dreamily before closing the door behind him. As he stepped off her porch, he turned to see her standing watch through the window. He waved before he made it to his own front door.

HIS ALARM WENT OFF AT FIVE-THIRTY, DISRUPTING hot dreams of the girl next door. He hadn't slept much, and now he was sorry he'd left her last night. He dragged himself out of bed and into a cold shower. As the sand washed from his eyes and the sleepy haze dissipated from his brain, the decision which had been taunting him since they'd shared a dance at his brother's wedding burst through the fog like a rocket.

I am going to marry Melissa Theroux.

Quietly obsessed with her all of his life, he didn't want a summer fling with her. He wanted forever. Yeah, he'd gone out of his way to seek out women who were nothing like her, in looks or in heart, only to be left disappointed. High-maintenance women never kept his attention for long. They threw themselves at him on a daily basis and, quite frankly, they bored the shit out of him. They were never what he *needed*.

Melissa was different, charmingly awkward at times but not when she was helping some poor creature, or when her temper flared — or when she was turned on. In those moments, she was confident, self-assured, and caring. She was real.

Ever since both of his brothers married Josh's two best friends, he didn't want to wait around for his own happiness. He suspected his sense of urgency was exacerbated by his nephews' births. However, deep down, he knew Melissa had always been the girl meant for him. How he knew this had more to do with his instincts rather than his feelings for her. He just *knew*.

Having come to the conclusion he was done being a bachelor, he threw on his jogging shorts, a shirt, and some running shoes before texting Melissa to see if she was up yet. As he put his keys in his zippered pocket, his phone chirped with her reply that she was on her way over. He smiled at his phone, tucked it in the pocket with his keys, and opened the front door where he found a ratty box blocking the front steps.

It was meowing in a pitiful but familiar way.

Melissa came up the walk as Josh opened up the box and lifted Ginger into his arms.

"Oh my God!" She reached for the cat and hugged the animal to her chest. Ginger purred but was totally out of sorts.

What the hell?

He saw the envelope at the bottom of the box at the same time Melissa went to reach for it. He grabbed her wrist to stop her. "Don't touch it. I'm calling Jarod," he seethed, barely containing his rage.

She warily backed away from his anger, but he didn't have

the capacity to soothe her yet. He took a breath through his nose and hit speed dial.

"This better be good," said a sleepy Jarod, the lazy bastard still in bed.

"The son-of-a-bitch left Ginger in a box on my front porch. There's a note at the bottom but we haven't touched it," he gritted out through clenched teeth.

Sheets rustled on the other end of the phone. "I'm on my way. Is the cat all right?"

"I think so. She's alive, but Melissa's checking her out now," Josh said quietly as he rubbed the back of his neck in frustration. She examined Ginger through teary eyes on the other side of the porch, still keeping her distance from Josh. It pissed him off even more.

"Melissa is at your house already?" Jarod had a teasing tone in his voice that Josh did not appreciate.

"Now's not the time for your teasing, asshole. Just get your lazy ass over here. I want to end this bullshit before I lose it." Josh clicked off and turned to Melissa. "How is she?"

She sniffed, which damn near broke his heart. "Dehydrated, listless, but she's purring. I need to get her to the clinic."

Josh clenched his fists. "I wanna go with you, but I have to wait for Jarod."

"I can't wait that long. She needs intravenous fluids."

Josh wanted to pull his hair out. The psycho was probably out there watching, waiting for Melissa to be alone, but one look at the kitten and he knew he couldn't keep Melissa here. He pulled her into his arms. "I'll be there as soon as Jarod is finished collecting evidence. Text me when you get there so I know you're safe."

"I will," she said distractedly as she continued to look at the cat.

Gently, he put his finger under her chin to get her attention. "Promise me, Melissa," he commanded.

She surprised him then. She leaned up and kissed his cheek. "I will text you as soon as I get there."

While she went inside to retrieve her car keys and the pet carrier, he made sure her SUV was devoid of intruders, then he escorted her to the driver door. Once she'd secured Ginger into the front seat and herself behind the wheel, he kissed her good-bye. He checked that no one followed her down their street, and when she finally turned the corner, he went back to the porch and stared at the dirty box which had contained his cat. He wanted to punch something — or better yet — someone.

Fifteen minutes later, his cell phone chirped, indicating she'd made it to the clinic, right as Jarod pulled up in his cruiser. "This shit's getting old," he deadpanned.

Josh said nothing while Jarod put on gloves and pulled a camera from his bag of tricks. He placed markers, took pictures of the porch, the box, and different areas of the front yard. Josh didn't understand everything his brother photographed but stayed quiet while Jarod worked his grid. Finally, Jarod was ready to examine the note. He reached in and opened it up. Instead of a word jumble this time, there were clippings of letters glued all over the page. He swore as he read the message and then raised worried eyes to Josh.

"What's it say?"

"'Stay away from what's mine. Making you disappear will be easier than the cat.'" Jarod placed the note on the porch and took more photos.

Josh kicked one of his patio chairs onto the lawn.

"Throwing a fit isn't going to keep her safe. You know

that," Jarod muttered as he looked through the lens. "Keep your head on, Josh. We'll get this creeper. Sooner or later he's going to screw up." He put the camera down and began to place everything he'd collected into evidence bags. "By the way, I've got some help from the U.S. Marshals."

Hands still on his hips, Josh looked at his brother. "Did you call them?"

"No," Jarod admitted. "Interestingly enough, Marshal McKinley is tracking the same professor Melissa put a restraining order on, and only the first name, Harold, is legitimate. This guy is a douchebag—the professor, not the marshal—because Melissa isn't the first woman he's harassed."

Josh swore under his breath. The catnapping and the message to Josh meant the suspect was nearby and watching, was much closer than anyone dared to think. He waited for his brother to explain further what he'd learned about Harold the stalker and the amount of danger he presented to everyone involved.

When Jarod continued with his work and didn't say anything, Josh lost his patience again. "Are you going to tell me the rest or just be a prick?"

Jarod put the evidence bags in his cruiser and turned to Josh. "I can only tell you we are doing everything in our power to get this son of a bitch. Marshal McKinley is an old buddy of Dane's." Jarod climbed into the cruiser. "Where's Missy now?"

"She took Ginger to the clinic."

"Alone?"

Exasperated, Josh explained, "I didn't like it either, but I had to wait for your slow ass to get here, and I couldn't stop her from taking care of the cat. She texted when she arrived. She's safe for now."

Jarod shook his head in disgust. "Stick close to her, Josh.

McKinley's been doing surveillance both here and around town. He drives a black pickup with Texas plates, so if you see it, *do not approach*. If Missy's being watched, we don't want to tip off Harold, understand?"

Josh nodded but didn't like it.

"I'll call you when I know more," Jarod promised as he started the car, then backed out of Josh's driveway, which was typical of Jarod. Just drop a bomb and leave.

CHAPTER 10

Mr. Right

Missy donned some scrubs from the supply closet to cover the shorts and shirt she'd thrown on for her morning jog. Ginger was resting quietly in a kennel with a saline drip attached to her leg. They'd taken blood samples. Doc concurred with Missy's suspicion the cat had been drugged. As soon as the toxicology results came back, she'd call Jarod.

First the chocolates, and now my cat.

She wondered what the note said. Another threat? And why had Ginger been delivered to Josh instead of her? Did her stalker know Missy considered Josh half owner? She eyed the patients waiting to be seen and wondered if one of them was her stalker.

"House of Stark?" she called out, reading the name listed on the chart. Sounding confident was a joke at this point, but she tried her best.

"Hey, Missy." To her surprise, Charlie Armstrong stood up with a carrier full of puppies.

"Hello, Charlie. Obsessed with *Game of Thrones*, I take it?"

"Only a little," he replied facetiously.

"Come on back," she instructed while she glanced at the chart. "Ah, vaccinations today."

Charlie placed the crate on the examination table. There were seven border collie puppies inside, in all their black-and-white fluffiness. As Missy readied the vaccines, Charlie handed her an envelope. "Camille's having a welcome home party instead of a baby shower since the twins are coming home tonight. Here's your invitation."

"Oh my. Thank you." She stuffed the envelope into her pocket to read later when she had time. "How is everyone doing?"

Charlie talked nonstop about his sister, the new babies, and how dopey Jarod, Jason, and Josh were around the twins. He even showed her all the pictures he'd taken on his cell phone. Charlie was pretty dopey about the babies himself. He couldn't hide his pride at being an uncle. "I hope we don't give the twins brain damage before they can walk. Don't cell phones give off a lot of radiation?"

She laughed outright, startling the patient she'd been examining. Charlie soothed the pup while Missy picked up a syringe. "Not enough to be concerned about. Here, hold her like this. Time for shots," she instructed.

The brief bright spot in her day darkened after Charlie left with the puppies. The toxicology results confirmed Ginger had indeed been drugged. Doc made the call to the sheriff's office. Missy would text the information to Josh later. She cursed herself for being a coward and not calling him, but she'd never seen him as angry as he had been this morning.

Josh was the "fun-loving" brother, not the menacing one.

That title was reserved for Jason. In her heart, she trusted that Josh would never turn the infamous King Brother temper on her, but the look in his eyes still frightened her. So, she'd texted him instead of phoning. She was busy anyway and didn't have time for a conversation.

By noon, Missy was filling her water bottle in the breakroom. Because of the chaos this morning, she'd shown up to work sans lunch. Her worry over Ginger ruined her appetite anyway. She was just screwing the lid on the bottle when strong arms wrapped around her from behind. "Have you eaten?" Josh said in her ear, his breath hot on her neck. Goosebumps formed on her arms.

She shook her head because her voice had disappeared with her appetite.

He turned her around and kissed her lips. "How's our kitten?"

"Better. I'm taking her home tonight. How did you get back here?"

"You think I've never been in the back of this clinic?"

She glared at him. He was joking, but she wasn't really in the mood.

He retreated a bit and said sheepishly, "Sorry. Are you hungry?" He gently moved the wisps of hair which escaped her sloppy ponytail out of her face.

"Maybe a little," she admitted, feeling better now that he was there. "Yeah, I could eat."

"Good! Get your purse, I'm taking you to lunch."

"I left without my purse or proper work attire. What you see is what you get."

He kissed her for real then. It turned into something a bit desperate until her sister's voice disrupted the interlude.

"Oh, *thank* God. I thought I was going to have to pull out

the big guns to get you two together." Marguerite laughed. "I'm hungry. Let's all get some lunch so you can tell me what the hell went on this morning."

"What are you doing here?" Josh asked accusingly.

Marguerite raised one of her finely plucked eyebrows. It was the look she gave Missy whenever her decrees were being questioned. "Checking on *my* sister. What are you doing here?"

Josh grinned evilly. "Checking on *my* girlfriend."

Missy missed the approving smile on her sister's face because she was too busy gawking at Josh.

I'm his girlfriend?

"How's Ginger?"

Coming out of her daze and not wanting to discuss the change in her relationship status with Josh to her busybody sister, Missy recounted the events of the morning as the trio rode in Josh's pickup to the diner. Josh held her hand the entire ride to Molly's, and she loved it.

"Declan says Harold has a history, Missy. He's dangerous," Marguerite said.

"Who's Declan?" Missy asked.

"He's a U.S. marshal," Marguerite answered with distaste and a dramatic eye roll.

"What's wrong with him?"

"Nothing," she huffed. "I'm sure he's a perfectly nice person."

"But you don't know for sure?" Josh teased.

"Of course I know for sure. He's an old friend of Uncle Dane's, so that makes him okay. How did this conversation turn into twenty questions about Declan McKinley?" Marguerite demanded.

Well, would wonders never cease? A man had finally rattled

her sister's cage. Missy sneaked a look in Josh's direction to see a dimple form in his cheek. "He's not interrogating you. Jeez, calm down," Missy scolded while stifling a laugh. "What did this Declan have to say about Harold's past?"

Back on track, Marguerite explained what the marshal had told her and Jarod. "Harold used a false identity when he was your professor. Apparently, before that, he'd harassed another girl who'd filed charges against him, too."

Missy sat stunned. Josh, strangely quiet, parked the truck at the crowded diner. Harold had definitely harassed her, but he'd backed right off after she filed the report. Missy thought him annoying, not dangerous — at least not until she'd moved back home. Things escalated here, but why? She said nothing more and hoped they'd change the subject once they got into the diner.

The restaurant was packed, but they found stools at the far end of the counter, two on one side of the corner and one on the other. Marguerite quickly took the single stool on one side, while Josh and Missy took the other two, making it easy to speak to each other without leaning over the person in the middle. Even so, Missy found Josh leaned into her anyway, and, God help her, she found herself leaning into him in return. He smelled so good, and he'd said she was his girlfriend. The thought was thrilling and something very new to her.

Marguerite poured sweetener into her iced tea. "Jarod handed me an invitation to the twins' welcoming party this morning. I almost snorted coffee out of my nose."

Josh laughed. Missy elbowed him in the ribs.

"Are you going, Missy?" Marguerite asked.

She pulled her own envelope out of her pocket. "Charlie gave me mine this morning. I haven't opened it yet."

"But are you going?" Marguerite insisted. "Oh, what I am

asking? Of course you are. We'll ride together." The decree seemed reasonable, but Marguerite normally liked to make an entrance. Missy squinted at her sister. Did she detect a bit of self-consciousness from Marguerite? What had Declan said to make her sister's notorious bravado falter?

"How about we do this," Josh offered. "Melissa and I will come and get you. That way I get to walk in the door with two beautiful women. I have a reputation to maintain, after all."

"You think I'm beautiful, Josh? Why didn't you say something sooner?"

Missy knew her sister was teasing, but it irritated her anyway. Josh could have anyone, including Marguerite, but his answer washed the irritation away.

"Because you already know you are, Marguerite, but not as beautiful as your little sister. No offense." He kissed Missy right at the counter for all to see. Public displays of affection were not something she was used to and definitely not good for someone with social anxiety. She wanted a hole to open beneath her and swallow her up.

"Stop it," Josh whispered in her ear. "If we move forward, you'll have to get used to me kissing you wherever I feel like it."

Marguerite laughed. "That's the answer I was looking for, Josh. Yes, I'd love for you two to pick me up. I'm in for the threesome."

Missy put her face in her hands and prayed no one heard her sister. Her prayers went unanswered, though, as the men wearing King Construction t-shirts sitting at the table behind them began to laugh heartily.

Josh dropped the girls off at the clinic before heading back to Jason's place. The men from the diner who'd laughed at Marguerite's innuendo were part of his brother's crew and had beaten Josh back to the work site. Jason was back to normal, thank God, except for the moony-eyed grin plastered to his face day and night. When he called Julie to check up on her for the eighteenth time, Josh swore he could see hearts and flowers coming out of his brother's ears. It was sickening.

He couldn't wait for it to happen to him.

They'd finished working by suppertime, and Josh was impatient to get home. He broke most of the speed limits on the back roads until he got to town. Seeing her CRV in the driveway, Josh wasted no time getting cleaned up before heading next door.

"Hey," she said when she opened the door. She'd changed into hip-hugging shorts and a t-shirt exposing the belly button jewel he'd seen before. His eyes zeroed in on the piercing before he caught himself and forced his eyes back to hers.

"Hey, yourself. How's our girl?" He could hear Ginger's unmistakable, stuttering purr coming from the kitchen.

"She's much better and glad to be home, I think. How could anyone drug and starve something as sweet as she is?"

"Monsters don't care about animals, Melissa." He scooped up the kitten and Ginger said hello with a raspy meow. Josh nuzzled the sweet kitten before putting her back on the floor so she could finish her dinner.

"Well, I've got half a mind to shoot him when I find him." Melissa went into the kitchen to add some more kibble to Ginger's dish, then pulled a plate of chicken breasts out of the fridge and set it on the counter. "Hungry? I was about to fix dinner."

"Sure, but first things first." He took her into his arms and kissed her like he'd been wanting to do all day. Warm and sweet, she tasted like heaven. It wasn't long before she wrapped her elegant arms around his neck and held on tight. Ten seconds later, she took over the kiss, and it was him being devoured. He let her have her way until the urge to pick her up overtook him. He carried her to the couch and gently laid her down, never breaking the kiss. She was as hungry for him as he was for her, but oxygen deprivation was affecting his judgment. He refused to make love to her for the first time on her sofa, where her roommate could walk in on them. He'd need a hell of a lot more privacy for what he wanted to do to her, and he needed to put on the brakes without hurting her feelings.

"I'm sorry, I only meant to kiss you hello," he whispered.

"I like the way you say hello," she answered sweetly.

Her shy admission surprised, and pleased, him. "I just like you."

A flare of awareness sparked in her eyes. "I like you, too, Josh." She proved it by stealing another kiss. The confidence in her touch nearly consumed him. Good intentions be damned, he wanted her right now, right here on the—

"Meow."

They came up for air to see Ginger sitting on the floor next to the couch, looking up at them with curious eyes. Her stop-starting purr was in high gear as she blinked golden eyes, and her tail swished back and forth as if she were interrupting them on purpose. Josh kissed the tip of Melissa's nose before sitting up to lift Ginger onto the couch. She happily burrowed between them, eventually settling herself into a ball to sleep. Though he was annoyed, he was thankful for the distraction.

Melissa followed his lead by sitting up and stroking the kitten's fur, drawing his attention to her hands. He wanted them on him. Damn, he needed to distance himself from her before he lost control. "Stay here, I'll go put the chicken on," he said, trying not to look as if he were escaping. He wanted her to trust him.

"Oh, you don't have to do that." She began to stand, but he stopped her by once again pressing his lips to her sweet mouth. He could not get enough of her.

"I promise, I'm a much better griller than Jason, so you can sit and relax for a bit. He headed out the sliding door to prep the barbecue before he could change his mind about keeping his libido in check.

Thankful to be out of her gravitational pull, he stepped onto the small patio off the dining room and started Lauren's old grill. Once it fired up, he closed the lid and surveyed the tiny plot of dirt filled with weeds. Most tenants planted tomatoes or flowers in this area, but Josh had neglected to do anything with it before he'd rented to Melissa. He felt like a horrible landlord. He made a mental note to hit a home improvement store for weed killer as soon as he had time.

Satisfied the ancient barbecue stayed lit, he went back inside to season the chicken and found Melissa fixing a salad. She smiled but said nothing when he returned. Was she back to feeling shy? Or was she relieved he'd stopped kissing her? She'd physically responded to him, but did she care for him at all? Had she cared for the other men she'd dated? It wasn't like him to question his abilities to woo a woman. Hell, even his brothers couldn't touch his charm. But damn, Melissa had always kept him guessing about her feelings, making him feel insecure in ways he shouldn't. She'd said she liked him, but was it more than physical? More than jogging in the morning and sharing a kitten? He wanted more, a hell of a lot more. He wanted what his brothers had, and he needed to prove to her she could trust him enough to give him her heart. He was up for the challenge of earning Melissa's trust. He'd keep his cool and not let things get too physical tonight. He needed to go slow. As much as Josh wanted to make love to Melissa, he wasn't sure if now was the right time. He had to get a leash on his desire before she got the wrong impression of him.

Ignoring his self-doubt, he grabbed the platter of chicken and headed back out to the grill. Ginger followed him outside and wound herself between his legs while he watched the flames kiss the chicken breasts, careful not to let them burn while they seared. When they'd had enough flame, he moved them up to the shelf, closed the barbecue lid, and turned down the heat. If he went back inside, he'd find Melissa and forget about the chicken. He knew it wouldn't be a good idea, so he played with Ginger for a few minutes before he checked on the meat again.

———

JOSH WAS AT THE GRILL STARING AT THE FLAMES when Missy set out the salad and place settings. She was feeling more and more comfortable around him, but conversation still didn't come easy. Physical attraction was the only thing they had in common. Maybe she should just roll with that? She had zero experience with men, other than a few disastrous dates in college, and Harold. Since nothing but a restraining order had occurred there, she didn't count her psycho professor as dating material.

If she were being honest with herself, Josh was the only man she'd ever been attracted to. He was handsome, strong, funny — God, he had a great sense of humor. But Missy had observed the types of women Josh dated over the years, and she wasn't like those bombshells. Marguerite was more to his liking. Even Angelica fit the bill. She looked exactly like every woman she'd known Josh to associate with. Missy was the polar opposite. Josh's attraction to her made no sense, but the more time she spent with him, the more she *wanted* it to make sense, and *that* had never occurred to her before because she never knew what to say to a man.

When he finally turned around, her heart skipped a beat. His blue eyes caressed her face before drifting down the rest of her body. No man had ever looked at her like that, and she wasn't sure if she should feel dirty... or bold.

"I want to kiss you again, but I don't want to burn the chicken." He laughed.

A nasty blush crept up her throat as a boldness she'd never known came over her. Laughing a little herself, she said, "I don't mind my chicken crispy."

"You don't know how happy that makes me." He wasn't laughing anymore.

Josh removed the chicken from the grill and brought it to the table, giving her time to think. Was she misinterpreting this whole thing? Was she just another conquest for him? Was Angelica correct when she'd said Josh wasn't sincere about his feelings?

She considered the situation for a moment. He'd never been disrespectful to her. In fact, quite the opposite, he'd treated her like no other man had before. He'd been there when she'd found Ginger and seemed as concerned for the animal as she'd been. He'd never blinked an eye about the cat living in his townhouse, or that she'd taken on a roommate without prior approval on her lease. He'd expressed his concerned about her mother's illness. He'd been protective about her safety, and his family had always treated her with kindness.

And when he said he wanted to kiss her, she felt the sincerity of his words in her heart, no matter what her brain tried to tell her. She couldn't be that far off, could she? The only other men who'd ever shown an interest in her had been in college. They'd been aggressive and looking for a good time, not a relationship. She'd seen through them and had no time for any of their trivial nonsense. She'd assumed with Josh's reputation, he'd be the same, but she'd been so wrong. Instead, he was gracious and caring, and it made her like him more than she'd like to admit. Fine, she'd secretly crushed on him for most of her life. If she wanted to get to know him better — really know him — then she had to take action. Feeling courageous, she leaned over and kissed his cheek.

"Thank you for not burning the chicken." The giggle escaped her when he suddenly grabbed her hips and sat her on his lap.

"Well, I'll be damned. You shocked me, Melissa," he said with a teasing glint in his eye. It was gone in a flash when he took her mouth again.

There was no more laughing. She melted, forgetting everything as the kiss deepened and grew. She worried briefly her inexperience would show, but the way he made her feel overshadowed her doubts about herself, as if she were more than the girl renting his townhouse next door... as if she were more to *him*.

His arms tightened around her body before he stood up. "What are you doing?" she whispered against his lips while looking into pretty blue eyes.

"I'm not hungry for food anymore. I'm taking you to bed." The resignation in his voice, made her doubt herself again.

"Oh." Still, a denial never occurred to her.

"Yes, 'oh.'"

She swallowed back the confession she knew she should make, not wanting to stop him from what she hoped would happen next. She was older than most women should be for her first time, and the thought made her feel like a loser, like the last person picked for the team. Even if she could voice the words, how would she say it? She hadn't saved herself on purpose, but she'd always wanted Josh to be her first lover, not because of his reputation around town, but because she'd always liked him. He was sweet and funny, and he cared about people even when he was pulling pranks on them. Rather than make an awkward attempt to warn him he was about to sleep with a novice, she smiled and touched her lips to his again, reveling in the masculine taste of him and formally committing the sin of omission.

She was quickly discovering that kissing was easier than talking anyway. He opened his mouth and her tongue automatically danced with his, sending shivers through her body. He took two steps at a time up the staircase while still holding her in his strong arms, wooing her with his strength. Once he hit the landing, he made a beeline for her bedroom, and not once did she think to stop him.

He kicked the door shut behind them and went straight for her unmade bed. Oh crap, her room was a complete disaster! The embarrassment of not keeping house vanished when he gently deposited her in the middle of the messy sheets and pressed his body against hers. She felt Josh *everywhere*. Desire sparked so strong he became her universe. Shyness fled as she wrapped her arms and legs around his body as if it were natural.

Ravenous for more, her body took control and she began to writhe. She was overheated though the air conditioner was on, and his subtle cologne drifted through her bedroom, mingling with her bedding. His hands explored her body, touching places never touched by a man before. When he reached her bellybutton, she felt his fingers swirling around her piercing.

"This little gem has been driving me insane, Melissa." Josh continued to play with the charm while he kissed her. "Do you have any idea how beautiful you are?"

She may be a virgin, but she wasn't ignorant about sex. Though his question thrilled her, she also knew these were the things a man said while making love. She offered no response to his nonsense about her looks and, not wanting to ruin the moment, she swallowed his white lies like a poisoned pill and enjoyed the vision of Josh King, in her bed, with sex on his mind.

Sex with *her*.

He would be her first, and she wasn't about to stop him with an argument over pillow talk. Besides, he'd already removed her t-shirt and was now fingering the front clasp of her bra.

She held her breath as he leaned down to suckle her neck. Her bra popped open, causing her to jump and exposing her to the suddenly cold room.

He didn't touch her breasts, but kept his vivid blue eyes locked with hers. Suddenly he knelt in the middle of the bed and with a jerk, lifted her up to sit on his legs so she straddled his lap. She thought he'd say something, but at the last second, he held her cheeks in his big hands to devour her mouth once more. His kisses made her lightheaded.

Then his hands began to explore.

Not wanting to be the only one without a shirt, she boldly fisted his t-shirt and dragged it up over his head. Skin-to-skin contact made her go a little crazy. She couldn't get close enough.

"Shh, slow down, baby. We've got all night," he soothed as he laid her back down. He took his time kissing her, slowing the pace but exciting her all at once. He kissed down her neck to her collarbone before trailing his lips where she wanted them most of all. When she thought she couldn't take anymore, he drifted down her sternum straight for her bellybutton. He tongued the amethyst jewel before clasping it with his teeth and gently tugged — like he'd done to both her nipples. She leaned her head back and groaned, not knowing how much more she could take.

When he unsnapped her shorts, alarm replaced her passion. "Josh," she whispered.

Should I tell him?

He looked up from where he'd been tormenting her belly. She saw only heat in his eyes and shallow breaths from his mouth. Had she aroused him that much? Would he be able to stop? Did she even want him to?

"We don't have to do this," he said with concern. "You say the word and we stop right now."

God, did she want to stop? There'd be no turning back once she was naked. Concern, respect, and caring — they were all there in his eyes. "No, I just..."

Climbing back up her body until he was nose to nose with her, he whispered, "Talk to me, Melissa."

She'd stopped him from taking the most important thing she could give, and now she wanted to kick herself. "I'm sorry, I don't want you to stop."

"I hear a 'but' in there."

She giggled at the double entendre but sobered quickly. She wanted it to be Josh. He wasn't in love with her but, so help her, it had to be him. "Please make love to me, Josh. I won't stop you again."

"Do you have any idea how long I've waited for you to say those words? Oh, God! Melissa..." He took her mouth again, only this time he was the one moaning. The fire in her blood ignited once more, and this time there was no going back.

CHAPTER 11
Morning After

All of Josh's plans to wait, to prove to Melissa she could trust him, went straight out the window the moment her sweet request to make love left her sumptuous lips. Damn it, no other woman heated his blood like Melissa Theroux. He kissed his way down her body, taking his time and counting the near-invisible freckles dusting her chest and soft shoulders. He felt her quiver, reveled in the gooseflesh covering her arms and her sporadic, panting breaths. When his tongue found the damn bellybutton ring again, he couldn't stand it anymore. He ran his finger under her waistband, feeling her suck in a startled breath.

He closed his eyes and savored the softness of her skin. When he opened them again, her violet eyes shone in the setting sun coming through the blinds, making him wonder what color they'd be at the height of her passion.

Determined to find out, he dragged his lips from one hipbone to the other before he stripped away her shorts, revealing delicate panties underneath, and grinned. Melissa had an inner vixen and an undeniable siren's call.

Staring at the masterpiece he'd unveiled, he vowed to protect her no matter what. God had never created anything more beautiful than Melissa Theroux, inside and out, but when she turned her head to the side and closed her eyes, he stopped.

"Baby, look at me," he begged, not recognizing the gruffness in his own voice. He swallowed and prayed he hadn't lost her. He waited for her to open her eyes, and when her gaze met his, he slowly stood up taking her pretty undies with him. With a wolfish smile, he tossed them to the floor and rid himself of the rest of his clothes. Her wary eyes drifted down his body until they landed on the part of him that demanded to be inside of her. He chuckled when the passion he'd been coaxing out of her turned into surprise. Something niggled in the back of his mind, something he'd suspected but she hadn't admitted to yet. If he was correct, he'd have to be extra careful with his passion. Not wanting to scare her off, he decided on a little levity.

He looked down at himself with mock confusion. "What? This isn't what you were expecting? I'll try not to be insulted."

Her eyes flashed up to his as redness stained her cheeks. Still she said nothing. Talking was overrated at a time like this, anyway. Slowly, he put his hands to her knees and drew them apart. He slid his hands up the inside of her thighs. So soft, so warm, and she was so ready. He climbed back onto the bed and didn't stop heading north until his body was cradled by hers. When she wrapped her long, silky legs around his hips, his blood heated to an unholy temperature and he lost his usual skill and finesse. Then her sweet mouth attached itself to his neck and her small hands did their own exploring. He groaned and hugged her body to his. God, he'd wanted her for so long.

She ground herself against him, making his plan to be

careful dissolve into nothing. He reached down to her core and found her hot and wet, one finger slipping inside with ease, small and tight. When he tried for a second finger, she tensed. The fog cleared a little as he realized he'd been right. The knowledge humbled him at the same time it amped up his need to claim what she was so freely giving to him.

"Melissa, Melissa," he whispered as her breathing increased and she ground herself into his hand. He replaced his hand with himself and looked into her eyes. "I love you." Then he began to push... right through a hymen.

If that hadn't jerked him back to reality, then Melissa freezing in pain did. The confirmation of her virginity shocked them both. He raised himself onto his elbows and stared at the woman he loved, the woman who'd just given him everything. Her face was turned to the side, eyes pinched closed, and her teeth bit into her bottom lip. He put his forehead to her temple and tried to slow his breathing. Other than that, he didn't move.

"Are you still with me?" There was no use discussing the obvious. She'd been a virgin and hadn't told him. What wasn't clear was whether she was injured. "Did I hurt you, love?" A tear slipped from the corner of her eye and his heart broke. "I'm so sorry, baby."

But when he tried to remove himself from her body, she squeezed him tight, trapping him with her legs. "Please don't stop, Josh." Her eyes remained closed. "Please... please don't stop."

"Are you sure?"

Finally looking at him, her deep purple eyes luminous in the fading sunlight, she ran her fingers through his hair and brought his mouth to hers. He loved it when she touched him, and he once again stirred inside her. She hissed in a breath.

"I've never been more sure of anything. Please don't stop loving me now."

"Never," he promised. "I'll never stop loving you." Slowly he began to move. He watched her closely, making sure he wasn't hurting her. He kissed her, caressed her, and as their bodies moved together, he patiently waited until her breathing sped up again and she began to match him thrust for thrust. A fine sheen of sweat began to coat her brow, her neck. He couldn't resist licking it, tasting her. He felt her passion grow, and when it finally crescendoed, he let himself go. "Melissa, oh God, Melissa!"

Arms giving out, he fell lifelessly onto her still-panting body. He nuzzled her neck, relishing the essence that was uniquely Melissa. He kept her close, not wanting to lose their precious contact. She still held him, calm and content.

He was absolutely spent.

Shifting to her side, he ran his hands along her face, wiping the damp hair from her temples. She was beautiful and she was his.

"You're incredible, you know that?"

"So are you," she whispered tiredly before her eyes slipped shut. He watched as her breathing evened out into sleep.

Incredible. Breathtaking. Earth shattering. It'd been a long time since he'd taken someone's innocence. Taking Melissa's brought out a possessiveness he'd never known existed. He was hers and she was his, even if she hadn't returned his admission of love, but she'd given him something he could never give back. At the very least, she trusted him, but why hadn't she told him? He prayed she felt the same way because if he had this all wrong, he didn't think his heart would survive the blow.

MISSY WASN'T ALONE IN HER BED. SHE WAS ON HER side facing the window with Josh plastered to her back. His cologne floated around the room while one of his hands coasted down her hip, swirled around her bellybutton ring, and then swooped down between her legs.

"Oh God," she moaned as his magic fingers began casting the spell which had kept her from getting any sleep the night before. "I don't think I can."

His chuckle tickled her ear. "Sore?"

"M-hmm," she murmured as her hips swayed to the rhythm he strummed, belying the denial she'd just given. He knew it, too, the scoundrel.

"Tell you what," he said as he rolled her to her back, his fingers not skipping a beat on the instrument they played. "Just lie still for a minute and let me do all the work." He tickled her lips with his tongue, cutting off her excuse that they should get up. Half an hour later, she didn't care if they ever left the bedroom.

———

MISSY WIPED THE STEAM FROM THE MIRROR AND tried to concentrate on her hair again. She didn't look any different than she had yesterday. She had the same tanned skin with freckles scattered over her nose and cheeks. Her eyes were still a weird shade of blue which changed with her moods. This morning they were a deep purple. Her hair was the same plain-Jane auburn it had been her entire life. She ignored her insecure thoughts, concentrating instead on weaving her hair into a single French braid down her back. Water dripped to the floor as she twisted three sections into the plait. She picked up her towel to wipe the ever-forming steam from the mirror.

"Can you hand me a towel, babe?"

Josh finally shut off the water and opened the shower curtain, blasting the mirror with steam — *again*! He was gloriously naked and wet, his big hands smoothing back his overlong hair from his face. She handed him the towel and stared in awe. His muscles moved seductively as he dried his face and his tattooed torso, then headed south. Her eyes followed that lucky towel before he wrapped it around his narrow hips. Lost in indecision, she wasn't sure if he looked sexier with or without the damp bit of cloth slung low around him.

"If you keep looking at me like that, you'll never make it to the clinic on time," Josh warned, interrupting her lustful perusal.

"Fine," she pouted. "I'll just have to dream about you all day." She slapped her hand to her mouth.

Holy hell, where did that come from? She cringed as his face split into a wicked grin before throwing his head back and howled with laughter.

"I should've gotten you into bed sooner, Melissa. I like it when you talk dirty." The towel around his perfect body began to tent.

Now red-faced, she opened the bathroom door and skedaddled down the stairs to the kitchen like a ninny.

Honestly, his stamina was astounding.

It was early, and she assumed Angelica was still upstairs. She'd been too preoccupied with Josh the night before to hear her roommate come in from her shift at the hospital.

God, she hoped she hadn't made a lot of noise. *How embarrassing.* Speaking of which, she couldn't get Josh's look of surprise at discovering her secret out of her mind. He hadn't commented on it this morning, so maybe it wasn't a big deal to him and he'd leave the matter alone. It was her business anyway, and she didn't want to discuss her lack of a love life with anyone, not even Josh. Maybe he hadn't noticed. She continued to live in that fantasy until he entered the kitchen.

"How does a beautiful, intelligent woman like yourself keep her innocence for so long, Melissa?"

He wrapped his arms around her waist from behind and gently bit her neck, making her heart rate speed up. His unique scent overshadowed the flowery soap from her shower. Maybe he didn't wear cologne at all, and it had been him all along? She didn't know the answer, but if she didn't get a handle on things soon, they'd be rolling around on the kitchen floor, and she couldn't remember the last time it had been swept.

"Now who's the one to keep us from work?" she asked.

"Who said anything about round... how many was that again?"

God, he was naughty.

She turned in his arms and pushed him back to arm's length. "Seriously, we're going to be late," she scolded. "Do you want coffee?"

"I want answers." He leaned on the opposite counter crossing his arms over his muscled chest. Oh, that chest, with its ridges and bumps, tattoos ranging from scary to funny, leaving her mouth watering and her body aching for more.

"Stop that."

"Sorry!" She spun around and poured coffee into two mugs. "Cream and sugar?"

"Yes, please. And get on with the 'splainin' cuz I'm not leaving until you do." He raised an eyebrow at her when she handed him the mug.

"Fine. What do you want to know?" She left him standing in the kitchen alone while she began the process of getting Ginger ready to leave. Food, water, carrier, kitty toys—

"Let's start with, why me?"

Was he serious? She couldn't tell him *that*. She tried not to blush but wasn't sure if she succeeded. Taking a page out of her sister's book, she brazened it out. "Why not you?"

"Don't screw with me, Melissa. What happened last night wasn't casual and you know it."

Oh no. He was angry.

"No one else has taken an interest in me that way," she mumbled. It was the truth, sort of. Harold had been interested in possessing her, but it wasn't love, which is why she'd slapped him with the restraining order.

Josh didn't look satisfied, making her confess, "And I know last night wasn't casual."

That seemed to appease him. He jerked her into his arms for another hot, deep kiss. "Not. Casual."

She smiled. "I gotta get going, Josh."

"I know. Here, let me help you."

As they gathered up her things, she wished she could tell him what last night meant to her, but nothing came out of her mouth.

He escorted her to the car, helping her get the cat carrier situated on the front seat while she climbed behind the wheel. She shut the door, and he leaned into the open window for a goodbye peck. "We'll finish this conversation tonight."

"Fine," she grumped before backing out of her driveway, knowing she wouldn't have anything brilliant to say tonight either. She gave one last look at Josh as he headed to his own townhouse wearing the same clothes he'd worn the day before. He tossed her his cocky grin before swaggering up his walkway. As she pulled away, she noticed the upstairs curtains in Angelica's room fall forward.

CHAPTER 12
The Body

"What's with the sappy grin?" Jason asked while he instructed Charlie and Marco on what to do with the sofa. Jason, Julie, and the twins were moving into their new house today. A room had been built for Charlie, but Julie's younger brother had opted to stay with James and Camille until he left for college. Josh was going to miss the kid in the fall, but meanwhile, Charlie and Marco were part of the moving crew.

Josh set down Jason's ottoman. "I'm just happy for you, brother."

"No, it's something else," Charlie said before he moved past him to the front door for more furniture.

"He's lovesick," Marco said with disgust. "He looks like you did right after prom."

"I did not look like that," Charlie argued.

"Dude, the unicorns coming out of your ass were rainbow colored and spewing gold sparkles from their horns," Marco said as they hopped off the porch and headed for the van. They were still bickering when they climbed inside to get the coffee table.

"I swear, I think those two were brothers in another life," Jason murmured. "Which brings me back to my own little brother. Spill it, Josh. Did you add another notch to your bedpost?"

Jason was only kidding, but damn it, Melissa wasn't another notch, and the jibe stung. He said nothing, hoping he wouldn't lose his temper and Jason would take the hint. His hope was for naught.

"What? No sex-ploits? You must've lost your touch. Maybe you should ask Melissa out instead of insulting the local ladies."

Josh shoved Jason against the wall, catching his badass brother by surprise. The big fat smirk fell off Jason's face, giving Josh a bit of satisfaction. "Do not talk about Melissa like that."

Charlie and Marco walked in with another armload, still bickering about prom. They were followed in by James and Camille.

"Good lord, what are you boys fighting about now?" Camille addressed the room at large with exasperation. "This is moving day, gentleman. Unless you all want to spend the rest of the afternoon helping me in the craft room, I suggest you knock it off."

His father chuckled. Camille's dictates were not to be ignored and they all knew it. No one wanted to spend time in her Room of Doom.

Josh let go of Jason, whose smile spread across his face. "Sure thing, Mom."

"Sorry, ma'am," Charlie and Marco said in unison.

"That's more like it. Now, let's get the rest of the crew in here so we can get this place ready for Julie and my grandbabies, shall we?"

Soon they were a well-oiled machine under Camille's supervision, furniture and boxes being placed in the correct rooms as they went. She'd asked a few of her event volunteers to help with the unpacking, and by lunchtime the house looked like a home.

The next item Charlie carried into the living room was Jessica. "Come an' get it!" she announced from the safety of Charlie's arms.

"Is Jujyfruit here?" Jason asked as he shouldered past them in the foyer to find his wife and kids.

Josh followed his family outside to the picnic table he'd built years ago. It still sat under the shade of an enormous cottonwood which still provided ample shade on a hot summer's day. It would be haunting in autumn when the leaves turned gold.

Lauren and a few ladies Josh recognized from church were setting up a buffet. Others brought folding tables, chairs, and picnic blankets. Julie left the twins in their car seats while Jason set up a portable playpen serving as a bassinet.

Josh looked around. "Where the hell is Jarod's lazy ass?"

Lauren grimaced. "He couldn't make it. He said there'd been a body reported in one of the abandoned motels just outside of town."

"A body?" His mind immediately went to Melissa. How long had it been since he'd seen her? Six hours? Had she been lured out on a call? He reached for his cell phone and tapped out a text.

"Don't you think if something had happened to Missy, we'd know it by now? Marguerite would be on a warpath." Lauren set out some food then stood in front of him with her arms crossed across her ample chest, emphasizing her growing belly.

"Yeah, you're right, Sassy. I just get," he trailed off.

"Obsessed?"

He looked at her from under his lashes sardonically. "Concerned."

She sighed in sympathy. "Have you asked her out yet?"

"Uh…"

"Josh, you're going to have to take control. Missy's a sweet girl and I know she likes you, but she's just, you know, awkward sometimes. But once she gets to know you, she'll be more comfortable in expressing herself." She patted his back and went back to setting up for lunch.

If she only knew how right she was, he thought as he made his escape. He didn't want to discuss last night with his family. They didn't need to know just how much he'd gotten to know Melissa, how comfortable she was with him. *Physically*. Things still weren't settled between them. She hadn't told him how she felt about him, and as the day wore on it ate at his psyche.

Once everything was ready, he fixed himself a plate and sat on the blanket next to his niece and nephews. Jessica sat cross-legged with a plate of macaroni salad, ambrosia, and half of a turkey sandwich. Though the sandwich looked small, when she picked it up, her little hands barely fit around the roll stuffed with turkey, cheese, lettuce, and pickles.

"Need some help there, princess?"

"Nuh-uh." She crammed a bite into her mouth. He watched closely for a moment. When he was satisfied she had her sandwich under control — and didn't choke herself — he dug into his own meal. Of course, Julie had outdone it. How she'd had time to prepare this much food with two newborn babies was beyond him. The woman was a superhero.

One of the twins cooed — Michael, he thought — and Josh made to pick him up.

"I wouldn't do that if I were you," Jessica warned around a bite of ambrosia. "Joojee don't like it when ya pick 'em up without askin' first."

Josh sat back, unsure. The baby looked fine, he wasn't fussing, just looking around. Maybe he didn't need to be picked up after all. Then Josh considered his niece. "Have you been helping with the babies, Jessica?"

"O' course." She raised her eyebrow at him.

Yeah, that was a stupid question. No wonder "Joojee" wants her to ask before she picks them up. He settled back down with his plate, content to sit next to the babies and Jessica under the shade of the cottonwood. Conversations took place around him, but he wasn't interested in engaging with anyone.

He wished Melissa was there to share the afternoon with him.

"How's your lunch, sweet pea?" Lauren clumsily sat her rounded self on the blanket next to Jessica, kissing the top of her head on the way down.

"Really good, Mommy."

Josh shared a look with Lauren. When it came to food, Jessica was the least picky kid he'd ever met. Neglect will do that to a child.

After thanking the many volunteers, Jason and Julie finally made it back to the blanket. "Did you two eat?" Lauren asked.

"We did," Julie said as she picked up a now-fussy Michael. Gabriel was awake now and starting to make some noise, too. Jason reached in to pick up his son. "And now it's time to feed these rascals." Julie kissed the baby in her arms before sitting him on her crossed legs and began to adjust her shirt.

Josh scrambled to his feet while Lauren threw her head back and howled. "Chicken bock bock," she called after him.

He didn't care. That was the last thing he wanted to see. He wandered around the crowd, shaking hands with people he knew, thanking them for their help. His parents were ensconced with an older group of people they'd known all their lives. Timbisha Township was a small but rich community of caring and loving people. How so much trouble had happened here in the past year was beyond him.

"Wanna toss the football around?"

Charlie studiously looked at Josh and away from the blanket where his sister was breastfeeding their nephews. He let out a hearty laugh. "Yeah, sure, kid. Bring it on."

Josh spent the rest of the afternoon playing yard games with Charlie and Marco, and occasionally Jessica, who thought she could keep up with the boys. Soon people began to disperse, but they still had a bit of work to do. Jason and Julie wanted to stay in their new home that night. It would've been one of the happiest days of his life except Melissa wasn't there to spend it with him. The melancholy the thought brought on surprised him and he hated it. Sooner or later, he'd get Melissa to admit her feelings for him. Then, they'd begin the rest of their lives together.

"Did you tell him you loved him back or did you leave him hanging?"

Missy moved her cell phone to the other shoulder and stared out the window in the breakroom. She hadn't confessed her feelings for Josh because she was a big sissy.

When she remained silent, Marguerite sighed into the

phone. "Oh, Missy. Men need to hear how we feel just as much as we women need to hear it from them." Her sympathetic advice was almost too much to bear.

"I was a little caught up in the moment," she admitted weakly. "You know, words failed me." *Like they always do.*

"I bet you were," Marguerite gently teased. "Have you talked to him since you left this morning?" she asked with concern now.

"No, he was helping the family with Jason's move into the new house today, and I've been slammed here. Actually, I need to get back to work. The schedule's packed and these animals aren't going to cure themselves."

"I know you care about him, Missy. Please don't be afraid to tell him. He won't laugh at you, I promise. I know his reputation doesn't help, but Josh is one of the good ones." The empathy in Marguerite's voice made Missy's lip quiver, but she viciously held back her tears.

"I'll try, Marguerite. Thanks for listening."

"Anytime, baby sister. I love you."

"I love you, too," she said quietly before ending the call.

She'd been able to escape to the breakroom briefly when there was a no-show in the schedule. Her mind had been racing since she'd left Josh that morning. When it came to men, Missy counted on her sister's advice, and she'd badly needed to talk to another woman about what had transpired. She hadn't told her sister every detail but, as always, Marguerite knew what she was feeling. It was a sister thing, something Missy counted herself lucky to have, even if Marguerite was a diva. Speaking of divas, she'd have to tread carefully where Angelica was concerned. She didn't seem to care much for Josh, and Missy didn't want to hear Angie claiming last night was a mistake.

She entered the waiting room and picked up the next chart.

As she was looking it over, two more patients entered the crowded space, excitedly discussing local traffic in Timbisha Township.

"I wonder where they were headed with such fanfare?"

"No clue, but something sure is up. The last time Sheriff King had that many emergency vehicles on the road, they'd found a body burned up at the Restful Night Motel. Remember that?"

"How could I forget it? I'm so glad Sheriff King got that drug business cleared up before anyone else got hurt."

The problem with small towns is everyone knew everything about everybody. She wondered how many tongues would wag when the news spread about her sleeping with Josh and what they would say about her loose morals. The thought was depressing, and scary. People would ask her questions about her relationship with the town bachelor and quietly pass judgments.

As the day wore on, she caught bits and pieces about the brouhaha. Mostly speculation on whether there'd been a terrible traffic accident on I-80 or if another murder victim had been found. The consensus was fifty-fifty either way and everyone would have to wait for the morning paper to be delivered the next day.

Missy hadn't heard from Josh all day, and now she began to worry about him. Had he been in an accident? A large portion of the townspeople who were usually able to volunteer had been helping with Jason and Julie's move today. Surely if something horrible had happened to Josh, everyone would know it by now. The Timbisha Township phone tree was more accurate than Reuters and the Associated Press combined, but still she worried.

At six in the evening, she looked at her watch and realized

the day had flown by. The charts were all gone and there were no more patients waiting to be seen. Though she'd been worried about him, she didn't text either because she didn't want to interrupt him when he was with his family. Wasn't there some sort of unwritten rule about not texting a man the day after you'd slept with him? She really wanted to know if Josh was all right, though.

Her hands started to sweat as she stared at the text screen on her cell phone. Josh's name was at the top, and her last message from him was still there. Should she ask if he was home? Would it be suffocating, like the little woman checking up on him? The anxiety gathered in the pit of her stomach, and she cursed her ignorance of social norms and the inability to communicate confidently with people. As she debated for the hundredth time, her phone pinged in her hand.

It was Josh.

Are you home yet?

Relief made her fumble her phone before she could tap out her reply: *Not yet but leaving the clinic now. Where are you?*

Leaving Jason's. You and Ginger meet me at my place? I'm hungry. ;)

A winky face? Now she laughed. *I'll see you soon.* In her rush gathering her things, she almost closed the door on the cat, which generated a disgruntled hiss from Ginger. The sun was nowhere near the horizon when she ran to the parking lot. It was still blazing hot in the sky, and her little CRV was like an oven. Luckily, she could roll the windows down with her key fob to let the hot air clear out before she put Ginger in the front seat. By the time she'd squealed out onto the main road, the air conditioner blew cool air around them, and both girls were happy to be going home.

"That's my suspect," Declan McKinley declared. "Looks like Schurke's been dead a while."

Declan and Jarod stood in the abandoned motel, a structure like so many other ruins dotting the Nevada desert, remnants of failed businesses long ago left to rot after the mines ran dry. Like the decayed building, Harold Schurke/Klein had once been a virile man. Now he was just another murder victim emaciated and lifeless, tied to an old bedstead in a forgotten motel. The slatted headboard was still sturdy, but the rest of the frame looked as old as the structure hiding it. Surely Harold could've broken free if he'd tried?

"Yes it does," Jarod murmured as he picked up an empty vial from the littered floor. "Ketamine."

"That would explain why ol' Harold here couldn't break out of this crumbling bed. His killer kept him weak." Declan surveyed the room with a critical eye. He was no crime scene investigator, but it didn't take a genius to note the scant amount of fast food wrappers and water bottles to understand the killer had barely kept his prey alive.

"The medical examiner will determine time of death, but it looks to me like this body's been here a while, weeks maybe." Jarod's brow was furrowed, but Declan agreed with the sheriff's assessment.

"Then who's been stalking Ms. Theroux?"

"My thoughts exactly." Jarod placed the empty vial in an evidence bag and headed back outside.

The stench of decomposition was strong, and Declan needed to get some air as well. He followed Jarod back out into the heat where he could breathe easier.

The death left more questions than answers. Taking

Schurke back into custody had been his assignment. Finding him dead should've meant Declan was done here, but the sheriff still needed help. Declan owed it to Bainbridge to find his niece's stalker. A copycat maybe? Who had kidnapped Schurke, then left him tied to a bed to die in an abandoned building in the middle of nowhere? It was all connected, Declan was sure. He and Jarod needed to find the missing piece to the puzzle.

His thoughts were interrupted by the ever-efficient elder Ms. Theroux's voice buzzing over the sheriff's mic.

"The medical examiner's on the way, Jarod. Any ID on the vic?"

A look passed between Jarod and Declan before the sheriff answered. "The body is too decomposed, so we'll need dental records to confirm. Marshal McKinley will have to wait for our people to process the body before he can leave Timbisha Township."

Declan puzzled at the comment, noting a twinkle in Jarod's blue eyes. What was his game? There was a pause before Marguerite replied, "Did I ask how long he'd be in town?"

Jarod chuckled. "She's so easy to rile up." He slammed the trunk after placing the evidence bags inside and turned to Declan. "It wasn't long ago she made my skin crawl, did you know that?"

"Uh, no." *And I don't really care, but,* "Are you sleeping with her now?" The thought pissed Declan off and he didn't like the feeling. It was nothing to Declan with whom Jarod cheated on his wife.

Jarod leaned his head back and laughed. "Hell no! I love my wife, dickhead."

Declan raised his eyebrows at the insult but didn't take

exception. Jarod didn't seem to notice and plowed on about his secretary.

"Marguerite isn't what she appears to be. I didn't think anyone could fill Lauren's shoes at the station, but I was wrong. Don't tell my wife this, but Marguerite's damn near irreplaceable. Her problem is she's got low self-esteem."

Declan snorted. "You're joking, right? That vixen has more self-esteem in her little finger than any other woman I've met."

Jarod tilted his head. "Huh. I pegged you to be a better judge of character than that, although Marguerite does put on an Oscar-winning performance to hide her issues. I can see where she'd trip you up. Anyway, I didn't believe it until I realized she'd been working undercover for her uncle on a case last year. When everything was resolved, I kept her on because she knew the job better than Lauren. My biggest fear is losing her to the field."

Declan rolled his eyes. Blondie in the field? That busybody would alert every criminal in her wake she was undercover.

"I know you don't believe me, but I also know you have the hots for her." Straightening from his relaxed position against the cruiser, Jarod leaned into Declan's space. "It's no skin off my nose if you want to get to know her better, but know this. I consider her a part of the family because she helped save my wife and daughter from a madman. Not to mention my brother has his sights set on her little sister, so if you hurt her, you and I will have a problem. Understand?"

Declan smiled. "Loud and clear, Sheriff." He'd seen nothing but polite tolerance between the sheriff and his secretary, but now the man was championing her? Declan's curiosity was officially piqued, and since he had reason to stay in Timbisha Township, he'd determine what Marguerite Theroux was like for himself.

He'd already done a little digging on her. Why he'd run the background check was beyond him, but what he found left him with more questions than answers. She was twenty-six and earned a degree in criminal justice and business administration. Upon moving back home, she immediately went to work for the sheriff's department. The mysterious part was there was nothing else on her, but he attributed it to her uncle. Even though Dane Bainbridge was retired, he was still well connected in the bureau. Declan had decided not to investigate her further until Jarod mentioned her work undercover. If she'd played a role in the undercover operation, why had she gone back to work for Timbisha Township instead of pursuing a career in the field?

Declan sighed. He didn't have time to ponder the life choices of Marguerite Theroux. His target was dead, and now he had to find a killer before anyone else got hurt. One thing was for sure though. Marguerite was dangerous to his concentration. He needed to stay the hell away from her.

CHAPTER 13

Babies

"There are a lot of cars here." Missy was relieved her voice didn't quake at seeing so many people in attendance.

I'm not doing any public speaking, for crying out loud, just idle chitchat.

Nope, didn't help. She started to sweat.

"It's going to be fine." Josh pressed a kiss to her temple. He'd been doing it a lot lately, kissing her whenever he felt like it, holding her hand, and whispering things into her ear to make her blush — and not from anxiety.

The man was shameless.

"Take a deep breath, Missy. You've got this," Marguerite said from the backseat.

"I know." Missy waited, wondering why her sister wasn't getting out of the car.

Josh sat patiently, not saying a word.

Finally, Marguerite asked, "Is that Declan's truck?" with a tinge of apprehension in her voice.

Josh murmured, "This should be fun," before he unbuckled his seatbelt and opened his door. Missy followed suit, only to be helped out by Josh. When Marguerite still hadn't moved, Josh opened her door and said jauntily, "Come on, Magpie! The party's inside!"

"Don't call me that!"

Missy rolled her eyes. Poking fun at her sister wasn't going to make anybody happy, but the ornery dimple showing in Josh's cheek said he really didn't care.

Scoundrel!

Jason and Julie's new house wasn't what Missy had expected. She'd envisioned a mini version of the King estate, but this home had two stories with a wraparound covered porch in the Arts and Crafts style. Light, earthy greens blended with stone and wood. The front yard was shaded by an old cottonwood tree, and new sod had been laid within a two-rung, split-rail fence. A friendly gate opened to a walking path leading to the front porch steps, where a sign invited guests to *Just Come Right In*.

Cozy furniture had been set out at different points around the porch, and a swing was adorned with pillows. Can lights and fans dotted the ceiling about every eight feet or so. Craftsman-style porch lights in stenciled metal and colored glass hung from the walls bordering the door, reminding Missy of the one and only trip her family had taken to Disneyland.

Josh reached for the heavy oak front door. It opened to an oversized, square foyer leading in three directions. To the right was a vast living room with a floor-to-ceiling stone fireplace, and to the left, a large formal dining room. Straight ahead lay two more paths, one to the back of the house and the other up a grand staircase.

People crowded into every room. Missy tried to breathe, but she felt the telltale signs of a panic attack slithering up her spine like a serpent waiting to snatch her ability to speak.

Please don't introduce me to anyone, please don't introduce me to anyone, please, please, please!

Marguerite took her hand. "Breathe," her sister whispered. "You've known most of these people all your life."

Josh put his arm around her and gave a reassuring squeeze. "I'm not going to leave you alone for a second." He kissed her forehead to seal the promise.

She knew she was being silly. She wasn't afraid of these people. She was afraid of embarrassing herself by saying something stupid. It'd been like this nearly all her life, from her first day of elementary school, when she'd asked Mrs. Wilson why Mr. Wilson didn't sit with her at church anymore, to the day of her gaffe at the clinic when she'd commented about putting a cat to sleep and made its owner cry.

Just as Missy was considering making a run for it, Camille entered the foyer to greet them. Missy noted the surprise in the older woman's eyes, directed at Josh, who still had his arm around Missy. Camille's smile widened into something knowing, which embarrassed Missy even more, and she prayed she wouldn't say something idiotic to Josh's mother.

"I'm so glad you could make it," Camille said smoothly, but not unkindly, before briefly hugging Missy and Marguerite. "You're just in time. The twins are awake, and Julie's bringing them downstairs now."

"Hello, Mother. Good to see you too," Josh said sarcastically.

Camille stopped in her tracks, turned around, and gave him a quick kiss on the cheek. She whispered in his ear. Mother and son chuckled conspiratorially before Josh dragged Missy to the back of the house. Camille and Marguerite veered off to the dining room, where her sister fit in with everyone. Missy tried not to be envious of Marguerite's social skills.

Toward the back of the house, the space opened to a great room connected to a large kitchen. Hardwood floors ran throughout the house, and the room felt light and airy. Another stone fireplace took up most of one wall and was flanked by built-in bookshelves. The kitchen contained a mixture of wood, tile, and marble with a huge butcher-block island in the center, where the food was laid out to perfection. Most of the guests gathered around it.

They'd just stepped into the family room when a pocket door to the right slid open. Julie walked out with both babies in her arms.

Is that an elevator?

Josh snickered and leaned in to explain. "Jason insisted on a lift. He didn't want anyone falling down the staircase in the middle of the night. Since there are two babies instead of one, Julie agreed."

"Honestly," Missy said. "I wish my mom had one. It'd sure make things easier for her. If things get worse we'll need to move her bedroom downstairs." Thinking about her mother's illness caused her mood to sink even further.

"How's she doing?"

"Marguerite's there most of the time unless she's at work or with me, like today. They need breaks from each other, but..." Missy didn't want to think about the disease progressing. She'd lost her father at a young age, and now she was losing her mother.

Thankfully, Marguerite found her way into the great room and changed the subject.

"This house is amazing." Her stunned expression was comical.

Josh said, "Come on. You've been to my parents' house."

Marguerite rolled her eyes at him. "That's not a house, it's a freaking mansion, but this," she gestured with wide arms, "is a home."

"Thank you, Marguerite," Jason said, sneaking up behind them. "After trying to explain what we wanted, Josh kept insisting it wouldn't work, but I proved I'm the better designer."

"Dream on, asshat. It's totally my design after listening to *Julie's* preferences, not his." He gestured with this thumb at Jason, "and the big oaf knows it."

Missy giggled at Josh's disgust with his brother.

"Oh yeah?" Jason argued. "You told me an elevator was out of the question, but after *I* tweaked the plans, you had to admit I was right."

"Gentleman, would you please zip it? There are guests who need to be tended to. We need more ice, Josh. Could you get some from the garage?" Camille said while holding one of the babies. "Missy, this is Gabriel. Would you like to hold him?"

Missy looked for help — any help — but found none. Babies were not her thing. Kittens or puppies, yes, but human offspring? The last thing she wanted was to hold that baby and have it scream its angelic head off. "Uh, I should help Josh with the ice, Mrs. King."

"It's *Camille*, dear, and he doesn't need help," she said as she thrust the baby into Missy's arms.

Missy froze.

Please don't scream, little man.

To her amazement, Gabriel cooed sweetly and blinked giant, baby-blue eyes at her. She felt something stir in the vicinity of her heart. Gabriel's little face bore a resemblance to Josh.

Missy melted.

She looked up to let Camille know she'd be all right with

the baby, and her eyes collided with Josh's as he returned from his errand. The world around her stopped. In the back of her mind, she heard something begin to tick in her body, and she was afraid to name what it was because she was much too young for *that*.

"Oh my," Marguerite whispered.

"Uh huh," Camille said with the same knowing smile Josh sometimes wore.

It completely unnerved Missy.

"Mrs. King," Marguerite said quietly, "you're the smartest woman I've ever met."

Camille tutted. "I know what my boys need, dear. Now, there's someone I'd like to introduce to you." Camille hooked her arm through Marguerite's and left Missy locked on Josh's stare as she gently swayed baby Gabriel back and forth.

MELISSA ROCKING HIS NEPHEW IN HER ARMS NEARLY brought Josh to his knees.

"I'm sorry I left you after I promised not to, but my mother can be very persuasive."

Melissa nodded her beautiful head. "So I've discovered." She broke their connection to look down at the baby in her arms. The move almost made him groan. When he leaned in to kiss her, his knees were nearly knocked out from under him, literally this time.

"Hunkle Josh! You're here!"

Relieved the powerful spell had been broken, he picked up Jessica because, honestly, when the little imp was around, it was hard not to. "Did you say hello to Melissa?"

"Nope. Hi Missy." Jessica got comfortable in Josh's arms. "Didya ask 'fore ya picked him up?"

"Uh," Melissa looked at the baby in question, "no, your grandma handed him to me."

"It's okay, then," Jessica said with approval, making Josh laugh.

"What's the plan, princess?"

"Oh! Well, first we getta eat lunch. Joojee made it so it's gonna be yummy," she said with conviction. "Then Joojee and Huncle Jase are gonna open baby presents." She ended by clapping her hands twice in excitement.

"You love presents, don't you, Jessica?" Josh laughed.

"Yep!" She kicked her feet. "I gotta go grab a plate 'fore they're all gone. Come on!" She tugged Josh's arm as she turned back to Missy and said, "You're gonna hafta set him down. He's not big enough for grown-up food."

Josh didn't bother containing his laugh, but he did stop Jessica from tugging on his arm. "I'm going to help Melissa with Gabriel, and then we'll get our lunch. You better go grab a plate, though, because I see that Charlie's already in line."

Jessica sucked in a breath. "Oh no! He's gonna eat up ever'thing. Char-LEE!" she shouted as she ran to the buffet line.

When Josh turned around, he found Melissa trying not to laugh and losing the battle as she struggled not to disturb the baby. He tried to help her, but they were laughing so hard they both looked ridiculous.

"Here, let me take him," he said, a bit out of breath.

"No, I'm good," she wheezed, finally finding her breath. "But you'll need to be on plate detail. I can't hold a baby and food at the same time."

Satisfied that she'd finally loosened up, he led her to the buffet line. Juggling two plates wasn't easy and neither was finding two seats together, but he rounded up a place in the dining room. Melissa kept his nephew tucked in her arms while they ate. People occasionally stopped by to comment on the baby and say hello. Conversations were easy when it came to babies, even if you weren't an expert. So far, Melissa didn't appear bothered by her nerves. Josh would have to find a way to thank his mother.

Suddenly, Marguerite flopped down beside them. "Your mother is an evil woman, Josh King." Her cheeks were flushed beet red.

What the hell? "Why?"

He was about to object to her insult of his mother but she interrupted. "Look, I know the woman doesn't like me, and your sisters-in-law can't stand me either, but ambushing me with *that man* is pretty cruel, even for them."

Her eyes welled with tears, so Josh bit back his rebuke.

"What man? What happened?" Melissa asked.

Marguerite swiped angrily at a tear which had successfully fallen down her cheek. "McKinley," she hissed. "I've just spent the last half hour being interrogated by the marshal."

"Interrogated about what?" Josh was lost. Glad to be sitting, he'd never thought to see a day when Marguerite Theroux got rattled by a man.

She continued as if he hadn't said anything. "He knew things about me, about us," she said to Melissa, "things he shouldn't have, like our birthdays, where we went to school. You know, personal stuff."

"But... why?" Melissa asked as she moved Gabriel to her shoulder. He'd begun to fuss, and now the baby rooted around with his mouth, causing Josh to look for Julie in a panic.

"I have no idea. I'm sticking with you because I do *not*

want to be near that man again," Marguerite said while Gabriel put hickeys on Melissa's shoulder.

"Oh!" Melissa said. "I think I'd better find your momma, little man."

Josh helped her get up and led her into the great room, Marguerite practically stepping on Melissa's heels but she got sidetracked to the kitchen.

They found Julie on the couch, blanket over her torso and a baby already attached.

Oh man, why is this so uncomfortable?

"I've got him," Jason said as he took the baby from Melissa's arms. "Josh, why are you blushing?"

The bastard knew why, but Josh needed to suck it up.

"It's hot in here. Why didn't you turn on the air?"

"I did," Jason said distractedly as he took Gabriel to the couch where Julie was finishing up with Michael.

"Wow," Melissa whispered, "Julie's incredible. I couldn't imagine dealing with twins, but she's so calm, and so happy." Melissa had a dreamy look in her eyes, the same look she wore for him when they were alone.

"You looked good holding my nephew." There was no denying their deepening connection. For once, getting emotionally involved with a woman didn't have him looking for his running shoes.

He grabbed her hand and brought the back of it to his lips. When pink filled her cheeks, he grinned. "Don't get all panicky. As soon as Julie's finished they're going to open their mountain of presents, and then we can go home."

"I'm sure Marguerite will be relieved."

"Why do you say that?"

Missy pointed with her chin to the other side of the room

where a very put-out Marguerite stood next to an older man Josh didn't recognize.

"That's Declan McKinley, the marshal I was telling you about." Jarod had sidled up next to them.

"Marguerite doesn't care much for him," Josh said with a grin.

"Oh, she likes him. She just doesn't know it yet." Jarod took a bite of a cookie. "I think he likes her too, but he's holding back for some reason. Could be the age difference, or maybe it's his friendship with Dane."

From his vantage point, Josh could see Marguerite fidgeting and looking at everyone around her except the man trying to engage her in conversation. When Marguerite caught Josh's eye, she said something to Declan, and quickly made her way over to their little group.

Josh grinned at Melissa. Marguerite didn't yet realize she had a shadow as McKinley followed her over. Marguerite gave them all a relieved smile as Jarod reached past her to take Declan's hand. Marguerite startled at finding the marshal behind her, and Josh had to stifle his laughter over her appalled face.

"Glad you could make it, McKinley. This is my little brother, Josh."

Josh reached for the older man's hand. "Nice to meet you."

"Same here," the marshal said before turning to Melissa. "You must be Marguerite's little sister. It's a pleasure to meet you. Your uncle and I go way back, ma'am."

Josh noted how Melissa's hand shook before Declan's big one enclosed it in a handshake.

"Nice to meet you too," she whispered. Josh immediately put his arm around her waist in a gentle show of support but didn't push her. Her discomfort pained him, and he wanted to take it away.

"I see you've met the incomparable Marguerite," Josh said.

The incomparable bombshell in question glared at him.

"Yes, we've met," she bit out.

Jarod said, "Now, Marguerite, that's no way to treat the man who's been keeping tabs on our siblings."

Josh felt Melissa stiffen. "Yes, Marguerite said something about that earlier."

Marguerite answered for everyone. "It's okay, Missy. Declan's been helping Jarod locate your stalker is all." She gave a slight shake of her head to both Jarod and Declan which Josh didn't like one bit.

He didn't like secrets.

With Melissa's stalker on the loose, he needed to be informed. Hadn't they all learned that lesson several times over already? Jarod would be filling him in ASAP, but now they had a baby shower to witness.

An extra sofa had been moved into the crowded family room to accommodate their guests while Julie opened presents. Josh sat so close to Missy she might as well have sat on his lap. Marguerite was smooshed against Josh's other side, creating a hunk sandwich.

Familiar faces reminded Missy how appropriate the name *family room* was for this space. Though everyone attending may not have been related by blood, the feeling of camaraderie and fellowship almost made Missy feel melancholy because her ill mother was at home, but thankfully, not alone. Uncle Dane offered to take care of her while Missy and Marguerite attended the baby shower. When Missy protested, he simply hugged her. "You need to go. Josh cares about you, and Julie and Camille would be upset if you stayed home." Then he looked at Marguerite. "Make sure she goes, young lady."

"Yes, sir."

For years now, Uncle Dane had mentored Marguerite. Missy didn't fully understand what Uncle Dane had required of Marguerite last fall, but she did know her sister had played an integral role in closing down a drug ring in Timbisha Township. Missy couldn't have been prouder of her sister, but she'd also feared for Marguerite's safety.

"Hey, you still here with me?"

She turned her face to his and got snared in his delicious gaze again. God, it almost hurt to look at him, especially since their noses almost touched. "How could I not be?" She gave him a peck on the nose. Growling, he hugged her impossibly closer.

Jessica said something funny, and the room exploded in laugher. The adorable girl was in charge of handing the next gift to be opened to Julie, taking center stage.

With her eyes, Missy followed the twins, who were being passed from guest to guest. There was so much love in the room Missy found herself smiling just because, and then it hit her.

She was completely comfortable with Josh. Her anxiety was gone. She wasn't sweating and at total ease. She squeezed Josh's thigh, earning her another kiss, this time on the cheek, and she didn't feel a speck of embarrassment.

That's what he did for her. He made her feel like she belonged.

It wasn't until all the gifts had been opened and everyone began meandering to different parts of the house again that she noticed Declan had been standing behind Marguerite the entire time. She gave her sister a glance and noted her controlled annoyance.

"I'm going to grab us something to drink," Josh said. "Do you want anything special or just water?"

"Water would be great," she said when he stood up. Once he was gone, she turned to Marguerite. "All right, spill."

Her sister huffed. "Is he gone?" she whispered.

"Mm-hmm." Declan had wandered into the kitchen behind Josh.

Marguerite faced her on the couch. "You know the marshal is here looking for a fugitive, right?"

"No, I thought Uncle Dane brought him in to help find my stalker."

Marguerite shook her head. "His fugitive turned out to be Harold Schurke. Since his case and yours seemed to be connected, he stayed to help. Anyway, Jarod and Declan found a body the other day, and they aren't saying who it is. Jarod claims they haven't ID'd the victim yet, but I know better. He's keeping something close to the vest and Declan's in the middle of it. I'm guessing the body is the marshal's fugitive, but they're shutting me out and won't confirm."

"Marguerite, if his fugitive is dead, and that fugitive is Harold, then why is he still here? The case should be closed, right?"

Marguerite threw her hands in the air. "That's exactly my point! Why is he still here, Missy? And why the hell does he keep 'running into me,' as he likes to call it and asking me all kinds of personal questions?"

Duh, he's attracted to you, sis.

But did they have another stalker in town — one with a badge? Or was Marguerite being overly dramatic? Missy mentally rolled her eyes. Of course her sister was being dramatic. She just didn't know what Marguerite's objection to Declan was. He was attractive and seemed nice, but then Missy wasn't a good judge of character, except when it came to Josh.

That dreamy feeling started taking over...

"Owie!" Marguerite slugged her in the arm.

"Will you focus on *my* problem, please?" she said. "Trust me, if you want Josh, he's completely yours. Now stop staring at his ass and help me!"

"Keep your voice down," she hissed. "I don't understand your problem, Marguerite. Tell Declan you aren't interested. He'll back off. They always do for you." Bitterness bled into the last part.

Her sister ignored it.

"I have, Missy, but he won't back off."

"Tell Jarod he's harassing you."

Marguerite scoffed. "I would if I didn't think Jarod was encouraging the jackass."

Missy tried not to snicker and failed miserably.

"It's not funny!"

"I know, sorry." Missy took a breath and concentrated. She needed to figure out what exactly her sister's problem was with the marshal before she could advise her. "Where is he?"

"Talking to Mr. King." Missy didn't miss the fact that her sister was completely aware of where the man was and to whom he was speaking.

"So avoid him until we leave." At Marguerite's eye roll, Missy forged on. "Look, we can't solve this problem today, but I don't want you to be miserable either. You already know where he is, so just make sure you stay away from him."

"Thanks for nothing," Marguerite said as she stomped off to the kitchen, right where the marshal and Mr. King were speaking, next to a plate of cookies Marguerite feigned interest in.

Missy shook her head at her sister as Josh returned with a bottled water. "I think Marguerite and the marshal are going to end up together," he said without preamble.

"No, she doesn't like him."

Josh's evil grin spread across his face. "Honey, I know women, and I've known your sister all my life. Trust me, she wants him. She's just fighting her feelings right now."

Missy didn't want to talk about her sister anymore. "What's the plan?"

"For the rest of the day?"

"Mm-hmm." She wanted to kiss him... and do other things.

The evil grin turned sensual. "Did I create a monster?"

Missy's eyebrows shot up before she took a shaky breath. "Maybe, but I don't want to insult your family. This has been a lovely day."

"I love seeing you happy, Melissa." He was the only person who didn't shorten her name. In the beginning she thought he did it to annoy her, but now she realized it was out of respect. It made her special to him. She was taking a big chance on him. No one had ever made her feel this comfortable outside her own family. She took a breath and said what she felt in her heart.

"I love that you can make me happy."

He immediately pressed his amazing lips to hers, but Jason's deep voice didn't let them get too carried away.

"Get a room, will ya? There are children present."

She sat back guiltily, but Josh didn't let her get far. "He's joking," he whispered in her ear before turning to his brother. "Like you're any better."

Jason only chuckled. "Listen, people are starting to leave, but I'm going to barbecue later. Do you two feel like hanging around?"

It sounded nice, but—

"Normally I'd say yes, but we've got to get Marguerite home to relieve Dane. Missy's mom isn't doing too well lately." Josh saved her from having to explain things. "And we need to check on Ginger."

Aww!

"Thank you for a wonderful time, Jason," Missy said without feeling the least bit awkward.

Jason drew her into a hug, surprising the new confidence right out of her. "We're so glad you came. Don't be a stranger, okay?"

"I won't."

Josh pulled her away, and together they said their goodbyes, collected a very relieved Marguerite, and were out the door in a flash. She couldn't wait to be alone with him. She wanted to take a chance on him, wanted to trust him, and Josh was making it very easy for her to let down her guard.

CHAPTER 14

Pretty

"I'm going to say hello to Mom and then we can go," Melissa said, opening the passenger door while Marguerite climbed out of the back seat of his pickup.

"Hold up, ladies, and I'll come in with you. I haven't seen your mom in a while." Josh hurried around the truck to help Melissa out, and close the door for Marguerite.

"Mom would love to see you," Marguerite said. "I'll go make sure she's presentable. It's been difficult for her to get out of bed lately."

He mumbled okay under his breath, troubled Darla Bainbridge-Theroux's cancer had progressed. He took Melissa's hand and together they followed Marguerite up the front porch steps, where Dane stood with the door open to welcome his nieces home. "Hello, young lady," he said to Marguerite before kissing her forehead and then hugging Melissa. "Hey, Josh. Everything go smoothly at the party?"

"Right as rain. Sorry you missed it," he said quietly when he noticed the sadness in the older man's eyes.

"Darla and I had a good time today," Dane answered before calling out, "didn't we, Sis?"

Darla sat on the sofa in a pretty red robe which looked too hot for this time of year, but the thinness of her face told how much the cancer had ravaged her body. Her smile hid how sick she really was, and her polite demeanor covered up the sadness in her dark eyes. "Yes, we did, Dane."

She reached out for Marguerite, who kissed her mother on the cheek before excusing herself from the room. Darla held her hand out to Melissa, who sat down next to her. When her eyes met Josh's with surprise, she smiled wide with joy. "Josh King! I haven't seen you in forever!" She tried to stand, but Josh rushed to her.

"No need to get up, Mrs. Theroux." He bent down to hug the woman, taking care not to break her. Damn, she was skin and bones underneath the robe. "It's real good to see you, too."

"Camille was here the other day, and we were talking about you. I understand you and my daughter are sharing a kitten."

"Mom was here? You two aren't trying to play matchmaker, are you, Mrs. Theroux?" He ignored Melissa's surprised gasp and Dane's chuckle. Marguerite returned from the kitchen with several glasses of iced tea on a tray.

"Of course she is." Marguerite placed the tray on the table and distributed the glasses. "Camille and Darla strike again."

"And you're next, my dear. Time's a wastin', so I'm not going to beat around the bush with you. Tell me all about this Declan character."

"Oh, Mother!" Marguerite said with disgust while Josh nearly spit his tea back into his glass. "No, no, and no. You and Uncle Dane are terrible." She put her glass down and hugged her mother then blew a kiss to Melissa. "I'm going upstairs to do some research. Josh, thank you for driving me to the party." She turned on her heel and jogged up the stairway.

Dane merely chuckled, but Darla's face turned grim. "Stop laughing. I have to get her settled."

"Mom, please don't talk that way." The fear in Melissa's eyes nearly broke Josh's heart. It was clear Darla didn't think she'd survive her illness. "Marguerite's having a hard enough time with everything. Leave her alone about men."

"Did you meet him?" Darla asked, ignoring everything Melissa said.

"Briefly, but if Marguerite doesn't like him, you should leave it to her to decide what to do. You can't make someone fall in love, you know."

Josh agreed, and to add some levity to the conversation, he decided to satisfy his curiosity about Melissa's feelings. "She's right, Mrs. Theroux. I've loved your daughter for years, but she's yet to tell me she loves me back."

Melissa turned two shades of red, and Dane's eyebrows crawled up his forehead.

"Too much?" Josh asked.

Dane cleared his throat. "A bit."

Darla broke the silence by sitting back into the couch with relief. "Well, I'll be darned. Josh King, the ladies' man of Timbisha Township, is in love with my daughter." A single tear dropped down her cheek. "Young lady, I'm happy you two dropped by, but after that pronouncement I think it's time you took your man home and put his heart at ease, don't you?"

"Yeah, I think maybe you're right." Josh didn't miss the breathiness of her voice, or the way her knees shook when she stood. "Love you, Mom. Bye, Uncle Dane."

"Mrs. Theroux, it was good to see you," Josh reiterated.

"Please, call me Darla. After all, I'm hoping you'll be family soon." Darla winked at him, and Josh smiled in return. He had a feeling Darla was as shrewd as his own mother.

"I'll walk the two lovebirds out," Dane said, his deep voice rasping. Josh took Melissa's hand, and they followed Dane to the front door. Josh turned to shake the man's hand, but Dane insisted on following them all the way to the driveway.

"Did your brother tell you about the body they found?" Dane said without preamble.

"No, why?" Josh's gut tightened. *Another body? When did his small town become so dangerous?*

"Marguerite told me a body was found and they assume it's Harold. Uncle Dane, what's going on?"

Melissa's distress only amped up Josh's feeling of doom and his natural instinct to protect. He held up a hand and looked at Melissa. "Wait, why didn't you tell me?"

She shrugged. "There wasn't a chance at the party."

"Damn that Jarod," Dane griped. "Look, I don't know why Jarod's decided to keep this a secret, but I feel my niece needs to know that she is still in danger. They found Harold Klein's body. He'd been kidnapped, tied up, and drugged. His killer is still on the loose."

Josh relaxed. "Well, if Klein's dead, then Melissa's stalker is gone, right?"

"Not necessarily. The body had been there a while. We don't know who's responsible for harassing you and Missy."

Josh met Melissa's wide eyes and cursed. "You called in McKinley to protect Melissa, didn't you?"

Dane reached up and scratched the back of his head. "That's the odd thing. I called McKinley to check up on a specific cold case from a few years back, a fugitive on the run named Harold Schurke." Dane looked at Melissa, and Josh swore he was fighting something. "He'd been convicted of many things, but the worst was sex trafficking. It wasn't until later McKinley discovered the guy was posing as a professor under the alias Klein."

Josh narrowed his eyes. "If Harold died before Melissa started receiving her 'gifts,'" and here Josh used finger quotes, "then who are we supposed to be looking for?"

Dane gave a hard stare. "We don't know."

When Melissa said nothing, Josh put his arm around her. "I won't let her leave my sight until we get this mess cleared up. Thanks for the head's up." He shook Dane's hand after Melissa hugged her uncle. If Dane was worried, then Josh was too. He trusted the man's instincts.

The ride back to the townhouses was quiet. He'd hoped to have a serious talk with her, but now she was troubled over some unknown creep, and the mood had soured.

"I don't want to sleep alone tonight."

Josh reached across the armrest and grabbed her hand. "You were never going to, Melissa." *Like she'd had a choice.* He'd told Dane he wouldn't leave her alone and he meant it. He lifted her hand to his lips. "We'll grab Ginger first, and then we'll go to my place."

She held onto his hand with both of hers, and he could feel a fine trembling in her body. He hated to see her so scared. He wouldn't let anything happen to her but he needed to figure out a way to keep her safe while he was at work. He'd call Jarod and let him know Dane spilled the beans before giving him a piece of his mind. It wouldn't do any good keeping that secret anyway, and Josh was certain that Dane was counting on Josh to blab. Jarod and Dane were usually at odds with each other, and now that Dane's niece was in danger, their animosity would only amp up. Josh was disgusted with his brother. You protect family no matter what, and Jarod should've known better.

Josh parked in his driveway without lifting the garage door. He didn't want anyone to have access to his townhouse while he helped Melissa gather her things and the kitten.

Both townhouses were dark. "Is Angie still at work?"

"Probably. They've got her on a strange schedule." Melissa put the key in her front door and turned the knob. "Do you think she'll be safe here alone?"

Josh didn't hesitate. "For tonight, she should be fine. I'm going to set both our townhouses up with alarm systems tomorrow. I never thought I'd have to do that in Timbisha Township, but I'm not taking any chances. I'll grab Ginger while you get what you need for an extended stay. I don't want you alone." He kissed her soundly and then turned her toward the staircase.

Josh didn't like the creepy feeling sliding up his spine. He was sure he was being watched. The sooner they were in his own townhouse, the sooner he could start building his relationship with Melissa and keep her safe.

MISSY FLIPPED THE LIGHT ON IN HER BEDROOM AND rushed to fill a bag with enough for an extended stay —whatever that meant. *I've loved your daughter for years, but she's yet to tell me she loves me back.* With Josh, a girl never knew if he was being serious or not, but they definitely needed to talk about their relationship. Missy was finally ready to do that.

Then there was the information Uncle Dane imparted to them before leaving tonight. How many people hated her that badly?

She hefted her bag over her shoulder, retrieved her favorite pillow, and met Josh downstairs. He was cuddling Ginger in his big arms while the kitten purred to her heart's content, and Missy's heart swooned.

"Ready," she said breathlessly.

He held Ginger as he took Missy's bag from her shoulder and slipped it over his own. "You have your keys?"

She held them up and followed him out the door, making sure to turn the deadlock. Angelica had a key, so Missy wasn't worried about locking her out. It was still early, but Angelica wouldn't be home for a few hours. Night hadn't fully descended on them, but the front of the townhouse was already shadowed by the setting sun.

"I should install some floodlights, too," Josh said quietly as they stepped up onto his front porch. He handed Ginger over to her so he could work his own lock, and within seconds they were inside. "I'll get us a couple of beers. I think we need it."

She trailed him into the kitchen, where he placed her bag on a small dinette table. Ginger meowed and stretched before hobbling to the kitchen to beg for kibble.

Josh immediately complied with the cat's request, then popped the tops off of two bottles and handed a beer to Missy.

"Thank you."

"So polite," he murmured before taking a big swig. "Television or talk?"

Now *that* made her laugh. "We should probably talk, don't you think?"

"Kiss first?"

"Kissing is just a distraction," she scolded, half hopeful he'd kiss her anyway. She got her wish.

He took her mouth quickly before setting her back on her

feet. "There, now tell me you love me too, so we can move on from all this awkwardness."

She swallowed hard. "I love you too."

If the situation hadn't been so serious, the look on his face would've had her rolling on the floor with laughter. His mouth hung half open, and his eyes were so wide she thought they might fall out of his head. When he still didn't answer and the pain of rejection began to bloom in her chest, she took a step back. The move startled him because he yanked her to him, kissing her as though the sun rose and set in her mouth. She was consumed by his reaction and, God help her, she wanted to be consumed. Forgetting about their much-needed conversation, she poured her heart and soul into their kiss, hoping there wouldn't be any more need for talk. She was quickly discovering nonverbal communication to be easier anyway. She'd show him how she felt, and trust Josh to understand what she was saying.

He didn't disappoint her. Before she could come up for air, he was already climbing the stairs with her in his arms.

JOSH HAD NEVER FELT A CONNECTION THIS STRONG to anyone in his life, not even with his brothers. His friendships with Julie and Lauren had been strong, but once they'd married his brothers and became his sisters-in-law, the feeling turned familial, which was completely different from what he was feeling for Melissa.

Melissa belonged to him and he belonged to her. *Lenny Kravitz had it right,* Josh thought as the song played softly in the background. She made his life complete. He'd fought for years to put her out of his mind by going from girl to girl, then woman to woman, but none of them compared to *her*.

"I love your voice," she mumbled sleepily.

Had he been singing along?

"I just love you, baby." He gently rolled her over from their spooned position to see the face he loved so much. "I'm serious. There's no one else but you."

She caressed his face with her delicate hand, an elegant finger tracing his cheekbone and then his bottom lip. Her purple eyes were dreamy and soft when she said, "You already know there's never been anyone else for me."

And then she giggled.

"Thank God. The idea of you being with another man brings out the green-eyed monster in me."

"But your eyes are such a pretty blue," she said with a teasing voice.

"Pretty? Girl, no one calls me pretty without paying a price." He captured her mouth to prove just how pretty things were between them.

"Eggs and bacon?" Melissa asked from the open refrigerator the next day.

Josh looked at his watch. "It's twelve-thirty. How about we head over to Molly's for a burger, then hit Neil's Building Supply for some floodlights. Maybe see if they've got information on alarm systems."

"Sounds like a plan to me. After that, I want to check on Mom again, if we have time before you install the lights," she said as she bent to refresh the water in Ginger's bowl.

"How's she doing?"

Melissa stood over the cat as she drank from her dish. "Perfectly healthy."

"No, silly, not the cat. Your mother."

Melissa blinked sad eyes and folded her arms protectively over her chest. "She has an appointment with the oncologist in a couple of weeks. We'll know more then." She forced a smile, dropped her protective stance, and sauntered up to Josh, who immediately hugged her. She hid the pain from him, but he didn't take offense. God forbid, if one of his parents or brothers were sick, he didn't know what he'd do.

By the time they got to Molly's, there weren't many seats to choose from except for two at the far end of the counter, but Josh preferred it that way. He could see most of the restaurant and whoever came through the door from that vantage point. They'd just been handed their menus when Angelica walked through the glass doors with Marco, who immediately raised his hand to Josh.

"Hey man." He slapped a palm to Josh's and waved to Melissa.

"Well, hello there, you two," Angelica said. "Missy, you didn't come home last night," she accused while wearing a vixen's smile which annoyed Josh. Marco seemed completely enamored by the older woman. He'd have to set the kid straight.

"Where's Charlie?" Josh asked.

"Pizza Factory. We'll hook up later when his shift ends," Marco said. "I'm just escorting this lovely lady around town today for her errands."

Josh noted, without comment, how the kid kept zeroing in on Angelica's chest. Yep, he'd definitely need to have a long talk with both boys about the trappings of older women.

"What errands are you running?" Melissa asked.

"Oh, this and that, you know. I'm out of some personal items. My schedule at the hospital is so erratic I need to get my shopping in when I can. Marco followed me to the garage. It's still not fixed properly. What is it with small towns, anyway?" She looked put out until her ice-blue eyes landed on Josh. "Can you talk to Gil for me?"

Her singsong voice grated on Josh's nerves, but one look at Melissa and her pleading eyes had him agreeing to the task. "Sure thing, Angie. I'll give him a call tomorrow. They're closed on Sundays."

"Figures," she grouched. "I can't keep hogging all of Marco's time, even if he is just so adorable." She looped her arm through the boy's elbow and gave him a squeeze. Josh didn't miss how Marco stood straighter.

"Oh, it's my pleasure, Miss Daemon. Anything you need, I'm here to help."

"Speaking of, I'm starving and that booth just opened up."

It was directly behind Josh and Melissa, so throughout lunch Josh could hear Angelica's coquettish voice ringing through the diner. Every now and then, she'd say something funny and ask, "Remember that, Missy?" distracting them from their own conversation. Her behavior was odd, but Josh understood some women were needy.

Apparently, Angelica was one of them.

"Maybe I should go home tonight," Melissa said quietly as she folded her napkin and set it on her empty plate.

"Maybe, but you're not going to." He leaned in and kissed her earlobe. Goosebumps became visible on her bare arms, and he loved that he was responsible for them. "Besides, do you really want to?" He raised his eyebrow at her.

She giggled. "No, not really. Ginger and I want to be with you," she said so quietly he'd barely heard it. He was about to kiss her full on the mouth when an arm not belonging to Melissa slid across his shoulders.

"How about if I run my errands and pick up something yummy to fix for dinner tonight?" Angelica said.

Melissa jumped away at the same time Josh shrugged off Angelica's arm from around his shoulders. "Sorry, Angie, but Melissa and I have plans for dinner. Thanks for thinking of us, though." He emphasized the word *us* so there'd be no mistaking they were a couple. A flash of anger came across Angelica's face before she smoothed her features into a knowing smile.

"I get it, third wheel and all." She sighed heavily. "All right, you two. Have fun tonight. I guess Marco and I will have dinner alone then. Toodles," she said with a wave of her fingertips as she and the fawning Marco walked out the door.

Melissa shook her head. "There is no way in hell I'm going to let her have dinner alone with that boy."

Josh agreed. "Don't worry about it. I'm sure Marco's going to have a rush of calls this evening from people in need of the *Timbisha Township Taxi Service*." He winked.

Melissa threw her head back and laughed. "Perfect. No one gets embarrassed, and he earns some money."

They paid their check, and as they walked out the door she said, "You're pretty amazing, Josh King."

It was Josh who puffed up his chest as they strolled to his pickup. "No, but I'm certainly glad you think so." He couldn't *not* kiss her, with her violet eyes shining up at him and the sweet smile which hadn't left her lips since they'd woken this morning inviting his to touch hers. She was his, damn it, and he planned on keeping that smile on her face for the rest of their lives.

They were still kissing in the parking lot when the cat calls from patrons floated to his ears. "Maybe we should get going before the sheriff arrests us for lewd behavior." He nipped her earlobe and didn't miss her excited intake of breath.

"Yeah, maybe. Or we could go back to your place."

It was him who gave a startled gasp at her brazen words. More turned on than ever, he lifted her into the passenger seat. "I like the way you think, babe."

He didn't waste any time getting back to his townhouse.

To hell with the errands. He'd pick up the floodlights and security alarm tomorrow while she was safe at work. He had better things to do on a Sunday afternoon anyway.

CHAPTER 15

Blocked

Missy had barely gotten out of her car when Josh took the cat carrier from her hands and dragged her inside. "Wait! I need to shower!"

"Shower with me after I make love to you."

"Yeah, okay," she agreed breathlessly.

Josh had met her every evening after work for the past week and dragged her willingly to his townhouse. She'd barely set foot in her own place, let alone spoken to her roommate. Angelica had left her a few nagging texts about not seeing Missy in a while and wanting to catch up on her life, but Missy couldn't resist being with Josh.

Marguerite sent texts complaining about not being in the loop, and was also concerned about their mother. Darla's illness was stable, but she wasn't getting better either. Missy opted out of lunches with Josh to spend them with her mom but twice he'd shown up at her mother's with food and spent time visiting as well.

He'd become Missy's obsession.

If she wasn't with Josh, she was thinking about him and

the things they did together when they were alone, or what he said to her when they couldn't be alone. Some of his texts were downright naughty, but she didn't dare erase them. She only prayed no one else would ever read them.

Love letters her father wrote to her mother were kept in a box on Darla's dresser. But these days, people didn't write letters. They texted.

Josh's naughty, heartfelt messages were his love letters. He was never shy about what he wanted or how he felt. At first, Missy thought their erotic nature was just Josh being *male*, but then he'd check up on her mother while Missy was at work. He held Missy's hand, opened doors, and asked her about her day. They talked nonstop about silly things, and he always listened to what she had to say.

Her limited experience with men had left her a bit jaded. But since moving home, Josh had shown her she'd been unlucky. He was a good man, and she was thankful he'd come into her life.

She trusted him.

She was in love with him.

"I put dinner on low. How does chicken chili sound? It's Julie's recipe."

"Anything you made sounds wonderful. I'm a terrible cook."

He smiled while trailing his fingertips down her cheek before kissing the tip of her nose. "Well, between Julie and my mother, I've had good teachers."

"Does your mother know you think Julie is the better teacher?"

"Yes. Julie isn't just the better teacher, she's the better chef. Why do you think they went into business together?" He kissed her quickly and hopped out of bed, throwing on some gym shorts which hung low on his hips, emphasizing all the fine ridges and bumps that made him interesting to look at.

He caught her enjoying the view. "Stop that. We'll never eat dinner if you don't." As if he couldn't help it, he kissed her again before quickly escaping the bedroom.

Missy rolled over onto her back and stared at the ceiling. As lovely as this relationship had become, she needed some boundaries. She'd basically been living with Josh for the past week, only running home to grab things here and there. She even showered in his bathroom. If she wanted to go home to get dressed, she couldn't because she no longer had any shampoo in her own shower.

God help her, she'd even brought over some feminine hygiene products and tucked them into his bathroom cabinet!

Things were moving way too fast and she loved it, but she needed to be sensible.

I'm the responsible sister, after all.

Wasn't she?

They needed to talk.

She got herself up and threw on a pair of Josh's boxers and one of his t-shirts. Again, this was another part of their week-long routine. Did he do this with all his girlfriends? Thinking of Josh with other women made her angry, so she shoved those images away and jogged down the stairs to follow the enticing aromas of garlic, basil, and cumin all the way into the kitchen.

"Oh my goodness, that smells divine."

"Wait 'til you taste it." He lifted a spoon out of the slow cooker and blew on it before lifting it to her lips. It was white and creamy, and when it hit her tongue she thought she'd died and gone to heaven.

"Mmmmm," was all she could get out. As soon as she opened her eyes, he'd filled up a bowl and handed it to her. She wasted no time setting it on the kitchen bar. He handed her a spoon and a napkin before filling his own bowl and placing it next to hers. He took a couple of beers from the refrigerator before joining her.

She didn't speak until half her bowl was empty. "What's in this?"

"Love," was his answer as he continued to eat. His dimple was showing.

"Well, I'll take a second helping, if you don't mind. Want me to refill you, too?"

He winked and handed her his bowl. "Do you want to come to Reno with me this weekend?"

"I'm on call all weekend and the Ferreros' mare is about to foal, so I can't leave. Why are you going to Reno?"

"Charlie. The family's heading there to pick out a place for him. He wants to live in the dorms, but if Mom has her way, we'll get him an apartment near the university instead."

"Your mom will win, won't she?"

"Of course. I'm mainly going for moral support."

Going a whole weekend without seeing him would suck, but the time away would give Missy the break she'd been thinking she needed in order to get her priorities straight.

"Hey, you all right?" he asked with concern when she set his bowl back down in front of him.

"Yeah." She took another spoonful of the delicious chili. "I'm going to miss you is all," she admitted with a shrug, hoping she didn't sound too pathetic.

"Woman, you'll be on my mind twenty-four seven, but Charlie is a huge part of my life, and I don't want to disappoint him by not going."

"My goodness, I would never ask you not to go! It'll give me time to think about things."

"Think about what?"

She swallowed another bite. "Well, honestly, Josh, we can't keep going on like this. I need to go home sometimes." She hoped he understood.

"You go home."

"I haven't been home in over a week, and your overfilled laundry hamper is proof." It was true. Neither of them had done laundry, and with a week's worth of their clothes spilling over the edge, his bedroom was beginning to look like a college frat house.

"I'll do a load tonight." His dismissive attitude was puzzling.

"That's not the point. I need to check my mail, pay bills, clean up at home, clean Ginger's cat box, and go grocery shopping."

"Angie can go grocery shopping."

"Josh, all I'm saying is I don't live here. I live next door."

He shoved his bowl away and turned toward Missy on his stool. He moved her bowl back, braced both his arms around her hips, and leaned in. "What if you lived here instead?"

Shock stole her breath, and she swore she felt her jaw hit her knees. "I... I,"

"Look, don't say anything. Just think about it. I'm not screwing around with you, Melissa. I've waited for you forever, but if you're not ready right now, that's fine. But know this. You are, and will always be, my forever. I love you, babe."

He used his thumb to wipe a tear from her cheek before kissing her sweetly. Her heart filled up with joy. As usual, her tongue tied in knots as it tangled with his. Her heart wanted what he was asking for, but her head screamed, *slow down*. She'd always been practical, and she wasn't sure if moving in with Josh was the smart thing to do. Part of her believed he was worried her stalker would show his face again, but since the death of Harold, there'd been no other incidents.

As usual, Josh's physical persuasion had its usual effect on her libido, and her objections and fears melted away under his gentle touch. No, she didn't need to go home tonight or any night soon, not with the way he loved her now.

SATURDAY MORNING, SHE WOKE UP ALONE WITH A feeling of dread. Well, not alone, she realized, as three pink kitty paws poked out from under the blankets near her pillow. Missy reached out and tickled the fluff between the pads of Ginger's toes, chuckling when the kitten kicked out three quick times before burrowing deeper under the covers. Missy reached under the blankets to give the kitten some love before she hopped out of bed and headed for the shower.

Alone.

She missed Josh. She hadn't showered without him in over a week and it felt weird. They'd decided to stay the night at her place since he'd be gone all weekend. She barely remembered him kissing her goodbye in the wee hours of dawn.

She turned off the water, dried off, braided her hair, and got dressed. Ginger now sat on top of the comforter waiting for her.

"Are you hungry?" Missy asked, and the kitty immediately hobbled to the edge of the bed and bounded off with as much grace as her three healthy legs allowed. She began her motorboat purr and followed Missy downstairs.

"Good morning, sunshine," came from the kitchen. Angelica stood at the stove scrambling eggs.

Missy smiled. It was like old times. "G'morning. Do you have to work today?"

"Nope, got the whole weekend off, can you believe it?"

That was surprising. New nurses rarely got the weekends off, but Angelica was pretty persuasive. "No, I cannot because I'm on call all weekend."

Angelica's shoulders drooped. "What's that mean?"

Missy poured herself a cup of coffee. "If someone has an emergency, I have to help them."

"Oh, goody. We can still go shopping."

Missy eyed her friend. "You understand this is Timbisha Township and not Los Angeles, right? The best we have is a Walmart Supercenter."

"Well, we'll have to make the best of it. What do you say?"

"I thought I'd head over to Mom's for a bit. Wanna come with me? My mom and sister would love to meet you."

"Sure," Angelica said. "Let's see how the day goes. Nothing is set in stone, right?"

"Right." Missy didn't like to make plans when she was on call anyway.

"Oh, I almost forgot. Gil called and my car is ready!" Angelica clapped her hands together. "I called Marco to give me a ride, but apparently he's gone to Reno to help his friend find a place to live."

"Charlie?"

"Yeah, didn't Josh tell you?"

"No, he... I didn't know Marco was going. I thought it was just his family."

"Huh. Well, Marco didn't say anything about Josh going with them either, so maybe he didn't." Angelica shrugged her shoulders.

"Then where would Josh be?" Missy thought Angelica was being ridiculous, but she held her tongue.

"Who knows? You know how men are. Maybe he wanted to go fishing or something with his brothers and didn't tell you because he thought you'd be mad. Men lie all the time, Missy. They don't like to hear women nag. Josh is used to living a bachelor's lifestyle. He probably resents having to account for his whereabouts." Angelica smiled, as if what she said made perfect sense. "I'm going to get changed. We have a lot to do today!" She jogged up the steps to her room, leaving Missy questioning everything.

Do men lie to women even if they love them? She was too young to remember what her parents' marriage had been like except for the happy times. Had her father lied about silly things to her mom? She'd have to ask. Marguerite would know.

However, Angelica made a good point about Josh not having to be accountable for himself. He had a reputation, and he hadn't denied being a ladies' man, so maybe he wasn't in Reno? She picked up her phone and noted he hadn't checked in yet. Was he driving? She looked out her front window and didn't see his pickup, but that didn't mean he hadn't left it at his parents' estate while someone else drove. Maybe she should text him now?

"Are you ready?" Angelica startled Missy so badly she felt her heart skip a beat.

"Yeah, um, let me get my shoes and my keys."

"REMIND ME AGAIN WHY YOU THINK WALMART ON A Saturday is a good idea?" Missy drove around the parking lot twice before she landed a spot, in what felt like, a mile and half away from the front doors.

"Certainly looks like this is where all the action is," Angelica said without apology.

"Wait a minute. I thought you *needed* to go shopping?"

"Of course I do, and so do you. You haven't been home in a week, and since everyone will be here, it's as good a place as any to meet people." She winked her heavily lashed eye and stepped gracefully from the car.

Missy rolled her eyes and slammed the door. The July sun burned down on them like a blast furnace. She squinted through her cheap sunglasses and followed Ms. Bubbly Britches into the Timbisha Township Zoo, aka *Super Walmart*.

Missy found the last cart available, which needed a front-end alignment, and shoved it through the front doors. If they purchased any soda, they'd have to carry it out themselves to prevent it from blowing up from the jostling. At least the cart didn't squeak.

They zigzagged their way through the crowd without running anyone over until they reached the health and beauty department. "Maybe I should hang out here with the cart while you get what you need," Missy suggested. There was no way to push a cart down the aisle, not with everyone jammed in there.

Angelica agreed, but she took her time with her selections, mostly because she had to fight her way to what she wanted. Meanwhile, Missy was jarred, bumped, and almost run over by a large woman in an electric scooter.

An anxiety Missy hadn't experienced in over a week crept up her spine as person after person strolled by; some smiling and some frowning, some mumbling social pleasantries, and some baldly telling her to get the hell out of their way.

By the time Angelica placed her items in the cart, Missy was sweating through her deodorant and needed to get some air.

"Let's head over to the ice cream department," Angelica said as she grabbed the front edge of the cart and shimmied Missy along the crowded aisles to the other side of the superstore.

The wider aisles of the dairy department provided more space for people to crowd around the glass cases. Missy parked the cart at the department's edge, near the yogurt, while Angelica perused the ice cream selections. Missy wiped sweat from her brow and tried to work past the haze of the panic attack threatening to bring her to her knees. When a small hand slid into hers, she immediately calmed down and looked into the familiar blue eyes of Jessica King.

"Missy!" the little girl said excitedly. "Are ya gettin' popsicles, too?"

"Hello Jessica. My friend is getting ice cream," Missy tried to remain calm.

"Oh, jeez, don't tell her that. She'll want some too." Lauren King pushed her cart up next to hers. "Hey, are you all right? You look pale, Missy."

"I-I'm fine." She wasn't and she wanted to cry. "The store's really crowded today."

Lauren dug in her purse for a baby wipe. "Here, this should help."

"Thank you," Missy mumbled as she swiped it across her forehead.

"Maybe we should find someplace to sit." Lauren grabbed Jessica's hand and began to search for a bench through the crowded store.

"Oh, she's fine," Angelica said with an armload of ice cream containers.

Missy noticed Lauren's scrunched-up brow before she reached out a hand. "You must be Melissa's roommate. I'm Lauren King, Josh's sister-in-law."

"Sorry, I should've introduced you," Missy mumbled, feeling more and more inept.

Concerned now, Lauren insisted, "I really think you should sit down, Missy."

"Oh, no need. We're about done here anyway," Angelica said happily. "I'm a nurse and I've known her for years. She's fine. Aren't you, Missy?"

No, but she didn't want to embarrass herself even more. "Yeah, I'm good. Nice to see you, Lauren."

As Angelica pulled the cart away, Lauren fished her cell phone out of her purse. Maybe she was texting Josh. The thought rubbed her the wrong way. Maybe the sheriff's wife knew exactly where Josh was and had no qualms about texting him. Missy inhaled as she wormed her way through the masses to the checkout stands. Angelica babbled nonstop about God knew what. The stress of being in such a mob left Missy hard of hearing, and all she wanted to do was go home. Unfortunately, they still needed to pick up Angelica's car before visiting Missy's mother.

She focused on her mom in an effort to help calm herself. She reached into the cart once Angelica had paid and opened a bottle of water. She drank the whole thing before they'd made it back to the car. All she could think about was Josh, and wondered why she'd opted to stay in town without him.

JOSH TRIED TO CALL MELISSA'S PHONE SEVERAL

times throughout the road trip to Reno, but he got the same message over and over again.

"The number you have dialed is not available..."

He'd spent most of his waking hours with Melissa. Now he hated being without her even for a second, let alone for three and a half hours on the road. It was becoming increasingly difficult to keep his annoyance in check. Marco and Charlie had been horsing around the entire trip. He was stuck between them in the back seat while his parents rode up front. He should've ridden with Jason and Julie, who were caravanning behind them in their newly purchased Suburban.

By the time they reached the hotel, Josh was ready to pummel both boys. So, to blow off steam, he did, which started a wrestling match in the grass next to their parking spot, followed by his father yelling at all three of them to "knock that shit off."

I'm losing my damn mind.

"Have you gone crazy?" Apparently Jason thought so too.

"Almost," he muttered as he stood up and dusted the bits of grass and dirt off his jeans.

"He can't get a hold of Missy," Charlie explained.

"Why not?"

Charlie shrugged before Marco put him in another head-lock. Camille rolled her eyes and skirted past them to get to one of her grandbabies. "Did you try calling Marguerite, honey? Missy might've gone over to Darla's."

Josh put his hand on his head and sighed. Yeah, that was probably where she was, but it didn't explain why he couldn't leave her a message or send a text.

"If everyone is finished playing patty-cake, I'll go get our rooms and meet you in the restaurant," his father said with irritation before he stormed into the hotel lobby.

"Which restaurant?" Marco asked. "This hotel has, like, a bunch." The comment made Josh groan again. He was not in the mood for this, and now he wished he'd just stayed home.

"She's fine, Josh." Charlie put a hand on Josh's shoulder. "Maybe her inbox is full, or maybe you've kept her so busy she forgot to pay her cell bill?" Charlie winked at him before pretending to sucker punch him in the stomach.

Julie rubbed a fussy twin's back. "I'll call Lauren when we get settled and see if I can find out anything." She leaned over to kiss his cheek before setting the baby in a stroller.

"Maybe she's in the middle of a pillow fight with her hot roommate and decided she doesn't like you anymore." This from Marco, who wore an arrogant smirk which needed removing. Josh moved closer and both boys took off down the parking lot, Josh hot on their tails.

BY SUNDAY EVENING, JOSH WAS IN THE FOULEST mood of his life. Not only had he not been able to reach Melissa, but he'd been dragged to every part of the university, toured each dorm room, and looked at no fewer than thirty apartments. Charlie and Marco had been excited, and normally their antics would've made him laugh along with them, but his head had not been in the right place.

The conversation he'd had with Lauren worried him even more. She'd witnessed Melissa having a bad anxiety attack at Walmart. She'd been with Angelica, whom Lauren didn't approve of. Lauren didn't approve of a lot of people when it concerned the family, which was nothing new. However, she'd also found out Darla wasn't feeling well and Melissa spent most of the weekend working on-call for the clinic.

It would explain why Melissa hadn't called him but didn't explain the continued bad connection. It was almost like he'd been blocked from her phone.

Why the hell would she block me?

In order to save Charlie and Marco's lives, Josh rode home sitting between the twins instead of those dorks. It was a much more pleasant trip, even if they had to stop more often so the babies could be fed. It gave him a chance to stretch his legs and calm his rage before he got home and busted down Melissa's door to find out what the hell the problem was. He wasn't used to feeling this impatient, and he was usually fighting other people's anger instead of his own.

At one point, he'd actually called Jarod to find out if she'd been reported missing. His brother laughed and patched him through to Marguerite, who'd assured him she was fine.

Why haven't you called me, Melissa?

When they finally reached the estate, Josh hugged his family, punched Marco in the shoulder, and put Charlie in a headlock and noogied some hair off his scalp before he high-tailed it to his pickup and sped down the driveway. He needed to know if she was all right.

He needed *her*.

When he reached their row of townhouses, his disappointment became acute. No one was home. It was late Sunday evening and he hadn't eaten since Reno, but he didn't care. Where the hell was she?

He got back in his pickup and drove to Darla's house. Marguerite's sporty convertible was parked in the driveway, but there was no sign of Melissa's CRV. He went to the door anyway.

"Well hello, handsome," Marguerite said as she opened the screen door for him. When she got a good look at him, her demeanor changed from flirtatious to concerned. "What's wrong?"

"You tell me."

Her eyebrows raised to her hairline, and that's when he realized he'd shouted. "Sorry," he said, clearing his throat. "I haven't talked to Melissa all weekend."

"I see. Have a seat and I'll get us something to drink. You look like you need it."

"No, please, I just need to know what's going on."

"Josh, have a seat." She brooked no argument, and having no other choice, he sat on the couch.

She returned with two bottles of beer, handed him one, and sat down next to him. "I can assure you she's fine. I have no idea why you can't get through to her, but I talked to her this afternoon. The Ferreros' mare is having its baby, but there are complications, so she's been out there all day."

He took a deep breath through his nose before he took a swig from the bottle. "Lauren said as much."

"Lauren?"

"Yeah, she said she'd run into Melissa at Walmart yesterday. She was with Angelica."

Marguerite hummed under her breath and took a pull from her own drink. "Josh, my sister loves animals. She always has and she always will. She also isn't as shy as everyone assumes. She just gets tongue-tied a lot and has issues expressing her feelings."

"She communicates fine with me." *When we're alone.* Marguerite didn't need to know all the details.

"She communicates with you the only way she knows how and, believe me, I love that you two have that." She smiled. "She loves you, Josh. She just has to deal with her own feelings right now. It's new to her."

"You're right," he said sheepishly. "I'm sorry I bothered you so late."

"Oh, Josh. You're not bothering me, especially if you're concerned about my baby sister. You love her and I couldn't be happier for you." She leaned in and hugged him like a sister would and it made him smile.

Happy she accepted him as a brother, he kissed her cheek and returned the hug. "Thank you, Marguerite." He leaned back against the couch. "Now, tell me how your mom is doing. I've been incredibly rude tonight."

Marguerite's face went from happy to sad in a flash. "The cancer's progressing. There's nothing anyone can do."

"Does Melissa know?"

"Nope, and Mom wants to keep it that way. So you'd better not say anything or I'll have you beat up." She was a good actress, but Josh could see her pain through the smart aleck remark.

"I won't. You and your mother need to come clean about it, though."

"Thank you. When the time's right, we'll fill her in. But even Uncle Dane thinks we should keep it under wraps, and we trust him."

They sat in companionable silence, sipping on their beers. The TV was set on a twenty-four-hour news channel, and Josh tuned out the droning arguments.

Maybe he should let Melissa come to him when she needed to. Marguerite was correct about her little sister being stronger than she appeared, but she'd been dealing with a stalker, a new career, and a very sick mother in a short time frame. Throw in a new relationship and you had a recipe for a breakdown, or a breakup, and that just wasn't going to work for him.

She needed his support, not his pressure.

CHAPTER 16
Mickey Finn

Silence.

Missy hadn't heard a peep out of Josh in a week. She didn't understand it. She'd been overly busy with work and had put in long hours driving around the countryside tending to foaling mares, sick cows, and even an arthritic African lion living in a private zoo ten miles out in the desert.

That had been interesting.

After verifying the lion had its proper papers, she treated the big cat with a steroid and instructed the owner to keep the cat warm, which wasn't a problem in Nevada summers, but high desert temperatures could drop below freezing in winter. He assured her the lion's enclosure was heated. She left instructions for a proper diet, exercise, and massage if the owner felt adventurous. The owner laughed and said, "This ol' boy is my buddy. We get along just fine."

Missy rolled her eyes at the ancient hippy and wished him luck. Then she called Marguerite to let her know they might need to check on the man periodically to make sure he didn't become lion food.

Angelica, on the other hand, had been a constant presence. She fixed breakfast every morning and had dinner waiting when Missy got home at night. The sudden change in her hospital schedule seemed odd, but Missy had been too busy to question it, not to mention fighting the horrible realization Josh had been using her all along.

"A tiger doesn't change its stripes," Angelica said in a singsong voice as she served Missy a bowl of cereal.

"No, I guess they don't." She pushed the colorful marshmallow charms around in her milk.

She left for work soon after and noted Josh's pickup sitting prettily in his driveway. He hadn't called or texted.

Maybe he's found a new girlfriend.

Josh kissing another woman filled her mind and pierced her heart. She cried so much she thought she'd run out of tears, but she was wrong. Viciously, she swiped at one on her cheek before anyone noticed and took the next chart off the counter.

Though the clinic was busy, the day dragged on. When the sky began to darken and the last patient had been seen, she packed up Ginger to visit her mom. She didn't want to know if Josh was home or not. Her mother had been tired lately, causing Missy to worry.

She found Darla home alone on a Friday night. Frowning, Missy grabbed Ginger's carrier and headed for the front door, which was unlocked. Her mother was sitting up on the couch.

A good sign.

"Hey," Darla said weakly. "What are you doing here?"

"Ginger wanted to check on you," Missy said, using her childhood excuse to help her cope with unpleasant things.

"Ginger, huh?" Her mother reached a bony hand out to pet the kitten, who immediately started purring and hobbled onto the sick woman's lap.

"She likes you, Mom."

"Yeah, I like this sweet baby, too." Darla studied her daughter and frowned. "Oh, my darling girl, what's wrong?"

Missy let the tears flow as Darla held out her hand. "Josh isn't speaking to me anymore."

"Whatever do you mean?"

Missy explained what had happened and Darla tsked. "Melissa Ann Theroux. You find that boy right this second and talk to him in person. He's been coming to see me all week, and talks about you nonstop. Have you even bothered to call him?"

Missy sat back at her mother's censure. "No," she admitted. "I didn't want to smother him."

Darla shook her head. "Calling is not smothering. It's common courtesy to let the people we care about know we're all right. Now give him a call. I know he's worried sick about you."

"He is?" Hope bloomed in her chest. She took out her phone and dialed his number, but it was immediately disconnected. "He hung up."

"I don't think so, honey. Something's going on, and you need to see him face to face. You don't need to keep your sick mama company on a Friday night. Go on home and put Josh's heart at ease, will you?"

Missy sniffled. "I will, Mom." She smiled a watery smile, hugged her mother, secured the cat, and headed home. Suddenly she couldn't wait to see him.

As she drove through the back roads to the townhouse, she racked her brain to figure out why he'd ignored her all week and came up with nothing. When she got home, her bubble burst. Josh's truck was nowhere in sight. Angelica's car was gone too, but with all the time off she'd had Missy guessed she was finally scheduled to work.

Ginger wandered over to her bowls and batted them around until Missy changed out the water and poured in some fresh kibble. The cat purred her content and dug in.

There was leftover pizza in the refrigerator, so Missy took out the box and a can of soda, then tromped up the stairs to her room. Too tired for a shower, Missy shrugged into her jammies and flopped herself on her bed to pig out. After taking a big bite of pizza and washing it down with pop, she tapped the Facebook icon on her iPad.

It wasn't long before the same photo kept showing up in her newsfeed. It was of Josh and Marguerite kissing on her mother's sofa!

What the hell?

Missy continued to scroll and found someone else had posted the same picture plus another. The pictures were taken well past Darla's bedtime because the ill woman spent most of her waking hours on the sofa.

And the truth crashed down around Missy.

They'd both lied to her.

Josh had used her to get to Marguerite, and her sister who'd crushed on Josh years ago participated in the ruse. As she continued to scroll, new photos were popping up of Josh and Marguerite hanging out at Blue's Whiskey Bar.

Missy dropped the iPad back onto her nightstand and closed her eyes. Josh and her sister were out together now. She'd feared losing Josh to someone beautiful. Her fear had been realized with her own flesh and blood. The tears wouldn't stop as she curled herself into a ball and cried.

Two hours later, Angelica slammed the door downstairs and yelled out to her.

"I'm here," Missy said meekly, wishing the pain of betrayal would go away. When Angelica flung open the bedroom door, triumphant about something, Missy knew she didn't want to know.

"I told you tigers never changed their stripes, and here's the proof!" She hopped onto the bed with bare feet and dropped down beside Missy, holding out her cell phone.

"I already know, so leave me alone."

Angelica frowned. "You do?"

Missy pulled the sheet over her head. "Mm-hmm."

"Well, did you see the part where Josh gets in a fight with that marshal who's been hanging around town?"

Missy sat up. "McKinley?"

"One and the same," Angelica said quietly as she searched for the offending videos on her Facebook app. Soon, twangy music blared out of her phone as the video began to play. "Come on, you gotta watch this."

Fine. She sat up to watch, waiting for the rest of her heart to be broken into tiny pieces.

The small screen showed Marshal McKinley approaching an extremely drunk couple on the dance floor. Josh and Marguerite were barely recognizable, and completely lit. Missy glanced at the clock, and it wasn't even midnight yet. Marguerite rarely drank, and Missy had never seen Josh so inebriated.

When McKinley reached them, Josh took a swing at the marshal and Marguerite fell to the ground.

"Apparently, they were arrested right after this was taken," Angelica said.

"What? Marguerite could lose her job!"

"I know. It looks like it was quite a spectacle. Look at some of the comments on this post."

They were all about how the two most notoriously single people in Timbisha Township had finally gotten together and what a mistake it was.

"Why didn't they just get a room and get it over with?"

"Neither of them will do any real time. One is the sheriff's brother and the other is his secretary. Goes to show what kind of cops we have in this town."

"She's always been a slut. Maybe now she'll have some shame."

"Never thought Josh would stoop so low."

"Man Whore and Blondie together at last."

As angry as she was at her sister, Missy knew Marguerite would never survive this kind of ridicule. Not only had Josh duped Missy into giving him her virginity, but he'd also ruined her sister's reputation for good. There'd be no coming back from this. Small towns could be judgmental and critical at the worst of times, and this was definitely the worst time for Marguerite.

"I need to see if she's okay."

"Who, Marguerite? After what she did to you? Oh, honey, you need to let her sober up first before you unleash that temper of yours. She needs to pay for what she did. Josh too. I'm just glad you found out before you got in too deep with that creeper." Angelica put her arm around Missy. "You'll be fine. They've shown you their true colors, and you have nothing left to fear. You've got me to look after you."

Missy held on to Angelica and cried it all out. When she was done, she vowed to never give her heart to another man, especially one as good looking as Josh King.

No matter what he said to her.

JUST KILL ME NOW.

Josh groaned as he carefully rolled onto his back but stopped moving when his stomach protested. Carefully he opened his eyes, then quickly slammed them shut as lightning pierced his skull, frying his foggy brain.

"You'll live, but you're still an asshole." Jarod's voice hurt his ears.

"Go to hell," Josh rasped before he took the minuscule pillow from behind his head and threw it at his brother. "Where am I?"

"Well, shit-for-brains, you're in the Timbisha Township drunk tank."

Josh swore foully under his breath before confronting his brother. "The hell you say, Jarod." If he could move, he'd punch his jerk of a brother in the face.

"The hell if you aren't. You and my secretary made quite the spectacle of yourselves last night."

Was he serious? "What'd you do to Marguerite?"

Jarod opened the cell and stood over Josh, blocking the killer sunlight which threatened to melt Josh's skull. "When we suspected she'd been drugged, McKinley took her to emergency."

"Well, why the hell didn't you take me to the hospital?"

"Because I didn't want you to kill the doctors and nurses, that's why, you batshit-crazy degenerate."

Josh prayed for patience — and for the room to stop spinning. "What time is it?"

"A little after one. You've been in a crazed stupor all night. Want to tell me what the hell went on last night?"

Josh tried to recall anything of the evening before and came up blank. "I have no idea."

"How did you get to Blue's?" Jarod sounded pissed, probably thinking he'd driven drunk.

"I drove there after work. The guys were heading over for a quick one before going home for the weekend. Since Melissa still isn't speaking to me, I thought, why not?"

"So you took drugs and drank yourself into oblivion? This isn't a country song, Josh. And as *my* brother, I'd expect better from you." Jarod was shaking his head in mock disgust.

"Don't be a prick. You know I don't do drugs, so screw off." His stomach lurched and he shut his mouth, refusing to lose his stomach in front of his smug-faced brother.

He felt something cold touch his arm. "Take it," Jarod said.

"Circumstances being what they are, I don't want to drink anything I didn't open myself."

"It's a little late for that, baby brother," Jarod said on a frustrated sigh. "Here, let me help you sit up."

At the first tug, Josh knew he was going to puke. Now he knew why they put toilets in these cells. When he finished embarrassing himself in front of Jarod, he took the bottle of water and placed it on his aching head. "I honestly don't remember much after I finished my first beer." He'd watched Ernie, the bartender, pop the top, so he knew the drink hadn't been tainted. He explained this to Jarod, who nodded but didn't say anything else. It was his way of letting Josh sort things out for himself. He'd said his goodbyes to his crew after throwing a round of darts. "I ordered an ice water after the beer," he said.

"Fits. You usually do when you bet."

Josh nodded. "Yeah... that's right. Jimmy challenged me to

a game." It was getting a little clearer. "That son of a bitch owes me fifty bucks."

Jarod snickered. "Okay, so you stayed long enough to hustle your crew. Did you have more than one water?"

"Maybe," Josh admitted. "I didn't feel like leaving." He took a tentative drink of water and felt the cotton melt a little in his mouth. When the first sip stayed down, he took another, and then another until the whole bottle was empty. Jarod stayed with him the entire time, took the empty bottle from him, and tossed it in the trash can sitting outside of the holding cell.

"I'm taking you home to The Estate. I don't want you alone in your house right now."

"Shit, Jarod, did you freaking book me?" The thought of having a record for drunk and disorderly really pissed him off, especially if it was his brother who'd done it.

Jarod sighed. "I should've, the way you were carrying on. Once McKinley rushed Marguerite to the hospital, I knew you both were in trouble, but for appearances' sake, I needed to bring you in. Understand?"

"Dude, the election isn't for another two years."

Jarod grabbed him under the armpit and hefted him to his wobbly feet. Josh was weak, but he took a deep breath and steadied himself. Jarod let him find his balance, and then with a little help, they made it out of the station house and into the blazing summer heat.

Josh thought he was going to lose it again but, thankfully, Jarod had parked close to the doors. They were driving down the road in no time, the air conditioner blasting frosty cold air into Josh's face. He leaned his head against the window and closed his eyes.

He must've dozed off because in the next moment they

were pulling into The Estate where their father stood waiting for them. Josh felt like he was sixteen again, getting busted for staying out all night without permission at a bonfire. James immediately opened the passenger door and helped Josh out. Good thing because he'd have face-planted on the first step. It seemed he was getting worse by the minute, and when they got inside, they made a beeline to the kitchen and the family dining room.

"Your mother and Lauren took Jessica shopping so she wouldn't have to see her Uncle Josh in such dismal shape," his father said with disapproval. "Son, I thought I'd beaten this out of you a long time ago."

Josh laughed. James King had never beaten his sons, nor anyone else for that matter. Oh, he'd threatened to beat them, and when they were little, they'd all had swats on the butt, but that had been enough to scare them into behaving themselves, at least for a little while. "Would you believe me if I said this isn't my fault, Dad?"

James looked him in the eyes. "Yes. I would, son." He patted his shoulder and brought over a mug of something foul smelling from the stove. "Drink it. You should be right as rain in no time."

A subtle chirp came from Jarod's pocket. He dug out his phone and swiped a finger across the screen. "McKinley, how is she?"

Josh and James listened to Jarod's half of the conversation while James attempted to pour more of the contents of the mug down Josh's throat. It was absolutely disgusting.

"They sure?" He paused. "Okay, when she wakes up take her statement and tell her I'll even let her file it herself if she wants to. Yeah, okay. Keep me posted." He shoved the phone back into his pocket and turned to Josh. "It was a combination of drugs, rohypnol and ketamine among them. By the time they got to the ER, she'd stopped breathing and they had to use the paddles on her." Jarod shook his head. "The one thing you and Marguerite truly have in common is Melissa."

"Where's Dane?" Josh asked.

James answered. "I sent him to the hospital to watch over his niece."

"Who's taking care of Darla?" Josh wondered if Melissa knew what had happened and if she cared.

"Look, you've been through enough today. I'm going to head over to Blue's Whiskey Bar and see if I can piece together when and how you were dosed. I don't want you to leave The Estate, Josh." Jarod gave him his cop face, and all Josh could do was laugh.

"Yeah, all right. I don't think I could drive anywhere anytime soon, anyway."

"He won't get past me, Jarod." Their father crossed his arms over his chest.

"I know he won't, Dad."

"Jarod," Josh called out to his brother's retreating back. When Jarod turned, he said, "Thanks, man."

Jarod nodded and walked out the door.

"How did you end up with Marguerite?" James asked.

"I have no idea. She wasn't at the bar when I got there, and I don't remember anything after I played darts." He explained what he remembered. Nothing else came to him. It was like there was a big, black hole in his memory.

"You know, the common theme here is ketamine," James said in a lowered voice which Josh appreciated.

"I thought the same thing. Dane was right about Harold not being Melissa's stalker," Josh admitted.

"You knew about that?"

"Yeah, and apparently so did you. Why the *hell* didn't you say anything, Dad?" Frustration didn't begin to cover how Josh felt at the moment.

James shook his head. "Dane told me how Jarod and the marshal wanted to handle things. Now that both you and Marguerite have been hurt, we're going to do things our way." Josh watched as his father dialed a number on his cell phone and went over Jarod's head by scheming with Dane Bainbridge.

———————

Tap, tap, tap.

"I don't think he feels good, Mommy."

"Jessica, honey, we told you to leave Uncle Josh alone. Come with me, now."

"But—"

"No buts, young lady."

Josh lifted the soaking wet washcloth off of his face and grinned. "It's all right, Sassy. The princess was only trying to help."

He opened his eyes to a very frustrated Lauren. "My goodness, Josh, you look like something the cat dragged in."

"Oh, Mommy, he don't look like a dead bird." Jessica's eyebrows were lowered over her eyes in the sweetest look of confusion. Josh sat up and hugged the girl to him.

"That's right, Mommy," he emphasized to Lauren. "I'm a helluva lot cuter than an ol' dead bird."

Jessica giggled.

He kissed her head. "Will you do me a favor, princess, and ask Grandma to make me an iced tea? I'm super thirsty."

"Okay, Hunkle Josh." She crawled off the bed and ran down the hall.

Josh made sure she was out of earshot before he explained everything to Lauren, who looked sick herself.

"Jarod's still at the hospital with Marguerite in the hope she can put some of the missing puzzle pieces together for us. Did you call Missy?"

Josh shook his head. "I've been either unconscious or too sick to make the call." *And too afraid it wouldn't go through.*

"Well, when you finally do talk to her, you're going to have your work cut out for you, Josh. Look." She handed him her cell phone, with Facebook opened, and Josh felt sick all over again.

"Has Jarod seen these?" Josh had an ominous feeling. Who the hell had taken those pictures?

"Yes, and my question is, what in God's name were you doing with Marguerite Theroux? I thought I knew you better, Josh."

"You think I'm sleeping with Marguerite?"

Lauren put a hand on his shoulder. "Honey, the whole town thinks you're sleeping with Marguerite. The photos are very compelling."

"Fuuu..."

"Watch your mouth. Tiny ears could be coming around the corner any second."

"Or your mother," Camille said dryly as she walked through the door and handed him a glass of iced tea.

"...udge." He smiled at everyone in the room.

Camille rolled her eyes. "I wanted to give you some aspirin but I have no idea what effect they'd have after so many disgusting drugs have been introduced into your system."

"Thanks, Mom." He took the glass and drank down half of the refreshing liquid in one gulp.

Jessica handed him the tattered blue blanket she cherished. "Blue will make ya feel better."

"Thank you, princess."

"Tell me why these pictures look so incriminating," Lauren persisted.

"I don't know, Sassy. It's not what you think, I swear to God." Josh leaned over with his elbows on his knees and put his face in his hands. How the hell was he going to fix this mess? More importantly, though, who the hell took those pictures? "I feel like I've been set up."

"Why were you at Darla's without Missy, son?"

"She's not talking to me and I'd hoped she'd be there. Marguerite's on my side, by the way."

"It sure looks that way to me," Sassy agreed sarcastically.

"Oh, come on! You know I love Melissa." Josh was sick of this crap. "I need to figure out who's setting us up."

His mother nodded. "Jarod's there now, and Dane knows the truth about how you feel about his nieces. I think you need to get up, get showered, and then get your butt over to Melissa's and explain yourself before things get any worse."

Josh cringed. "Don't even mention things could get worse." He wiped his hands down his face and took a deep breath. "Where's my truck?"

Lauren shared a look with his mom. "I think it's still in impound. I'll call Jarod."

Camille walked to the door. "And while she's doing that, you get yourself cleaned up. You smell like a bar bathroom after a busy weekend."

Josh stood on wobbly legs and handed the blanket back to Jessica. "Thank you, sweetheart. I feel better all ready."

"Welcome, Hunkle Josh." Camille picked up the little girl, promising she could help bake some cookies.

Josh stumbled into the *en suite* bathroom while Lauren argued with her husband over the phone. Josh shut the door, grateful for the silence. His head hurt worse now after learning about the photos. They were pretty damning, and he could only imagine what Melissa was thinking right now. Had she contacted her sister? What would Marguerite say?

After taking a quick shower — which did nothing to improve his mood — he wrapped a towel around his waist and went to find some clothes.

Once he'd brushed his teeth and combed his hair, he left the bathroom and heard bickering coming from the hallway. He opened the door to find Charlie and Marco going at it.

Josh rolled his eyes, and the motion nearly had him sitting down again. His head still pounded and the boys' bickering didn't help. "What are you girls fighting about now?" he said on his way to the kitchen. Food sounded awful, but maybe some toast would help soak up the remains of the crap still lingering in his system.

Charlie put his hands on his hips. "We aren't fighting."

"Yeah," Marco agreed. "We're discussing."

Josh stopped in his tracks and turned around. "You know that's exactly what my parents used to tell us boys when we were little. Are you sure you two aren't married?"

Charlie and Marco stared at each for a moment before turning back to Josh. "Yeah, we're sure," they said in unison.

Josh shook his head and continued down the hallway, both boys hot on his heels.

"Look, we need to talk," Charlie said.

"About you and Marguerite," explained Marco.

"Nothing to talk about," Josh mumbled as he entered the kitchen. He headed straight to the bread box but found only the heels left from the loaf. Irritated, he searched the pantry until he found some of Jessica's fish-shaped cheese crackers in weird colors. Why kids liked this stuff was beyond him. He stuck his hand in the bag and shoved a bunch in his mouth. Since his mouth had been filled with cotton only a short while ago, the crackers didn't taste like anything but dirt. Maybe another iced tea was in order.

He turned in time for Charlie to hand him a tall glass filled with beautiful golden liquid. "Hunffs," he said around the mashed-up mess in his mouth.

"You're welcome. Now, about last night. We think we know who took those pictures."

Marco nodded. "And we know why."

The boys nodded at each other in agreement before telling their story. Josh listened to their tale as he finished off the bag of crackers and two glasses of iced tea. What they said didn't surprise him. Women could be devious when they wanted to be, and there were a few devious ones in Timbisha Township. What he couldn't figure out was why anyone would want to hurt Melissa in the process, and to what lengths this particular vixen would go to get what she wanted.

"Have you told Jarod yet?"

"No, we thought we should tell you first since it's your face that's all over the Internet," Charlie said.

"I need to get to Melissa's." Josh groaned as he got to his feet.

"Missy's at the hospital," Marco said.

"How do you know?"

"Dude, I'm a small town taxi driver. I usually know where everyone is at any given moment." Marco jiggled his keys.

"Well then, taxi me to the hospital, will ya? I'm without wheels 'til I can get my truck out of impound."

CHAPTER 17

Frenemy

Missy stood in the doorway while her ill mother silently cried over Marguerite. Her sister never took drugs, and she'd never behaved as erratically as she had in those videos. However, between Josh's reputation as a hound and Marguerite's ability to get what she wanted, Missy was having a hard time not believing they'd betrayed her.

Movement down the hall caught her attention. Jarod and the marshal were deep in a quiet discussion. Seeing Jarod King only reminded her of Josh. Missy turned away from the scene, swallowing her hurt, and tried to focus on her own family.

"The doctors say she's going to be fine." Uncle Dane wrapped his arm around her shoulders.

"Why won't she wake up?"

Dane grunted. "It's possible she's had an allergic reaction to the drugs that were slipped into her drink. They're giving her something to counteract their effect. The doctors are hopeful she'll wake soon."

"Will she be okay?"

"Honey, we're talking about Marguerite." Though fear was still plain on his face, Uncle Dane gave her a reassuring squeeze.

"Why would Josh drug her?"

"Josh?" he said incredulously. "Melissa, that boy was doped up too."

"I saw the videos, Uncle Dane. I know you're loyal to the Kings, but I also know what I saw." Josh kissing Marguerite, dancing, partying, having a date together while Missy worked late. She couldn't get the images out of her head. She'd never considered herself a jealous person, but the green-eyed monster was in total control of her emotions right now.

"You saw what someone wanted you to see, Melissa Ann." He turned her to face him in order to meet her eyes. "Josh King loves *you*, not your sister."

"But Facebook—"

"Stop it." He gave her shoulders a gentle shake. "Did you forget you're being stalked? This has 'setup' written all over it."

"Miz Theroux." Marshal McKinley had approached them while her uncle gave her the *what for*. "I couldn't help but overhear you. Marguerite went to Blue's to meet me. I'd meant to be there sooner but I got tied up in something, and by the time I arrived, both she and Josh were lit up like firecrackers."

"I see." Another tear ran down her cheek.

"Do you? Because it sounds to me like you think your big sister has the hots for my little brother," Jarod said now. "I can assure you that's not the case, but even if she did, Josh has had it bad for you for a long time."

"Do you honestly think your own flesh and blood would betray you, Missy?" Dane asked.

"Do you honestly think I'd keep her on if she did?" Jarod asked. "Loyalty, especially to family, is a quality I value in my employees. Your sister has it in spades. No, Marguerite and I may not have gotten along at first, but she's as loyal to family as they come."

Of course, with so many handsome males and overwhelming emotions surrounding her, she lacked the ability to speak, so she nodded instead and looked back into her sister's room.

"Why don't you go sit with your mom? She needs you now." Dane hugged her close for a second and then gave her a little push into the hospital room.

Marguerite lay motionless and pale in the hospital bed, her makeup smeared away and her hair a wreck. If — *when*, she corrected herself — she woke up, she was going to be in a complete tizzy about her appearance.

Darla's frail hand clasped Marguerite's limp wrist, careful not to touch the IV needle inserted into her hand. Darla turned in her wheelchair as Missy approached the bed and revealed a ravaged, fear-filled expression. "Oh, Missy!" She lifted her arms out for a hug.

When Missy reached her mother, they both broke down in sorrow. "They said someone drugged her?" Darla cried. "Who would do this?"

"I don't know, Mom. Uncle Dane, Sheriff King, and Marshal McKinley are working on it." God, she hoped they found the person responsible.

Suddenly, her mother grabbed her face with both hands. "Dane explained to me about the photos on the Internet. You listen to me and you listen good, young lady. Your sister would never betray you, do you hear me?"

"Yes, ma'am." Her mother's grip was stronger than it had been in months.

"And don't believe Josh had anything to do with this. That boy loves *you*, honey, not Marguerite." Then she grabbed her in a fierce hug that would have hurt if the woman were healthy. Missy couldn't stop crying now.

They held each other as they watched Marguerite lying on the bed. A nurse came in to check her sister's vitals, and the men stood outside talking. It wasn't until the nurse simpered at one of the men that she realized Josh was present.

She turned in time for her gaze to collide with his. He was pale even under his tan, and his once-beautifully clear eyes were red-rimmed and bloodshot.

"Go to him," her mother said, and before she knew what she was doing, she was running into his arms.

"Oh, thank God," he whispered into her ear as he held her firm. He felt so good, and she'd missed him so much that all the angst of the night before and the pain of this morning evaporated into sweet relief. "I didn't do this, baby. You have to believe me." Warm hands on her cheeks, he held her face to his and looked into her eyes. "I love you, Melissa Ann Theroux. Not your sister, or anyone else. I love *you*." He stressed the last part, and everyone including her mother and her uncle heard him.

"I love you too."

He kissed her hard. Reality and embarrassment were too strong for Missy, so she ended the kiss on a laugh and gently pushed him back. She had so many questions, and before she knew it the anger was back.

"Why haven't you called me?" she asked through the doubt and pain. "Why, Josh?" she asked with force. All the men looked surprised, but she didn't care. "I waited a week for you to call. You were the one who left for the weekend, and then I never heard back from you. What the hell was I supposed to think?" she yelled.

Taken aback, he smiled. "I did call."

She didn't understand. She dug her phone out and showed it to him. "Really? Prove it!"

Chuckling as if her anger amused him, he shrugged and pulled out his own phone. "See for yourself, honey."

She grabbed it and scrolled through his call log and texts. He'd called more than a dozen times and sent her text messages, none of them appearing on her phone.

"What does this mean?"

"It means I've been blocked."

"But how?" She was confused. She'd never block him from her phone. She had a password, too, so no one else could've done it.

Some monitors beeped in Marguerite's room before they heard Darla gasp in relief. Missy's sister was waking up. The crowd in the hall moved into the room. Missy noticed Charlie and Marco when Charlie reached out a hand to her. "Can I see your phone? I have an idea how it was hacked."

She immediately gave it to him. "Hacked?" The idea of someone having access to her phone made her sick. All of Josh's previous texts and voicemails, the ones she'd kept of him expressing his love for her, were on her phone. She hadn't deleted them even when she'd thought he'd betrayed her.

"Yeah," Charlie mumbled as he concentrated on the phone while Marco looked over his shoulder and periodically pointed at something on her screen.

"While they fiddle around with it, maybe you should say hello to your sister," Josh whispered in her ear.

She turned and saw Marguerite sitting up but looked

peaked. Darla held a plastic cup with a flexible straw for her daughter to take a sip.

"What's with the peanut gallery?"

The whole room sighed with relief at her sarcastic tone, raspy and weak though it was. "We just wanted to see what you looked like hungover," Jarod said.

Marguerite's eyes widened before a hand went to her hair, and then an embarrassed groan issued from her mouth. "Get out so I can get dressed, will ya?"

"Not a chance," Darla said.

"Fine." She closed her eyes with resignation before she asked, "Jarod, please tell me you caught the driver of the truck that ran me over."

Everyone chuckled then. "No," he said, "there was no truck, but maybe you can fill in some blanks for us."

Her expression became grave. "I'll try." Her eyes went to the marshal. "You called me and wanted to meet at Blue's Whiskey Bar, right?"

"Right." He nodded, and Missy swore she saw regret on his face.

"I remember Josh playing darts." She looked to him for confirmation. "Jeez, you look like shit."

"Feel like it, too. Go on, because I don't remember seeing you at all. I barely remember the darts."

At his admission, Marguerite eyes widened, scared. She stared at everyone in the room, then at the IV in her arm, and a tear fell. "What's happened, guys?"

"You and Josh were drugged, honey," Darla said. "If it weren't for the marshal, God only knows what would've happened to you."

"SOMEONE'S JAILBROKEN MISSY'S PHONE," CHARLIE announced to the room.

"What's that mean?" Josh asked. He'd heard the term before, but he'd never taken the time to find out the ins and outs of a smartphone's operating system.

"Well, whoever did it installed spyware and apps to block callers. It also looks like they've forwarded all received messages to another phone," Marco answered.

"Yeah, I'm trying to figure out where, though," Charlie said in concentration as he manipulated the phone in his hands.

"That's why I couldn't get through to her." Josh was pissed. All this time Missy hadn't blocked him. Then he remembered the creepy warning he'd found in the box along with a drugged-up Ginger: *Stay away from what's mine. Making you disappear will be easier than the cat.*

"What is it?" Jarod asked going into cop mode.

Josh shook his head. He didn't want to spook the girls any more than they already had been. "Just thinking about past messages," he said to Jarod with meaning.

Jarod narrowed his eyes before he nodded in agreement. "Marshal, we need to talk."

"Got it!" Charlie announced. He handed the phone to Jarod. "Can you trace the number?"

"I can," Dane said.

"I think I can do it, Bainbridge," Jarod said with disgust. "Stay with your family. McKinley and I can take it from here."

"You two have been mucking this up from the beginning," Dane accused.

"Now wait just a damn minute," Jarod said.

"What the hell are you talking about?" McKinley asked.

"Guys! I think you all should go and work together.

Please." Melissa stood up. "My sister is in the hospital and my boyfriend has been drugged because of me. You all have talents and resources that you can pool together to find whoever is doing this before anyone else gets hurt. Now go!" She actually pointed to the doorway.

Damn, she's magnificent.

"Yeah, what she said," Josh agreed. "Seriously, Jarod, put away the territorial bullshit and work with them, will ya?" He couldn't fight the smile on his face because he loved it when his brother stepped in it. "If you don't, I'm telling Mom."

"You wouldn't dare."

Josh nodded. "And Lauren."

Jarod sighed with disgust. "Gentleman, follow me," he said, but before he left he went to Marguerite's bedside and hugged her, whispering something Josh couldn't hear. When Marguerite smiled and nodded, Jarod straightened and left the room, assuming the other men would follow. They did, but not without their own goodbyes to the patient. Josh didn't miss the longing in the marshal's eyes before he walked out the door.

"Crap, we forgot to tell them," Charlie said as he ran out of the room, Marco hot on his heels.

"Tell them what?" Darla asked.

"Their theory of who could be doing this," Josh said. If they were right, then he had to get Melissa out of her house. "Where's Ginger?"

"Home, why?"

"'Kay, hold on." Josh followed after the other men.

Charlie was just explaining everything when Josh caught up to them. "Marco takes her to work, but the other night he noticed she didn't go in."

"Yeah, so I followed her. She backtracked to a car I haven't seen before, a Land Rover, I think. Anyway, she took an old trail up the hill on the other side of town. I didn't follow beyond the old mining road in my car. It's my only set of wheels and how I make money, ya know?" Marco looked worried. "I think she's Missy's stalker, guys."

"Why do you think that?" Jarod asked.

"Well, she's always carting around vials of medicine in her bag."

Josh shared a look with Jarod, who glanced at McKinley, who was eyeing Dane.

"Marco?" Josh asked, "can you give me a ride to impound? I need my truck, and I need to go get Ginger and move her to my townhouse."

"I don't want you going there alone," Jarod gritted out through his teeth. "I'll take you, and while we're there, I think we should bring Angelica in for questioning."

The other men agreed.

"Charlie, you and Marco stay away from her until we can sort this out," Dane said.

"Yessir," both boys said in unison.

"I'm going to the personnel office downstairs and see what I can dig up there. You three go get the damn cat and take it to The Estate. I don't want you staying at either townhouse until we get this sorted out," the ex-FBI man said.

"Now wait a minute. I can take care of myself," Josh argued.

"Really? If she's Missy's stalker, then you're in just as much danger as Harold Schurke was, and you know how he ended up."

Jarod and McKinley agreed, which irritated Josh. He knew women and he could handle Angelica. "Fine, but I don't want Melissa there either. Mom will have to make her a room."

Dane cleared his throat in fatherly disagreement. "She'll be staying with her mother."

Properly chastised, Josh said, "Yessir."

However, Jarod interrupted. "No one's safe. I think Darla, Marguerite, and Melissa should stay at The Estate. It's more secure and we have plenty of room." He didn't bother waiting for an argument.

After saying goodbye to Melissa, Josh left with Jarod and McKinley to get the cat. Angelica wasn't home, and Josh assumed she'd gone to work or had a hideout in the hills. Ginger was happy to see him, and he quickly got her things together. He was back in the cruiser within minutes. "Don't you want to lift her prints or collect DNA or something?"

McKinley laughed. "You've been watching too many *CSI*s." Josh was about tell him to screw off when the marshal's phone rang. "McKinley," he answered.

After a few "i'zat rights?" and "no shits," the marshal put his phone away. "That was Bainbridge. Turns out Angelica Daemon is not, and never has been, an employee of Timbisha Township Medical Center."

"How can that be? She was Julie's nurse when the babies were born," Josh said.

Jarod swore.

McKinley said, "I ran a background check on her when I first arrived in town."

"Why?" Jarod asked.

"Because I was being thorough. Schurke was a fugitive, living under an assumed name, and Bainbridge's niece was being stalked. I ran checks on everyone associated with Miz Theroux, and wanna know what I found on Angelica? Zip."

Josh turned around in his seat. "That doesn't make sense. Melissa knows her from school. They were roommates."

"There's no paper trail on her from before her arrival at Melissa's school; no financials, no birth records. That's why I was late getting to the bar last night." McKinley shook his head. "Drop me at my truck before heading out to your estate, Sheriff. I need to do some follow-up. I'll hit ya back when I know more."

After they dropped McKinley off at his truck, Josh tried to talk Jarod into getting his own pickup out of impound. The stubborn jackass wouldn't go for it. "I think I'll keep it for a bit longer so I can keep my eyes on you. I don't need you doing anything stupid."

"I have to work, dickhead."

"Gimme a break, Josh! You practically work from home! But if you need to go somewhere work related, Dad can drive you." Jarod had an answer for everything. He was going to get his ass kicked — again. The sweet memory of overtaking Jarod last fall and bloodying his nose brought a smile to Josh's face, and he vowed to do it again soon.

Jessica was beyond thrilled at having Ginger at The Estate. After dropping off the cat and giving a brief explanation of the circumstances to Camille, Josh threw Jarod a dirty look before getting back into the cruiser.

"Since you've taken away my driving privileges, you'll have to be my chauffeur. Take me back the hospital."

Jarod must have seen something in Josh's eyes because the entire ride back to town was silent.

MARGUERITE HAD DRIFTED BACK INTO A HARD SLEEP. Missy watched her sister breathe steadily in and out and thanked God she'd be all right. The doctors believed

Marguerite's extreme reaction was due to an allergy. She hadn't been breathing when she was brought in, and at one point her heart stopped, necessitating the use of a defibrillator. The doctors had been lucky to raise her heart rate enough that intubation hadn't been required. Missy kept an eye on the pulse oximeter attached to Marguerite's finger. Her oxygen levels were normal now. The rhythmic beeping of Marguerite's heart monitor lulled Missy into a false sense of calm as her sister recovered.

"It's frightening how easily a person can be poisoned in public," Darla said. "Dane doesn't want us to go home."

Missy shook her head. "I need to take care of Ginger. I need to get ready for work once I know Marguerite is going to be all right, and you need to rest in your own bed. All your meds are at your house."

Her mother gave her The Look. "If your uncle said don't go home, then we don't, honey."

"Where are we supposed to stay?"

Darla sighed. "With James and Camille. Honestly, I'm not comfortable with it either." When Missy said nothing, her mother let the silence reign. Finally, she said quietly, "You know, I'm very proud of you for sticking up for your sister like that."

"Like what?"

"Like you were the woman in charge," she said slyly. "All your life, you've lived in the shadow of your big sister, who loves you with all of her heart. That's the first time I've seen you be so assertive. I'm glad you've finally found your voice."

"Mom, I've always had my voice."

Knowing what to say is my problem.

"No, you haven't. Oh, sure, we all knew you wanted to be a vet since you uttered the word 'puppy,' but you've never, ever taken the initiative and spoken your mind." She shook her head while hugging Missy. "And, oh, what a brilliant mind you have."

"Mom."

"Did you know you didn't speak until you were almost three?"

This was the first time Missy had heard this. She shook her head.

"Well... your big sister knew what you needed or wanted before anyone else did, including yourself. She was so excited to be a big sister, Melissa," she said, gazing down at her oldest child. "When your father and I told her we were having another baby, she jumped up and down and said 'baby' over and over again. When we found out I was having another girl, Marguerite told us that your name was Missy."

"You let a two-year-old name me?" Missy asked dryly.

Darla conceded with a laugh, "We'd already picked out the name Melissa Ann, so when she called you Missy, it stuck." She shook her head at the memories. "I was so angry with you when you thought Marguerite had stolen Josh. She would never, ever, EVER do anything to hurt you, but I was relieved when you stood up for her today. It was what I needed to hear to know you love her as much as she loves you."

Missy stared at her sister. "Even when she's bossing me around, I always feel like she knows me best."

"And you know her, I expect. Now, what are you going to do about all this Facebook nonsense?"

Missy looked ill. "I don't know, but I'm sure I'll figure something out."

"I'll help you," Josh said as he came into the room and took a seat next to Missy. "Between my brother the sheriff, Marshal McKinley, and your ex-FBI uncle, I'm sure we can get the social media giant to take down those posts. Maybe they can even help track down where they originated."

"Not bad, handsome," Marguerite croaked from the bed. "You should ask your brother for a job at the station."

"Yeah, no thanks," Josh drawled.

Everyone immediately went into caregiver mode after Marguerite woke up.

"Are you thirsty?"

"What can I get you?"

"Do you need the nurse?"

Marguerite smiled at all the attention. "Yes to the water, please, Mom."

Darla handed her the cup. Missy noticed how dry her sister's lips were and dug into her pocket.

"Here's some lip balm," she said, handing it to her.

"A godsend, thank you."

When the nurse came in, Missy said, "I thought for sure Angelica would be taking care of you today."

She immediately felt Josh stiffen next to her.

The nurse attending Marguerite frowned. "Who's that?"

Now Missy was puzzled. "My roommate. She's a nurse here."

"Well, maybe we haven't been on the same shifts," the nurse said as she turned her attention to her patient. "Marguerite, your vitals have been stable for a while. Do you feel like eating something?"

"Yes, but I'd also like to pee," she said, looking at the IV in her arm. "I think my bladder is going to burst."

Missy and the nurse helped Marguerite to the restroom while Josh volunteered to take Darla to the vending machine and back. Getting up seemed to have motivated Marguerite, and she requested to get dressed.

When Josh and Darla made it back to the room, Marguerite had donned some sweats and sat grimacing at her lunch. She looked much better and was beginning to demand to be released.

"Seriously, I think I just needed to sleep all that crap off and get some fluids in me. I'm fine." She pushed the rest of her mushy hospital food around on the plate. "Can we stop by Molly's and get a burger?"

"I'd call ahead, but I don't have a phone anymore," Missy said.

"I'll do it," Josh volunteered. After taking everyone's orders, he called them in, and by then the nurse was there with the release forms. Missy was the only one with a car, so they all piled into the CRV and picked up dinner. Making an executive decision, Missy drove to her mother's house — earning a glare from Darla — but it would be easier on her mother if they all stayed there.

"Have you heard from anyone?" Missy asked the car in general.

"No," Josh said. "Have you heard from Angelica?"

"I don't have a phone, remember?" When he didn't look at her, she asked, "What aren't you telling us?"

"Dane checked her records. Angelica doesn't work for the hospital."

"You mean she was fired?"

"No, I mean she's never worked for the hospital." He still wasn't looking at her.

"Hang on," Marguerite said. "I think that's what Declan wanted to talk to me about last night."

Marguerite's use of the marshal's first name didn't escape Missy's notice, but she avoided commenting on it. "Why?"

"Some memories are coming back, but it's still fuzzy. He

said he needed to talk to me about your roommate, that he needed more information or something."

"Makes sense since her history only goes back a few years," Josh said.

"Are you saying Angelica is responsible for drugging you two?" Missy racked her brain. What had Angelica said? *Tigers never changed their stripes*, and that she herself would look after Missy. She told everyone, and they all sat stunned.

"If she were posing as a nurse, she would've had access to all kinds of drugs," Marguerite said.

Josh agreed. "Yep, and she knew our routine and when to nab Ginger."

Missy tried not to be sick. "Angelica never cared for Ginger either. I should've known then something was off."

"My dear lord," Darla whispered. "Honey, you've been living with your stalker this whole time!"

"No, the chocolates were the first incident. She wasn't living with me then."

"True, but she could've been holed up somewhere watching you," Marguerite said angrily from the backseat.

"There's something else," Josh said. "She has another vehicle, Missy."

"How do you know?" Missy asked him.

"Charlie and Marco told us. Apparently, Marco followed her one night after he dropped her off at 'work.'" He motioned with air quotes.

"Jeez, is that kid a stalker too?" Marguerite asked dryly.

Josh laughed. "No, but he's got the hots for her, so when she didn't go inside the hospital like she was supposed to, he followed her."

It made perfect sense even if Missy didn't want to believe it. "She helped me with Harold, too."

"Maybe Harold wasn't stalking you at all." This from her mother who'd been quiet for a long time. "Maybe Angelica wanted you for herself." No one said a word as they processed this disturbing theory.

After arriving at Darla's house, Marguerite carried in the food, appearing stronger than she'd been all day. Meanwhile, Josh and Missy helped Darla out of the car and into the house. Once everyone was settled at the small dinette, Missy's mind began to recall all the problems she'd had since moving back home.

Angelica's surprise arrival had felt weird from the beginning, but because Missy had been anxious about her new job — and her incredibly sexy landlord — she hadn't put too much thought into Angelica's behavior. She paid her rent in advance and spent money like she had a lot of it. She had to be getting an income from somewhere, and Missy said as much to the group.

Josh shook his head. "The marshal can check on it. With Harold's death still unsolved, maybe she's tapping into his accounts to pay for whatever it is she's got planned for you."

"No," Missy said thoughtfully. "Angelica had money to spend when we were in college, too. Maybe she's living off a trust fund." When everyone turned to stare at her, she said, "What?"

"If she's pulling money out of a fund, we can track it." Marguerite tapped on her phone's screen. "Hey, Jarod, it's me... Yes, I'm home... Yes, I'm fine, will you listen a sec? Okay, tell Dane and Declan to check for any trust fund babies who've gone missing. Because if Angelica doesn't have a job, she's got to be drawing cash from somewhere, right?" She paused. "You bet." She hung up and put her phone face down on the table, then took a bite of her burger.

"Well, what'd he say?" Josh asked impatiently while Marguerite took her time chewing her food.

"He said he was on it. We'll know soon enough. Between the three of them, they'll find out who the hell Angelica Daemon really is," she said with confidence before inhaling another bite.

CHAPTER 18

Women

Flower wallpaper dotted the walls, and a pink chenille bedspread covered a full-sized bed with iron rails. Teen idols adorned the walls in between pictures of family, farm animals, and a *Twilight* movie poster.

"I'm exhausted." Melissa pulled her t-shirt off and flung it on the floor. "What are you doing?"

"Making sure there isn't a long drop down from the window," Josh said.

"Why?"

"Because I'm in a teenaged girl's bedroom, and I don't want her father to catch me playing doctor, that's why."

Melissa stopped unbuttoning her pants and stared at him. "How many windows did you sneak out of in high school?"

"Too many to count," he said wickedly. He took her in his arms and she immediately rewarded him by putting her sweet lips on his. "Now that's what I'm talking about."

"You said you'd behave. The walls are thin in this house."

Josh had pleaded with her to stay at The Estate, but her concern was for her mother and, frankly, she'd been right.

Simply visiting the hospital had taxed Darla, who was seriously ill. He felt ashamed he'd let his libido effect the safety of two women who weren't in the best of health at the moment; Darla and Marguerite.

"And I will behave, as long as you let me hold you all night." He even crossed his heart.

"Deal." She smiled as she shimmied out of her pants, leaving her wearing nothing but matching panties and bra, which had him regretting his promise.

He'd just taken off his own shirt and was about to unsnap his fly when Marguerite's curse filled the house and Melissa's bedroom door flew open. Marguerite stood gaping angrily and holding out her cell phone.

"Have you seen this bull?"

Josh saw the picture of himself with Marguerite and sighed. "Yep. Now get out."

"Josh!" Melissa scolded him. "She's my sister."

"I know who she is, and one day she'll be my sister-in-law, if I'm lucky." Both sisters went all soft and said "aw" at the same time, and he forged on. "But right now, Marguerite, this is old news and I'm tired, so go." He tried to close the door on her, but she skirted around him and flopped on Melissa's bed.

What. The. Hell.

"Get real, Eye Candy, I have a situation here!"

Josh rubbed his hands down his face and sat on Melissa's vanity bench. When it didn't collapse under his weight, he looked over at the sisters. Melissa, who now wore nothing but her sexy panties and bra, sat on the bed next to Marguerite, who wore skimpy pajamas. Suddenly, Josh flashed back to his second year of college and a very pleasant incident involving the Myers twins. Shaking his head, he leaned down, elbows to knees, and put his face in his hands.

"Marguerite, between Uncle Dane's connections and the efforts of Marshal McKinley and Jarod, we're going to find out where the photos came from and get them taken down. Until then, we just have to hold tight." Melissa took the phone out of her sister's hands. "Now, I need for you to go to bed. *You've* been through hell today, *Josh* is recovering too, and *I'm* tired. Screaming all night about Facebook isn't good for Mom either, right?"

Marguerite smiled sheepishly. "No, you're right. I'm sorry I barged in. Goodnight, you two." She stood to leave but then stopped in the doorway. "Don't do anything I wouldn't do," she said with a smirk before shutting the door behind her.

Josh chuckled. "You handled her nicely."

She rolled her eyes and pulled down the covers. "Yes, I did. Now turn out the light and come to bed," she said around a yawn.

He did as she ordered, sliding in beside her. Her warm body was a balm to his weary soul. All the drama of the past week and the heartbreak of last night melted away as she pressed against his body. He tightened his arms around her. "I love you so much."

"I love you, too."

SUNDAY MORNING LIGHT FILTERED IN THROUGH THE blinds in Melissa's old bedroom, striking Josh right in the eyes. Remnants of the Mickey he'd been slipped still polluted his system, making it difficult to open his eyelids. After finally cracking a very dry one open, he read the clock.

8:30 am

Melissa lay spooned against his back, her long, elegant arm

draped over his middle, and he felt her soft breaths blowing between his shoulder blades. The ceiling fan gently pushed warm air around the room. Sometime in the night, Melissa had kicked off the blankets so they could hold one another without sticking to each other, literally.

He laced his fingers with hers and dreamed about a future when he could wake up like this every morning. He brought her hand to his lips and kissed it before tucking it up against his heart.

Melissa began to wriggle and then she yawned. "What time is it?"

"Quarter to nine."

She let go of his hand and rolled onto her back, stretching her perfect body against his. Unable to stop himself, he rolled over in a flash and pinned her down with his own hungry body and kissed her as if they were alone in the house.

Damn.

When he came up for air, her purple eyes were luminous and her sweet breaths were coming faster. All he wanted to do was spend the day like this.

But they couldn't.

Melissa grinned evilly and ground her hips up against him. "If you need to take a shower, you'd better do it now before Marguerite gets up and sees you... awake." She frowned before admitting, "I really wouldn't want her to see you like this, Josh. Get moving."

And she slapped his ass!

"Well, aren't you the demanding little thing," he said with a laugh. "Hell, where're my clothes?"

He scrambled out of bed and dragged on his jeans. He tossed his t-shirt over his shoulder, and headed for the door where he gave her one more longing look. She was so perfect it actually hurt to leave her.

"If you don't stop that, I'm not going to let you get your shower," she said in a warning tone.

Josh knew even if they did throw caution to the wind and wound up making love in her childhood bedroom, she'd regret it, and he was damned if he'd let her regret a single moment with him.

"Tonight," he promised before he shut her door, looking for signs of life in the hallway. He was relieved to make it undetected into the bathroom.

JOSH FOUND THE THEROUXS SITTING AT THE DINETTE after his shower.

"There's toast and bacon on the counter." Melissa handed Josh a cup of coffee.

"Thank you." He kissed her a bit indecently for company, but no one batted an eyelash. "Any word from Jarod or Dane?"

Marguerite harrumphed. "I received a text from *Declan*," she said with disgust. "Apparently, he's checking on something up the hill behind the hospital while Jarod and Uncle Dane research other leads. No one's seen Angelica since Missy left to visit me at the hospital yesterday."

"I can't believe it's her. I thought I knew her better," Melissa admitted, her voice rife with disbelief.

Josh filled his plate before sitting down next to her. "How are you feeling this morning, Mrs. Theroux?"

Though she was sitting up in her wheelchair, dressed and apparently ready for the day, her pallor had a gray tinge to it, and her eyes looked a bit more hollow than they had a week ago. He was sure the stress and worry over her daughters were the culprit, but she covered it with a cheery smile. "I'm happy my girls are home safe. Thank you for asking, Josh." She took a sip of her coffee and shakily placed the heavy mug back on the table. "What are your plans for today?"

Melissa answered while he chewed a piece of his toast. "I need to replace my cell phone. It's the only way my patients can get hold of me in case there's an emergency."

"I'm sure Dr. Brown has been notified of what happened," Josh said. "Maybe you should wait until Angelica is in custody before you go back to work."

"Better yet," Marguerite intoned, "why don't you just call him from Mom's landline? I think she's the only person left in Timbisha Township, besides businesses, who still has one."

Mrs. Theroux laughed at her daughter's sarcasm. "It's better to have two phones. What if the North Koreans shoot down our satellites? Cell phones won't be any good then, now, will they?"

Josh was about to argue how cell phones work with towers and not satellites when his own phone beeped.

A text from Jason.

"What's it say?" Melissa asked warily.

"Jason invited us up to their house for a picnic lunch."

"Oh, that sounds nice," Mrs. Theroux said.

"What time?" Marguerite asked.

"Noonish. My family's very casual, especially on a Sunday after a bunch of drama," Josh drawled.

Melissa laughed. "What should we bring? It seems your family is always feeding me and I never contribute."

"Oh, you don't need to bring anything," Josh said dismissively.

"Yes, we do," all three women said in unison.

Just then the front door opened and Dane stepped into the house. "Good morning," he said in his usual gruff baritone. "Any of that bacon up for grabs?"

"Of course, Uncle Dane." Marguerite handed him a plate then poured the man a cup of coffee. "Any news?"

"Yup. We found out who Angelica Daemon really is."

"You were right, Marguerite." Uncle Dane took a sip of his coffee before he continued. "Angelica's living off a trust fund."

"I can't believe this," Missy muttered.

"Couldn't put my finger on it," Josh murmured to himself, "but I knew something didn't feel right with her."

Dane continued as if no one had acknowledged his announcement. "She's also the person who accused Harold Schurke of sexual harassment and got the ball rolling in his criminal conviction. She disappeared right after he escaped custody." Her uncle seemed pretty cavalier about this revelation, but Missy guessed in his line of work, he'd seen worse things.

"Angie convinced me to get the restraining order against him," Missy said. "If she knew who he was, why didn't she just turn him in?"

"McKinley has a theory," Dane said. "He believes it was Angelica who harassed Schurke, and when he turned down her advances, she suffered a breakdown."

Josh squinted at her uncle. "How does he come up with that theory when Schurke was convicted of fraud and sex trafficking?"

Dane took another sip of coffee. "Her real name is Angela Dunne. That's where he gets the idea."

"Wait." Marguerite held up a hand. "Are you telling me this trust-fund psycho is the heiress to Dunne Technologies? The brat who was famous for being famous all those years ago?"

"The very same," Uncle Dane confirmed. "It's why we couldn't trace her back to her finances. She's drawing money from a cash fund, *and*," he drew out for emphasis, "her family has known she's unstable for years. Their private investigator lost track of her right about the time she enrolled at Missy's university and assumed the name Angelica Daemon."

"Why didn't they fill out a missing person's report?" Josh asked.

"She was still drawing directly from her trust fund until that time. Rather than open up their private lives to a scandal, they kept quiet until Angelica came of age and withdrew the whole amount for cash."

Missy shook her head and leaned back in her chair. "All this time I've been living with a sociopath."

"Looks that way, honey." Uncle Dane shrugged and took another sip of coffee.

"So now what are we supposed to do?" Josh asked. "Clearly she's dangerous and Melissa can't be left alone, not while Angie's still out there somewhere plotting God knows what. She's made it clear she can get to us if she wants to."

"Dunne Technologies. That's how she knew how to mess with my phone," Missy said, the answer finally coming to her. She was still stunned that her best friend would do this to her.

"We'll wait until she makes a mistake because they always do. We'll get her," Dane said, answering Josh's question.

"Uncle Dane, you can't be serious. We can't put our lives on hold," Missy said. Darla was sick, Marguerite had a career and Missy had a future to build with Josh. Were they supposed to put it all aside because her so-called friend was really her enemy? No. Missy had been living with social anxiety all of her life. Josh was hers. She wasn't going to give him up for some crazy bitch with a mental problem. "I'm not going to hide while we 'wait for her to make a mistake.'"

Josh put his arm around her and said, "No, none of us are." He looked at Dane for confirmation. "Are we?"

Uncle Dane sighed. "Look, Josh, you have to deal with your father and Jarod. Neither one of them is going to let you out of their sights until Ms. Dunne is apprehended." He leaned on the table and glared at Missy. "And it's for damn sure I'm not going to let either of my nieces out of *my* sight. So we have a lot of talking to do, don't we?"

Marguerite had been uncharacteristically silent through all of this, and Missy turned to her for help. "Are you going to stand for this?"

"Yes."

"What? Don't tell me you're going to hide too?"

Marguerite shook her head. "Angela Dunne is used to getting her way, Missy. I remember reading all about her in the tabloids. Uncle Dane's right. If she's fixated on you, then everyone in your life is in danger. Look what happened to me and Josh."

"I agree with your sister, babe," Josh said, resignation clear in his voice. "We need to think this through. Angela Dunne's been living an assumed identity for years, all to get back at the man who spurned her. I assume she's responsible for the man's death?" he asked Dane.

"We think so, yes."

"So she's capable of anything," he began, ticking the list off on his fingers. "She's spoiled. She's petty. She couldn't gain

Harold's attention so she accused him of sexual assault and chased him when he escaped, and then eventually killed him. She kidnapped Ginger and hacked your phone. She threatened me and then drugged us." Here he pointed to himself and Marguerite. "Why did she do all that? Why is she so fixated on you?"

"I have no idea," Missy said, but she desperately needed to find out. "Maybe I should try to find her?"

"No!" everyone shouted at once.

"You will not go after her," her mother commanded. "That's final."

JOSH STILL DIDN'T HAVE HIS TRUCK AND HE NEEDED more clothes if they were going to the barbecue at Jason's. Ginger was still at The Estate, so they decided to take a ride out to his parents' home. Missy sat in the passenger seat of her own vehicle and glared at Josh.

"I could've driven."

"I know." He reached out and took her hand. His touch, his nearness... just the man himself made everything clearer. He calmed her nerves while exciting her senses. Josh King knew how to please a woman in every way, and he did it with little effort.

Relief washed over Missy when they finally turned onto The Estate's long driveway. Jessica was chasing something in the grass while Lauren held a video camera. Once Josh had parked, they both followed the sound of the child's laughter.

"Hey, you two," Lauren said in greeting.

"Hey back, Sassy Pants," Josh said as he enveloped the pregnant woman in a hug. They'd been friends for a long time, Missy knew, before they'd become family, and their close relationship made her smile. Missy's smiling face got squashed when Lauren greeted her with the same enthusiasm as she did her brother-in-law.

"Thanks for letting us borrow your cat. She's quite the character." Lauren held the video camera up to them. "We caught her stalking Charlie's socks this morning, stealing Jessica's teddy bear, and hiding in the smallest spaces in the craft room. She's really funny."

"Oh my goodness, I hope she hasn't been any trouble." Missy hated being without Ginger for more than a day, but she hated it more if her babysitters had been terrorized.

"Ginger's funny," Jessica giggled. "She likes to play with me."

Josh reached down and picked up the little girl. "Everyone likes to play with you, sweetheart."

"Watch out, Hunkle Josh! Ginger's gonna getcha!" Jessica pointed to a clump of grass a little taller than the rest.

Missy had to cover her mouth to keep from laughing. All that could be seen of the kitten were two tufts of fluffy, ginger-colored fir above her eyes. As soon as Jessica called out, Ginger made her move, and in a flash, she was stuck to Josh's thigh, three legs clinging to his jeans by sharp claws.

"Holy crap, I've never seen her jump that high," he said incredulously.

"She's been doing that all morning, and I have the scratches to prove it," Lauren said, laughing. "Every time someone picks up Jessie, Ginger makes a climbing post out of them."

Missy was astounded! Her sweet kitten clawed her way up Josh's pant leg, maneuvered around his delectable behind and, with three quick hops, landed on Josh's shoulder.

"She's part monkey!" Josh's mouth hung open as Jessica

petted the kitten between her soft ears. "That really didn't feel good."

"'S okay, Hunkle Josh. Mommy has stuff for scratches. Daddy didn't use up all of the yellow tube."

"I got it on film, too," Lauren said conspiratorially.

"That's how she survived so long on her own," Missy said with admiration. "Didn't you, my wild tiger?" She lifted Ginger from Josh's shoulder, and the kitten's purring stuttered and rumbled as Ginger licked Missy's ear. "I've missed you, sweet girl."

"Let's head inside and we'll get Josh all doctored up," Lauren said, preceding them through the front doors. "How's your sister doing, Missy?"

"She's better, but not great." Missy knew the two women had a rivalry of sorts dating back to their high school days, but she appreciated Lauren asking all the same.

Lauren nodded with a troubled frown. "Camille's making lunch. She'll be glad you finally came home, Josh."

"That's right," Camille said from around the corner. "Soup's on in five." She hugged Josh around her granddaughter, who was still in his arms, and when she turned to Missy, her face lit up in a sincere smile. "I'm so happy to see you. How are Darla and Marguerite?"

"Better, thank you."

Camille nodded. "The more important question is, how are *you* doing, my dear? Between Dane, Jarod, and that McKinley fellow, we've had quite an earful regarding your roommate."

Missy looked to Josh for some help because, honestly, she didn't want to talk about how duped she felt.

"We're both adjusting to the news, Mom. And thank you

so much for wondering how I'm doing. After all, I'm the one she drugged, remember?"

Camille rolled her eyes. "Such a drama King."

"I TALKED TO JAROD THIS MORNING," LAUREN SAID as they all sat around the dining table. "Marshal McKinley believes Angelica is holed up nearby, someplace she can keep tabs on you undetected, which means she's getting around security cameras. He wants to set a trap for her."

"Oh, hell no, Lauren. Traps need bait. He wants to use Melissa, doesn't he?" Josh couldn't believe this.

"Well, in a sense, yes, but she'd never be without protection."

Yeah, famous last words.

"Traps never work, and if Angelica has a background in tech and is smart enough to use security systems to her advantage, she'll see us coming a mile away." He sat back crossing his arms over his chest..

"I don't know all the details, they're still finalizing the plan. Sheesh, don't shoot the messenger," Lauren huffed.

"I thought I knew her, and in a way I still do," Melissa said quietly.

"What are you thinking, dear?" Camille asked.

"I think she truly believes she's trying to save me. From what exactly, I'm not sure. Maybe from being hurt by people I care about?" Her face flamed red when she glanced at Josh.

"Go on," he encouraged. He loved seeing her confident, even with a blush.

She cleared her throat. "I don't think *I* should be the bait."

She looked directly at him, and that's when he realized she was throwing him under the bus.

Josh sighed in resignation. "All right, what do you want me to do?" They stared at each other for a moment before they both grinned.

"What is going on, you two?" Lauren asked with suspicion. "It's like you're reading each other's minds."

"Not quite," Josh answered. "But we're getting there." He reached for Melissa and kissed her hand. "We *are* getting there, aren't we?" he whispered.

"I certainly hope so," she whispered back.

"I'll call Jarod and see if your plans will mesh together with his. Don't be surprised if Dane and Dad have something to say about it. I'd feel better if neither of you went anywhere near that loon." Lauren left the table to make the call.

"Son, I agree with Lauren. I don't want either of you anywhere near this person."

"Mom, by now she'll have figured out we're on to her and she's gone to ground. Anyone close to Melissa poses a threat. She'll have to come after me again, which is when we nab her." Josh was sure this would work. He knew women, even crazy ones like Angelica. She wouldn't quit until she had what she wanted, which was Josh out of the way and Melissa all to herself.

"We'll have to do this sooner rather than later," Melissa said. "I think she's regrouping. I'm beginning to remember odd things from when we lived together. If something didn't go her way, she'd hole up in her room for a while to think things through. Then she'd retaliate. When Harold asked me out the second time, she convinced me he was harassing me. Now I know it was out of protection of me and revenge against him."

"But, honey, she was lying even then."

"Yes, but it didn't matter. He had a record and she wanted to protect me from him. It's why she insisted on the TRO." Melissa nodded her head, as if she was just now coming to grips with the depths of Angelica's illness.

Lauren stepped back into the room. "They want you both to meet them at the station ASAP to go over your plans."

"Do not pass go, do not collect two hundred dollars, right?" Josh asked.

Lauren laughed. "You know my husband when he's in cop mode. He said, and I quote, 'Tell that shit for brains to get his ass down here and no stopping anywhere in between.'"

Josh rolled his eyes.

"Jeez," Melissa said under her breath.

His mother laughed and hugged Melissa. "You'd better get used to it. You're part of the family now."

When Melissa gasped, Josh scowled at his mother. "Can you not scare her off, please?" He kissed her cheek before they both left the house.

"Sorry about that," Josh mumbled as he took her keys out of his pocket.

"I'm not sorry about this," Melissa said as she snatched the keys out of his hands and ran to the driver's side of her car, a giggle escaping her lips.

"Hey!" He caught up to her in a flash and pressed her against the CRV, which was hot. At her yelp, he pulled her into his arms and kissed her with all the passion and angst stirring inside him. "You cheated."

"No, I didn't. I want you to trust me. Besides, it's still my car and I'm doing what Jarod asked. I want to get us to the station house without any detours."

"I can think of a great detour." He waggled his eyebrows up and down.

"Ha! Exactly. Now behave and get in."

"You know you're turning me on with this new confidence, right?"

"Josh, I always know what I want. I just have a hard time verbalizing it sometimes."

She drove down the empty two-lane country road leading into Timbisha Township with a twitch in her lip that had him wanting her so bad he was uncomfortable in his jeans. The sky was crystal blue and the sun past its apex. Warm air blew in from the open windows even though the air conditioner pushed cool air out of the dash vents. She'd just turned to speak when they hit something in the road.

The front tires blew out.

Melissa fought for control, but when she hit the shoulder, rocks and debris blew into the car, blinding Josh. He heard her scream before the CRV turned over, landing on the passenger's side with a crunch.

"Oh my God, Josh! Are you okay?"

She dangled above him in the driver's seat, struggling to get out of her seatbelt.

"Yeah, I think so. I'm stuck, though." He was more than stuck, but he didn't want her to panic any more than she already was.

What the hell did we hit?

He tried to wrestle himself out of his seat, but his right arm wouldn't budge and lancing pain radiated up and into his torso.

"Honey, I think my arm is broken. My shoulder's messed up, too." Shit, his cell phone was in his pocket. He tried to maneuver around to reach it with his left hand but the movements jarred his injuries too much, taking the air out of his lungs.

"Hold on, Josh. Let me get out of this seat belt," she said, struggling with her own predicament. When she was free of her belt, she flipped her door open and then turned herself in order to reach for his belt. She got it unhooked but suddenly said, "Ouch!"

"What?" he yelled, feeling useless and angry at his disabled position.

"I think a bee stung me." She laughed once, but when she turned to look at him again, her smile faded right along with the brightness of her eyes.

"Melissa, honey, what's wrong?"

Suddenly, her limp body was being pulled up and out of the car.

A disembodied voice from outside said, "Hold on, Missy. I've got you."

"Angie?"

"Yeah, I'm here to help." Her cherubic face came into view through the open door where Melissa had just been. "I'm always here to protect Missy from creeps like you, Josh," she said sweetly before disappearing again.

He listened in horror as Angela Dunne dragged Melissa away from the overturned Honda.

"Melissa!" He struggled harder.

"I'm sure the cavalry will be here soon enough to get you out, Josh," she said as she peeked back into the vehicle. "I'm sorry I won't be able to stay, but I have to get Missy as far away from you as I can. Can't you see how much trouble you've caused her?"

When she disappeared from view, he could hear more dragging and then the slam of a car door.

"Angela! Bring her back!" he cried in total frustration as an engine turned over and drove away to God only knew where.

CHAPTER 19

Krazy

Free of his seatbelt, Josh was finally able to dig his phone out of his pocket, but he still couldn't get out of the damn CRV. His right arm was trapped between the seat and door. He juggled his cell phone one-handed and successfully dialed Jarod.

"Come on, pick up," he muttered in frustration.

"Where are you?"

"Melissa's car rolled, I'm stuck, and she's been taken. I'm about five miles from town."

Josh yanked the cell phone from his ear as Jarod swore vehemently before his brother gave orders for an ambulance and tow truck. "We're on our way, Josh. Don't you hang up."

"Don't plan to."

"Tell me everything that happened," Jarod commanded.

While Josh recounted the last few minutes of his ride into town, he prayed Melissa would be all right. He didn't give a shit about his arm; all he could think about was her going limp and being dragged from the car. How the hell were they going to find her?

JOSH WAS LIVID. HIS ARM IN A SLING, HE PUSHED HIS way out of the ER and waited for Jason to pick him up to take him to the command center Jarod had set up at the station. His arm wasn't broken, but his shoulder had been dislocated and his ribs were bruised. They'd offered him a narcotic before they reset his shoulder, but he hadn't wanted to take anything. He'd been drugged enough lately.

All he wanted was to find Melissa.

"Spill it," Jason said when Josh got into the truck.

He retold the story, and by the time they reached the station, Jason was the one who was livid. "Why didn't anyone have eyes on her?"

"That's what I'd like to know," Josh said as he pushed his way through the plate glass doors. Marguerite was pacing back and forth behind the counter. "Where are they?" he asked her.

She turned bloodshot eyes to him. "In the back. I've been waiting for you." She nodded to Jason in acknowledgment, but otherwise she was angry professionalism. Josh understood her mood. She loved her sister, and what they'd been afraid of happening had happened.

Marguerite led them down a hallway to a small conference room packed with men Josh had never seen before. "Declan sent for a team," she answered his unasked question.

"Good. The more the merrier." Josh glared at Jarod, who'd just made his way over to them. "Melissa's been kidnapped. Where the hell is the FBI?"

"Dane's in contact with the feds and working with the marshals service. It's their show and out of my hands. That's why I asked you and Melissa to come here. There have been developments." Jarod let out a pent-up breath, and Josh could see his brother was barely holding it together.

"What's changed?" Jason asked.

"Toxicology came back on Harold's remains. He was drugged with the same chemical makeup introduced into your systems," Jarod said. "It's also the same drugs found in the chocolates sent to Missy. Apparently, Angela Dunne had sent drugged chocolates to Harold, too. DNA from a toothbrush at Missy's house confirms Angela Dunne was living there."

Marguerite put a bottle of water in Josh's good hand. "Drink it. You look like hell. I'd get you something stronger, but I think we both need our wits right now."

He watched the room buzz and the men make calls, draw on glass boards with colored pens, and click away on laptop computers. "Where the hell did she take her?"

"They're working on it." This from Dane, who looked weary. "Declan is good at what he does, Josh. He'll find her. He tracked Harold. He can find my niece." He put his arm around Marguerite, who put her head on the older man's shoulder for comfort. Josh was pretty sure he needed Marguerite's support more than she needed his.

"I've got something," a man rushed up to McKinley.

Josh couldn't hear what they said, but the way the marshal's eyes lit up gave Josh hope.

"All right, listen. We've got pings from Dunne's cell phone coming from this tower," McKinley said before indicating a spot on the map hanging on the wall behind the team. "I want searches in these areas of Timbisha Township starting right now."

The men grabbed what portable equipment they could, and Josh got out of their way when they all headed for the doorway.

"How do they have her cell number?" Jason asked.

Dane said, "They retrieved several numbers from Missy's hacked phone. Dunne covered herself with a few burners. Apparently, someone's using one as we speak."

"What do we do now, Uncle Dane?" Marguerite asked.

"Stay with Jarod and I'll find out what I can."

Josh followed Dane with his eyes as he conversed with McKinley. When Josh heard Marguerite's quiet sob, he took her in his arms for a reassuring hug. "I know," he whispered. "I know."

"Hey," Jason said quietly, "Charlie said something about Marco following Angelica up the old mining road behind the hospital."

Jarod nodded. "Yeah, McKinley took a drive up there, but he said he didn't find anything."

"Did he go all the way up to the mine site?" Josh asked.

"Yeah," Jarod confirmed, "he said there was nothing up there."

Josh met Jason's eyes. "Did he circle up to the top where the old office sits against the rock?" Jason asked.

Jarod pursed his lips. "I don't know. He reported no sign of human activity. I took him at his word."

"There's a building up there?" Marguerite asked as she wiped a lone tear from her cheek. "I've been up there more than a dozen times, you know, bonfires and such. I don't remember an office."

"It's up behind the mine a good quarter mile or so. None of us went that far at those parties, but a few of us rode our dirt bikes and quads during the summer. The old office is abandoned but well hidden. You have to know it's there in order to find it," Josh explained.

She nodded and then Josh noticed the wheels turning in her head, making him smile.

"Jason," she asked, "did you bring your pickup?"

"Of course."

"Then I think we all need to take a ride up to the mine, don't you think, Jarod?" She cocked her hip and raised an eyebrow. All trace of distress was gone and the vixen was back with determination in her eyes, making Josh feel a whole lot better.

Jason had already left the room when Jarod rolled his eyes and followed their middle brother out of the station and into the blazing sunshine.

"Where are you four going?" Dane called out as they hit the sidewalk in front of the building.

"To get my sister back, Uncle Dane. You coming?"

"Oh, hell," Dane muttered and hurried over to them. "Where?"

Jarod turned to Dane to explain the situation. Dane cursed like a sailor. "Fine, I'll let Declan know where you're heading and get a team to meet you up there."

Josh hopped up into Jason's pickup while Marguerite hugged her uncle. "Do you think that's where Angelica would take her? To an abandoned mine office in the middle of BFE?" Josh asked Jason before anyone else got in the truck.

Jason shrugged. "Who knows with a whack job like her, but it's a damn sight better than sitting with our thumbs up our butts doing nothing, right?" He started the engine and kicked up the air conditioning. "If she's got Missy up there in this heat, I'd rather take a chance on nothing than risk missing a chance to get her back, wouldn't you? Especially if the marshals aren't looking in the right place. How do we even know the cell phone they're tracking hasn't been given to someone else?" Jason muttered.

"Yeah, I thought the same thing."

Jarod and Marguerite climbed into the back of the crew cab and slammed their doors. "Dane's riding with McKinley," Jarod said. "They're going to lead us up. When I told Declan about the old shack, he confirmed he did not go that far up the hill."

"I'm calling the cell phone number they're tracking right now," Marguerite said as she put the phone on speaker.

"How'd you get the number?" Josh asked.

Marguerite smirked. "I asked the youngest marshal I could find for it." She winked, but the underlying anger told Josh there'd be hell to pay if someone answered. She was not happy with McKinley.

The phone rang a few times, and right before Josh thought it would go to voice mail, a voice whispered, "Marguerite?"

"Oh my God, Missy! Where are you?"

"Not sure," she whispered. "Angie's outside getting something out of her car. She doesn't know I'm awake."

"Keep her talking, I'm calling Declan now to get a trace," Jarod said.

"We're on our way, honey," Josh said.

Melissa started to cry. "I'll stay on the line as long as I can, but you guys have to be quiet, she's coming."

———

"OH, YOU'RE AWAKE!" ANGIE SAID WITH THE SWEET cherubic smile Missy had come to hate. What once was a sweet and caring friend had turned into a sinister monster with a lunatic smile.

"Y-yeah," Missy stammered. She had to keep calm. The cell phone was tucked into a crevice in the rock wall lining the back of the room. She prayed she didn't lose the signal or that her sister didn't screech into the phone and tip off Angie help was on the way.

"Here, have some water. I know you must be thirsty."

Missy bared her teeth in a semblance of a smile and took the bottle. It was likely the water contained more of the drugs Angie seemed to prefer, but Missy was so damn thirsty it was hard to resist.

"Here, silly." She took the bottle and Missy heard the snap of the cap as the bottle was opened for the first time. "It's clean, I promise."

Hating to be grateful, Missy said thank you and took a big swallow. It was ice cold and felt so good on her tongue she took another swallow before setting it on the blanket next to her. "Where are we, Angie?" She tried for sweet and curious, but Missy was so angry she doubted it came off as anything but antagonistic.

Angela, if she heard the rancor, didn't seem to care. "Somewhere I can keep you safe from all the people who want to hurt you."

Missy shook her head slowly. Did she dare argue? She really didn't care at this point. "The only person who's ever hurt me is you, Angie."

The blonde clucked her tongue at her and dug into the cooler, drawing out another water for herself. She took a big gulp and then sighed. "Not true. You don't know the lengths I've gone to keep you safe."

"Explain it to me then," Missy prompted to keep her from looking for the phone. Maybe, if she was lucky, Angie would confess all and Marguerite could record it on her end.

"Harold was going to hurt you. I couldn't let that happen."

"How do you know?"

Angie walked the small space, which was comprised of three shiplap walls attached to a rock face in the hill. All the walls contained broken windows, and around them sat broken office furniture from the early 1900s. Missy again wondered where they were when Angela looked out one of the windows and sighed.

"Because he'd already hurt me once. I tracked him to the university, you know."

Missy didn't answer. She'd heard Dane and Marguerite talking about interrogation tactics once. If you're quiet, the other person will keep talking. It worked.

"Harold was my high school math teacher. He said he loved me, but he didn't. He'd only used me and then kicked me to the curb. He was a predator, Missy, and he didn't deserve you." She spun on her heel then and came to kneel in front of Missy on the blanket. "He followed you here from school, but I was clever and followed him. He was going to hurt you."

She sounded so convincing. "How do you know that?"

"He sent you those chocolates. But I had to warn you, so I put the syringe in the box."

"Did you poison the chocolates, too?" Missy had to know if Angie really tried to kill her or if she'd warned her from harm.

"No, of course not! I'd never hurt you, Missy. You're my best friend."

Unsure what to make of all of this, Missy only nodded. "What happened to Harold?"

"Does it matter?" Angie asked as if he were of no consequence. "He's gone now and can never hurt you."

Feeling like she was getting nowhere, Missy changed the subject. "Exactly where are we?"

Angie again looked out the broken window and murmured, "This is only temporary."

Missy certainly hoped so, now that help was on the way. She'd heard Josh's voice in the background, which gave her hope. Knowing he was all right kept her from falling apart. The last thing she remembered before waking up in this awful room was him trapped in the passenger seat. He'd been injured and all she could focus on was helping him until she'd been stung. Now she knew it wasn't a bee, but a syringe.

Missy pulled her pant leg up to find the injection site and, sure enough, there was a bruise. She glanced up to find Angie watching her closely.

"I did it for your own good, Missy. You always find yourself in trouble, and can never get yourself out. You're weak. I was weak once, but I made sure to never get hurt again. I vowed to never let another man hurt a woman as I've been hurt. When I met you, it was like looking into a mirror." She touched Missy's cheek and Missy quickly leaned away from the touch, as if it would burn.

"You know, Angie, everyone is always underestimating me."

"Don't be like that," she said as if Missy were a child. "I know you're strong in your own way, but when it comes to relationships — when it comes to men — you're as naive as they come."

True, Missy had been inexperienced, but only because she'd been focused on school. She'd never cultivated social skills. She'd never needed to with Marguerite around. Her sister hadn't hogged the spotlight; she'd tried to make things easier on Missy.

"What's that buzzing noise?"

Crap, the cell phone! "I don't hear anything," Missy said, leaning back against the rocks where she'd tucked the phone.

Angela immediately pulled her away from the wall. She dug out the phone and stared at it like it was kryptonite. "What did you do?" She threw the phone against the wall, where it shattered.

As Missy stared at the fragments to her release, Angie swung a delicate hand and slapped Missy hard across the face, taking her by surprise and knocking her to the floor.

"After all I've done for you?!" Angie screeched. "You betrayed me, you bitch!"

As Missy tried to get her bearings, Angie tied her hands together with an old telephone cord she found on the floor underneath an ancient desk. She'd hit Missy hard enough that she'd seen stars. Unfortunately, Missy didn't regain her faculties until after her hands had been securely bound.

"Make any other moves and I'll have to give you this." She produced a syringe from her pocket. The last thing Missy wanted was to be drugged again, so she stopped struggling and glared at her captor.

"Good girl," she said to Missy. "This will all be better as soon as we can get out of this damn county. Another day or two and we should be fine, but we can't stay here any longer, thanks to you."

Angie began packing up the few items she'd brought in, and all Missy could do was sit and think about how she'd completely botched her own rescue.

"Drive faster, Jason!" When the line went dead, Josh couldn't breathe.

"I'm going as fast as I can without killing us, little brother," Jason said not unkindly as they bounced up the old dirt road.

Josh trusted that Jason knew exactly what he was going through. He glanced at his eldest brother in the back seat and saw the same emotions reflected in Jarod's eyes. Apparently, all three brothers had been destined to rescue their future brides from maniacs.

What the hell's happened to my safe little town? Josh scanned the countryside for the old mining office. It'd been years since he'd been up this far, but it was easy to see from the ruts in the road someone had been traveling this trail recently.

Marguerite was quietly praying, "Please be all right," over and over again under her breath. Her cell phone chirped. "Uncle Dane, what's happening?"

Just as she asked that question, a search and rescue helicopter flew past them on their way up the hill. She put her phone on speaker.

"Was that my helo?" Dane asked.

"Yessir," she answered.

"We triangulated her position before the line went dead. Hang back because the feds should be there already, coming from the back side of hill."

"Too late," Jason said as they crested the hill to witness the scene unfolding before them. Josh let out a sigh of relief. Two black Suburbans surrounded a silver Land Rover. The helicopter landed half a football field away from the marshals who were now entering the crumbling mine office. A few shots were fired and Josh jumped out of the pickup only to be tackled by Jason.

"Let me go!" he screamed, but his brother held firm.

"You know I won't, so stop struggling. Look," Jason said calmly. "they're bringing her out now."

Marguerite looped her arm around the brace on Josh's injured arm while Jason kept a strong hold around his torso. "We can't go down there until they've secured Angela Dunne." Marguerite's voice was calm, but Josh could feel how badly she trembled all over.

Josh nodded, respecting that she knew police protocol. When he relaxed his stance, Jason released him but stood close by for support. Jarod, that prick, had disappeared into the melee below.

It was Dane who carried Melissa out of the office while McKinley and Jarod wrestled a screaming Angela Dunne to the ground. The once-pretty blonde had transformed into a crazed lunatic shouting nonsense and obscenities at her captors. As soon as Dane cleared the site, Marguerite led Josh down the hill, Jason hot on their tails.

Melissa was talking nonstop by the time they got to her. "I couldn't get her to confess to murdering Harold, but she did admit she put the syringe in the box of chocolates. She'd always distanced herself from Ginger, surely that should've tipped me off but, nooo, I'm an idiot. How did I not see this coming? To think I actually believed Josh would ever hurt me? How could I have listened to her for so long? Please make sure she doesn't see the light of day until she's either cured of her mental disorder or dead, will you, Uncle Dane? Oh, Josh! Marguerite!"

Melissa jumped to her feet and rushed to Josh, nearly knocking him on his ass. Relief flooded his body and he held on tight with his good arm, but she wasn't finished talking.

"Oh my God! I thought I'd lost you! The last thing I remember is your face in pain! You're hurt! What's wrong with your arm?"

To shut her up he put his mouth on hers. Her response was immediate, and before he knew it, Marguerite was clearing her throat.

"Can I hug my sister, please?"

"Oh, Marguerite!" Melissa didn't let go of Josh entirely but brought Marguerite in for a group hug, making Josh laugh for the first time in hours.

"You know I like a three-way, but my shoulder isn't up for it."

At Melissa's gasp, he laughed. Marguerite shook her head, but a smile pricked at her lips.

"I like hearing you talk so much, baby," he whispered before kissing her again. "I just need to get used to it, is all."

A tear fell down her cheek. "I was so angry, Josh."

"Not scared?"

Marguerite huffed out a laugh. "Don't tell me you haven't been on the receiving end of my little sister's temper."

"I don't plan on ever making her mad, at least, not at me," Josh said with conviction.

"Oh yeah? What do you plan to do then, Josh?" Jason said behind them.

Josh turned in time to see the amusement in his brother's green eyes. "Same thing you did, you big oaf. I plan on marrying her."

"Yeah? Well, you need my permission first," Dane Bainbridge said in his rough, no-nonsense voice.

Josh looked into Melissa's beautiful eyes. They were shining violet today, which meant she was happy. "Maybe this should be a subject for another day."

Her chin wobbled as she smiled. "Maybe," she said, a bit of the shyness he'd fallen in love with returning in her voice.

McKinley and Jarod made their way up to the group. "That was fun," Jarod muttered.

McKinley wiped a hand down his face. "She won't be in jail long. Once her family knows she's in custody, they'll do anything to hide the scandal and get her released. I'll do what I can to get her institutionalized, but I'm afraid you might be looking over your shoulder for a while."

"You're so negative," Dane said. "My niece will be fine, I'll make sure of it."

"So will I," Josh confirmed. He wasn't ever going to let her go, and he wasn't ever going to let her be hurt again.

"Do you feel like heading back to the station and giving a statement, Missy?" Jarod asked. "I want to get this all on the record so we have enough ammo to give to the prosecutors."

"I'm ready."

There was nothing but confidence in her two-word statement. He'd never seen her so self-assured, so willing to speak. "I'll go with you," he said.

"You better."

Josh heard the command in her tone, which sounded like Dane and it made him grin from ear to ear.

As they stared each other down, a phone was thrust into Melissa's hand. "It's Mom," Marguerite said.

Melissa took it and assured her mother she was fine. She didn't stop talking until they'd reached the sheriff's station to give her statement. Josh held her hand the whole way. He couldn't wait to get her home. He had a proposal to make and he needed to make it right. Melissa deserved the best, and he'd damn well give it to her.

Jared interrupted his thoughts. "I need your side of the story for the record. You witnessed the actual kidnapping."

Josh hated leaving her, but he had to make sure Angela

Dunne was put away for a long time. He left nothing out, and refrained from decking his older brother when he attempted to blame Josh for not being able to keep Melissa safe.

"My shoulder's dislocated and several ribs are bruised. I was trapped between the seat and the metal post, you prick." Josh glared at Jarod, who wore his cop face as if he wasn't passing judgment. The bastard was and they both knew it.

Jarod turned the recording equipment off when the interview was over. He was stewing over something. Josh knew his brother well and could see that he needed to get something off his chest. Finally Jarod muttered, "I'm going to lose her."

Alarm shot through Josh's body. "What's wrong with Sassy?"

Jarod glanced up and gave him a disgusted look. "Nothing, you ass. I'm talking about Marguerite."

Anger brought Josh to his feet. "I knew you didn't really love Lauren, you son of a bitch! I knew you were only using her to take care of Jessica, you bastard!"

When Josh made a weak attempt to punch his oldest brother in the face with his left, Jarod rolled his eyes. He used a move Josh saw coming but couldn't prevent. He was shoved face first against the wall, his uninjured arm caught between his back and Jarod.

"Not this again, you stubborn jackass. I love my wife, for the fiftieth time. I'm losing my secretary again, goddammit!"

It was Josh who rolled his eyes this time. "Marguerite would never leave her mother, Jarod."

His brother released him. "No, she wouldn't, but I don't think Darla has a whole lot of time left and Marguerite has asked for time off."

CHAPTER 20

Proposal

Missy hugged her mother with everything she had. "Praise God you're all right," her mother whispered in her ear. "Praise God."

"I know, Mom." She withdrew from her mother, who sat on the couch next to her. Her color was better today, Missy thought. She waited patiently as Josh hugged her too and then took the recliner beside the couch which had been her dad's before he passed away.

"Marguerite says she's taking time off to drive you crazy," Missy said.

Darla harrumphed. "That girl. I told her I'm fine. She needs her job. She's good at it too, and I don't want to be a burden on my girls."

"Like we would ever allow it," Marguerite said as she set down a tray of iced teas. "You don't have a choice anyway, Mom, so just deal with it."

"Nice bedside manner," Josh said with a laugh.

Marguerite put her hands on her hips. "I'm a wonderful caregiver, Josh King."

Missy laughed. "Yes, you are, Sis, but you don't need to quit. I think between the both of us, we can help Mom." She looked to her mother for confirmation.

With a sad smile, Darla acquiesced. "As long as Marguerite promises not to quit."

Her sister sat on the other side of their mother. "How about if I ask Jarod to rearrange my schedule in order to be home with you more?"

"I think my brother would be relieved. He was in a total panic at the thought of you leaving," Josh said.

"Really?"

"Oh, Marguerite, as astute as you are about reading other people, you sure missed the boat on how much you're valued." Missy was tired of all the gossip and negativity which seemed to weigh down her sister.

"We're digressing," Marguerite said, glaring at Missy and making her laugh. "Mom, will it make you happy if I change my hours?"

Missy laughed at her grumpy attitude, and so did their mother. "Yes... fine," she said. "Now," Darla turned to Josh, "when are you marrying my daughter?"

"Which one?" Josh asked without missing a beat.

Missy hit him.

"Ouch! My shoulder still hurts."

Missy raised her eyebrows.

Josh sighed. "You know, I sort of wanted to make a big deal out of my proposal. I know it's not a secret anymore, but can a guy make a plan?"

"No," Missy said in unison with her mother and sister. It made her laugh to see him struggle. He was such a ladies' man, and deep down it made her happy she threw him off his game.

When she continued to stare at him, he gave her the wicked

smile he was known for — the one that made women do whatever he wanted — the one which said, *Trust me. I'll take care of you because I know what you want.*

Her heart fluttered and she reached for his hand.

He took it, pressing the back of her hand to his sexy lips, sending a hot rocket of lust zinging throughout her body.

"I promise it will be soon."

There was so much meaning in his words she wasn't sure if he referred to a marriage proposal or sex.

She was fine with either.

Her mother chuckled, which unfortunately led to a coughing fit sending Missy scrambling for the glass of tea on the table.

Once Darla finished with the drink, she took Missy's hand and held on. "I promise I'm not going anywhere until I see the two of you settled." Missy shared a look with her sister, who furiously wiped a tear from her cheek.

"Mom, I'm settled," Marguerite said. "The short hours are only temporary. Missy will be settled as soon as Josh pulls his head out of his butt and proposes."

"Why do you keep circling back to me?"

"Children," Darla scolded. "You're all my family and I need to know everyone has their ducks in a row. That's all."

The conversation ebbed and flowed, constantly circling back to what Josh's and Marguerite's plans were, but Missy knew it was a cover for the big ugly elephant in the room: her mother's cancer.

When Josh finally said it was time for them to leave, Missy didn't argue. She wanted to go home and sleep for a week, to shore up enough strength to get her through the next painful chapter in her life. Josh would be there to help her, and it made it easier to leave for the evening. "I'll check on you tomorrow," she said, kissing her mother goodbye."

"I'll be waiting."

Josh said something to Darla, and when he stood, her mother was smiling contentedly.

"Let's go," he said quietly, and Missy followed him out the door to his pickup, which Jarod had finally released since Missy's CRV had been totaled. That was another problem. How the hell was she getting to work tomorrow?

The townhouses were dark when they arrived, and Missy wondered which one they'd pick for the night. Of course, Josh pulled into his own driveway and shut off the engine. "Okay?"

"Definitely okay," she answered honestly. As long as she was with Josh, she was fine.

"When can we get Ginger?"

"We'll swing by tomorrow and get her." He opened the door. "My mother wants a family luncheon anyway, to celebrate Angela's capture."

It hadn't been that long ago when the thought of a social gathering would've made Missy want to puke, but now she realized she wanted nothing more than to visit with his family. "It sounds lovely."

He shut the door and locked all the locks, then turned to challenge her. "Really? No excuses not to go?"

"I wasn't *that* bad."

"No, you weren't, but I like this new confidence, baby." He kissed her again, and this time he didn't stop until the sunlight came through the blinds the next morning.

HE SHOULDN'T BE NERVOUS. HE KNEW SHE WAS going to say yes, but he still couldn't get his stomach to settle down.

Maybe I'm still feeling the effects of the drugs?

He'd called ahead, and Jason promised he'd help with the arrangements. He also enlisted Charlie and Marco to help, which was why Josh couldn't settle his nerves. Those two twerps couldn't be serious for two seconds, and a practical joke was always right around the corner. If Charlie screwed this up, Josh was going to beat the shit out of that kid for sure.

He wiped the steam from the mirror and dragged a razor down his cheek.

"Josh, there's no bar soap," Melissa said from behind the shower curtain.

"Hold on, babe." He ducked down and grabbed a pink box from under the sink, and slid the flowery bar into his hands. When he handed it to her, he held it just out of reach. "Kiss first."

Her smile was immediate, and she leaned over and pulled him back into the shower — shaving cream, towel, and all. "It's not fair you're dressed and I'm not."

"You call this dressed?" He looked down at himself. The soaked towel was now in a heap at their feet in the bathtub and most of the shaving cream had rinsed from his half-shaven face.

"No, I call this better."

God he loved her. He took his time with his second shower but made her get out with him so they could get to The Estate without any more "delays."

THE DRIVEWAY WAS CROWDED WHEN THEY PULLED in, and he waited for the telltale signs of distress that always came with Melissa's anxiety. She only smiled and seemed eager to get out the truck. As soon as they did, Jessica opened the side door and yelled, "Hunkle Josh! Is Missy gonna be my aunt?" Before he could answer, he caught Lauren waddling out the door to corral her daughter.

Melissa, God bless her, was laughing. He took her hand and led her into the house, where a scolding Lauren discussed the rules of politeness to a five-year-old imp.

"Oh, there they are," his mom said. Camille put down the platter she'd been carrying to give them both hugs. "Josh, your poor shoulder. How do you feel?"

"I'm good, Mom. Melissa's the one who got the drugs this time."

"I'm fine," she said before his mom could ask. "Thank you so much for inviting me. Looks like you've outdone yourself again."

"Well, Julie is back in action, so I can't take all the credit."

"How can I help?" Missy asked, and with that, Josh and Melissa were tasked with carrying bowls and platters out to the back patio. Jason manned the grill again, but this time, Julie was helping with the prep.

Charlie slugged Josh in the arm before hugging Melissa, and then he was off again. Josh narrowed his eyes at Charlie's back until he was out of sight.

"What's that look for?" she asked.

"Just wondering when the little shit's going to prank me."

The patio was set much like it had been the day Melissa saved the heifer, only different flowers were blooming now and more birds were chattering about. Every now and then hummingbirds zipped by dogfighting, and Josh assumed there was a nest nearby. Jessica led her mother to the table. Each of them held a bowl, Jessica's smaller one held lemons for the tea while Lauren balanced a large bowl of salad on her burgeoning belly.

"You sit here, Hunkle Josh." Jessica indicated with her chin. "Missy can sit next to ya."

"Thank you, princess." He took Melissa's hand and led her to the table.

"Are you sure there isn't anything else I can help you with?" Missy asked loudly, and a resounding "no" came from the family.

"Actually, yes, there is," Julie said as she handed a baby to Melissa. "Mikey doesn't nap as long as Gabe, which means he's going to want to eat soon, but if you hold him a while, I might be able to get this meal done before I need to feed him."

"Where's Gabe?" Josh looked around for the other baby and found him sound asleep in a portable crib in the shade by the sliding glass door. Josh was surprised the little guy could sleep through all the noise.

Marguerite arrived pushing Darla's wheelchair. Dane helped them maneuver over the tracks of the slider.

"Mom!" Melissa said. "What're you doing here?"

"Stay there, Missy. I want to hold that baby," Darla said. "Camille called and invited us to lunch. I'm having a good day and thought the company and sunshine would do me good."

Josh noticed the place setting next to Melissa had no chair, meaning they'd prepared for Darla's arrival. His plan was taking shape. Marguerite sat on the other side of Darla while Dane took his normal spot next to James and across from Camille.

Melissa placed the twin in Darla's arms, and the older

woman melted. "My goodness, it's been a long time since I held a human this small."

Marguerite leaned over to look at Mikey, holding a finger out for the baby to grab. "He is so little," she said reverently.

"There's another one over there," Josh pointed out. "Want to hold him?"

Marguerite's eyes widened. "Could I? I don't want to disturb him."

"Ya gotta ask first," Jessica warned as she climbed up into the booster chair next to Josh.

"I'm sure it's fine, Jessie," he laughed. He stood up to retrieve the baby when he was pushed back into his seat by Jason.

"I'll get him," the big oaf said before walking over and grabbing his son. He cuddled Gabe, who stiffened into a ball before relaxing back into sleep. Jason kissed his head then delivered the tiny package to a waiting Marguerite. Just as the baby was placed in her arms, Marshal Declan McKinley walked through the slider and stopped cold in his tracks.

Josh snickered. "He's a goner."

When Melissa gave him a questioning look, Josh lifted his chin in the direction of McKinley. Melissa's eyes widened, and then she turned to Marguerite.

"This oughta be good," Melissa said conspiratorially.

Josh held her hand under the table.

As Declan was shown his seat, Julie put the steaks on the table and announced, "Lunch is served." She sat down next to Jason and noticed her boys were not in their crib. "Oh, ladies, let me take them so you can eat."

"Nonsense," Darla said. "I'm sure you don't get to eat a hot meal very often. You help yourself, and Marguerite and I will take care of these little ones for you."

"Are you sure?"

"Of course," they said unison.

Josh laughed at their antics, but when Melissa leaned in and asked him a question, he got nervous all over again.

"Do you want children, Josh?"

She was serious, and he wanted to kiss her with serious intent.

So he did.

Until a throat cleared. It was Jessica.

"Sorry, princess."

"'S okay, Hunkle Josh. Daddy and Mommy do that all the time." Then she arched her eyebrow in a clear imitation of Camille. "But not at the table, right, Gramma?"

"Right, darling," his mother said with a wink.

"You didn't answer my question," Melissa pressed, and that's when he realized she wasn't embarrassed. In fact, she was almost taunting him.

"I tell you what, Melissa. I'll answer your question if you'll answer mine first. Deal?"

Her eyes turned violet and a smile danced on her lips. "Deal."

He never took his eyes off hers as he stood up, then knelt down beside her.

"Shit, are we doing this now?" Jarod said from down the table.

"It's okay, I have the camera," Charlie said.

"Will you two be quiet and let the man ask his question, for crying out loud?" Lauren said, clearly frustrated.

Marguerite's and Darla's eyes widened in surprise and amusement. Melissa started to laugh, and now Josh couldn't get his composure. When Michael let out a loud cry, he knew he had to get this show on the road before Julie had to breastfeed. Josh took Melissa's hand in his left hand, and withdrew a ring from his pocket with his right.

"Melissa Anne Theroux, would you do me the honor of becoming my wife?"

He couldn't keep pride off his face when she smiled with confidence and said, "Yes, I will." He placed the single solitaire diamond ring on her finger and helped her to her feet because he was about to get inappropriate at the table again.

When he'd started to feel as if they were the only two people on the patio, more than one person cleared their throats, and Melissa began to giggle.

"Now you answer my question."

"Do I want kids?"

"Yes, do you want kids?" She had a strange look on her face, one of happiness mixed with fear.

"Of course I want kids, especially with you."

She smiled the smile of a woman with a secret, and Josh thought his eyes would pop out. That's when he heard his mother say, "Oh dear, not another rushed wedding."

JOSH STARED JESSICA IN THE EYES.

Jessica stared right back, not flinching.

"Do you have any kings?"

Without looking at her cards she said, very seriously, "Go. Fish."

"Damn," he muttered.

"Hunkle Josh, you can't say that in front of me."

"Sorry, princess."

"Your turn, Char-lee."

This was the fourth game they'd played, and Jessica had

beat them three times in a row. She had three sets to their none, and Missy suspected the little imp was cheating.

They sat at a small table in the waiting room at Timbisha Township Medical Center waiting on Jarod and Lauren, who were currently occupied in one of the delivery rooms. Missy rubbed her abdomen and smiled.

"Got here as soon as I could," Julie said, pushing the double stroller. She looked tired but happy. "What'd I miss?"

"Lauren screaming it was all Jarod's fault," Charlie answered.

"And my brother apologizing a million times before telling her to breathe."

"Did she hit him?" Julie asked with concern, and Missy leaned her head back and laughed.

"It's not funny," Charlie said. "She's been exceptionally sassy these past two weeks."

Julie chuckled. "It's the hormones. They make you crazy, I swear." She picked up one of the babies and handed him to Missy, who accepted Mikey — at least she thought it was — without complaint.

"I can't wait for it to happen to me," she said dreamily. "Because then I get to hold my own one of these." She kissed the baby's cheek and smiled when he cooed.

"Melissa won't be crazy," Josh said, abandoning his game and sitting next to her and the baby on the couch. Jessica now had six pairs of cards in front of her and Charlie had two, meaning the girl was definitely cheating and they had let her.

"How do you know I won't be a craven loon?"

"Because you're carrying my child, and together we are not crazy." He kissed her cheek and held a finger out to Mikey. "Together we make sense."

Jason walked in at that moment to set them both straight.

"Hundred bucks says not only will Missy be a bundle of raging hormones, but you'll sleep at least three nights on my sofa when she kicks your sorry ass out for knocking her up before the wedding."

It turned out she hadn't been pregnant when Josh proposed, only late. Her OB/GYN believed it to be due to all the stressful shenanigans. Everyone had been happy to have as much time as possible to plan the wedding. Well, everyone but Josh, who wasn't happy about her not being pregnant, so...

He'd made sure she got that way.

"He has a point, you know. Me being pregnant complicates the wedding planning, and your mother and I are not happy." Missy slid a look in the direction of Julie, who was diligently not looking up from a nursing Gabriel.

"You started it by asking me that question and you know it," Josh said a bit sullenly.

"Honey, you threw away my birth control pills."

"They're bad for you anyway," Josh said with a nod and took Mikey completely away from her now.

Jason sighed. "Like I said, you'll be on my couch no fewer than three nights."

"What are berf troll pills?" Jessica asked as she counted out her winning hand of Go Fish.

Charlie laughed out loud. "Yeah, Josh, care to explain?"

"Shut up, Charlie."

And so were the conversations which took place among her new family. Missy had grown up in a house full of women, and now she was thankful to be included in this rich, humorous, and loving bunch.

"When does your sister leave?" Julie asked.

Marguerite had been recruited by their uncle Dane on another investigation. "I'm not sure, but I think within the week. Now that Mom's cancer is in remission, Marguerite felt she could go. It was hard when she put in her resignation."

Julie nodded. "Lauren said Jarod was beside himself. He's not sure what he'll do without a good assistant."

"That lazy ass will manage, I'm sure," Josh muttered.

Jason grunted his agreement, making Missy shake her head at them. "You know, you guys really love your brother. You're not fooling anyone."

"Who said we didn't love the prick?" Jason asked.

"But—"

"But what, honey? He's our brother. Just because he's a jackass doesn't mean we don't love him." Josh shook his head as if she didn't understand the nature of brothers.

She supposed she didn't.

Men were weird sometimes.

"Anyway," Missy returned to her conversation with Julie, "my sister will be working with Marshal McKinley."

Jason and Josh both laughed before Josh said, "We'll be going to another wedding soon."

"I can honestly say, you might be right, honey. I've never seen Marguerite react to someone like she does with the marshal." Missy would never forget the fight she'd witnessed between Dane and her sister over the arrangements, but it had been their mother who'd talked her sister into joining the task force. Missy suspected her mother had the same ulterior motives as Dane when it came to Marguerite and Declan.

"Oh, good, you're all here," Camille said as she and James entered the waiting room. "Any news yet?"

Everyone shook their heads and resumed their conversations. When Gabe was done nursing, Josh traded babies with Julie and Jason took his turn getting creamed at Go Fish. As the hours dragged on, Charlie called his old employer, Pizza Factory, and ordered dinner.

By midnight, Jessica had pooped out on the couch next to Josh, who'd also fallen asleep in Missy's lap. Julie had begun to pace, worried for her best friend.

"Should it be taking this long?" Charlie asked.

Finally, a very haggard Jarod walked into the waiting room with a huge smile on his face. He looked for his daughter and saw she was asleep. He lifted her up in his arms and she stirred. "Can I see Mommy yet?"

"Yep, and you know who else you can see?"

Jessica rubbed her eyes and smiled. "My new baby?"

"Yup. Your new *brother*." The joy in his face told Missy all the hormones had been worth it.

"Ima big sister!"

"You sure are, Darlin', and Mommy can't wait to introduce you." He took the little girl with him out of the waiting room.

"I guess we're all supposed to follow along," Jason deadpanned.

Camille and James didn't say a word; they just followed their son and granddaughter down the hall.

"Wake up, Josh. You have another nephew," Missy rubbed his head.

"I heard," he said through a yawn and sat up. He dragged his hands over his face before he stood up. "Come on, woman. Let's go home."

"Don't you want to see the baby?"

"I'll see him tomorrow."

Missy looked down the hall with longing. "Well, I want to see him."

"Aren't you tired?"

"A little," she admitted. "We've been there all dang day. It seems silly not to at least take a peek at the little guy and congratulate Lauren and Jarod."

"Fine," Josh muttered. "I'm warning you now, though, my mother will have us all sleeping in that room all night."

"No she won't."

"Yes she will, and no one sleeps with my wife but me," he complained.

Missy rolled her eyes and walked down the hallway. He was seriously irritating her now, and then it hit her. Jason was right. Josh would be spending a few nights on the sofa if he didn't change his attitude. She told him so, and that's when he caught up to her and pressed her against the hallway wall. "You make me crazy, you know that?" he said after he came up for air.

"You love me anyway."

"You're all I've ever wanted. You're my everything, Melissa."

She sighed. "Then let's go home. We'll see the baby tomorrow."

Relief on his face, he took her hand and walked down the hallway on their way out of the hospital.

He was all she'd ever wanted, too, and she'd be damned if she ever let him go.

Josh was her future, her family, her life, and she counted her blessings and thanked God for the love she'd been given. It had been a challenge but life was full of those, and she knew together they could face whatever life threw their way and come out on the winning side. She rubbed her abdomen again and knew it was the truth.

From Elise

Dear Reader,

Thank you so much for reading Josh's Challenge and I hope you've enjoyed the third installment in the King Brothers novels. Life got in the way at times, making writing Josh's story difficult, but also fun. These characters, especially Jessica and Ginger kept shouting at me and spurring me on at every keystroke! Hopefully, they gave you a giggle or two along the way. You may have noticed that a few characters are moving on to bigger and better things, which means they want their story told too!

Currently, some new personalities are yelling at me (when aren't they yelling at me?) so please turn the page for a sample of *Marguerite's Redemption*, book 4 in the *Trouble In Timbisha Township* series.

As always, you can find me on my website or Instagram. Message me, friend me, follow me, and let me know what you loved (or maybe what you didn't). Hearing from readers makes all of us authors better story tellers and I love hearing from YOU!

Sincerely and, as always, HAPPY READING!
 Elise
 http://www.elisemanion.com

PS. My gift to you is Julie's Chicken Chili recipe, the one Josh made for Melissa using a big helping of love. Enjoy!

White Bean Chicken Chili

1 lb boneless skinless chicken breasts, cut into cubes

*substitute two cans canned chicken if you're in a hurry

3 cloves minced garlic

2 cans white beans, rinsed

2 - 4 oz cans chopped green chilis

*I use mild but if you like the heat, spice it up!

1 tsp ground cumin

1/2 tsp black pepper

1 onion, chopped

1 tablespoon olive oil (if you use canned chicken, this isn't necessary)

16 oz chicken broth (I usually eyeball it)

1 tsp sea salt

1 tsp ground oregano

1/4 tsp cayenne (optional, but honestly this makes the dish)

1 cup sour cream

1/2 cup whipping cream

grated cheese, your preference, as garnish

In a large saucepan, sauté chicken, onion, and garlic in oil until chicken is no longer pink. Add beans, broth, chilies and seasonings. Bring to boil. Reduce heat; simmer, uncovered, for thirty minutes or until some broth has evaporated and you have a thicker soup. Remove from heat; stir in sour cream and whipping cream. Serve immediately. Garnish with grated cheese.

I've been fixing this dish for a few years now, sometimes substituting fresh chicken with canned when I'm plagued with plots and don't have time to mess with the meat! In this case, I add the broth first, then the chicken and seasonings and the beans last. The secret, I think, is to make sure the beans are rinsed. It's easy and yummy, and perfect on those cool fall evenings.

Excerpt from
Marguerite's Redemption

"*McKinley*!"

"I'm right here, honey." Gentle hands guided her back to her pillow.

Marguerite groaned as a dull ache coursed from her shoulder throughout her torso. She blinked her eyes open. McKinley fussed over her blankets until he sat next to the bed.

"Where's Uncle Dane?"

"ICU."

"Is he awake?"

He shook his head. "No."

Dread made everything hurt worse. She peeked around and noted her arm firmly packed into an immobilizing sling. Her eyes swung to McKinley to see he wore something similar, though not as padded. "Are you all right?"

Even as she asked, she knew he wasn't. Whiskers covered his cheeks and chin. His clothes were clean, yet wrinkled as if he'd slept in them. Dark shadows under his eyes screamed he hadn't slept well for days, yet he continued to just stare at her. "Where are we?"

Finally, he blinked. "University Medical Center." When she didn't respond, he clarified, "Salt Lake City."

"How long have I been out?" She didn't remember traveling here, or how she got the damn sling. God, was she wearing her clothes and, if not, where were they? Did her mother know?

The heart monitor started beeping and McKinley stood again. "Hey, you're okay. You're family should be here any moment. I made sure to get your things brought in, and your purse is there." He pointed to a cupboard across the room.

She swallowed. "Thank you."

He moved some hair from her forehead but grimaced before sitting down again. "You coded on the table. You've gotta stop doing that."

He referred to the bad reaction she had to being drugged the summer before. Not wanting to think about it, Marguerite steered the topic back to Monti.

"He got me when I left the bathroom. Thank God he didn't search for my phone. That's how you tracked me, right?"

Again, he nodded, and she noted his eyes were tight, lips pinched.

"I'm sorry, McKinley. It's all my fault."

"Don't. It's mine. I shoulda never let ya walk off alone," he said, the twang in his voice she hadn't heard in a while coming through loud and clear.

She wanted to argue but whatever they'd put in the IV kept her brain foggy. To fill the silence, he described everything she'd missed while unconscious. After he finished, she dozed off as her mind wondered what would happen now. Surely, there'd be inquiries and most likely she'd be released from her duties and sent home.

As she began to envision all the tongues wagging in Timbisha Township, familiar voices and the dull ache in her shoulder called her back to reality.

"Marguerite!"

She grimaced at Missy's attempt to hug her when she jostled her shoulder. "Ow."

"Oh, no! I'm sorry!"

Josh, never far from her sister, pulled Missy back. "Careful, sweetheart. Here, hold her hand. Is this okay, Magpie?"

"Yeah. And will you stop calling me that?"

"No." But his handsome smile didn't reach his eyes, telling her he'd been just as worried as the rest of her family.

Missy sniffed. "Uncle Dane's in a coma. Have you seen him yet?"

"Haven't been out of this stupid bed. Which reminds me..." She looked at the wires and tubes because her bladder screamed to be emptied.

"I'll get the nurse," McKinley said before leaving her alone with her family.

"Mom, are you all right?"

Her mother had taken McKinley's seat, a tissue clutched in her hands. "No, but I will be. Will you please come home now?"

It hurt to chuckle. "Yeah, I'm pretty sure I don't have a choice in the matter."

"Well, good because Jarod still wants you back, so you have a job. Isn't that right Josh?" Missy said as she hugged her husband.

Josh rubbed Missy's swollen belly. "He hasn't quit bitching about you leaving."

"Sounds about right," Marguerite muttered.

God, where's the nurse? She pressed the buttons on the side of the bed, trying to find the one to help her into a sitting position. Finally, the door swung open.

"Oh, wait, dear. Let me clear these IV lines out of your way."

Everyone stood back while Marguerite and her helpful nurse made their careful way to the toilet. There wasn't any sweeter relief when she finally sat down and let go.

Afterward, as the nurse helped her back to bed, Marguerite asked, "When the hell can I get out of here?"

"I'll check your chart, but don't count on leaving until tomorrow or the next day. You did a number on your shoulder, and the cardiologist needs to clear you. Are you hungry?"

On cue, her stomach growled.

"I could eat."

Unfortunately, she tried to shrug at her own comment but ended up groaning in pain, just as McKinley returned with Special Agent Lightfoot, who Marguerite had met at the beginning of this fiasco.

"I'm sorry to break up the party," Lightfoot said, "but now that Marguerite is awake, we need to clear up some business."

Everyone said their goodbyes and filed out. When the door closed Agent Lightfoot began his debriefing. Afterward, Marguerite signed her exit papers. Agent Lightfoot confiscated her electronics, wished her well, and left with McKinley at his side.

He shut the door without a backward glance.

Without saying goodbye.

Shoulder throbbing, and heart broken at her stupidity, she let her tears fall. Wallowing in self-pity proved cathartic and allowed her time to think.

In her heart, she knew she'd bounce back as always, but this time her arrogance had gotten people hurt, and ended her future in law enforcement. Of course, Jarod would always take her back as his personal assistant at the sheriff's station, but did she want to end up where she'd started? She supposed she could become a deputy in order to advance her career, but after her abysmal freshman launch into her dream job, the very last thing she wanted to do was go back out into the field with crazy-assed criminals, wearing a god-awful heavy uniform.

She glanced at her IV bag.

The drugs made me think it.

Closing her eyes, she dreamed of home in the fall, her new baby niece waiting to be born, and a life without danger.

A life without US Marshal Declan McKinley.

Acknowledgments

A special note of gratitude to Lynda Bailey, my partner in crime and all things Indie. Thank you for your patience, criticism, advice, and most of all, friendship.

You're the *Naughty* to my *Nice* ;)

Also by Elise Manion

Trouble In Timbisha Township Series

Jason's Princess; King Brothers Book 1

Jarod's Heart; King Brothers Book 2

Josh's Challenge; King Brothers Book 3

Marguerite's Redemption; Book 4

Applewood Series

Unwanted: Finding Where You're Loved